Metal Rose

By
Jessie Lovie Watt

Northern Lights Publishing

First Published in 2003 by

Northern Lights Publishing
Benholm Studios,
Ryehill, Oyne
Aberdeenshire AB52 6QS

ISBN: 0 9524413 14

Printed and bound in UK by
Antony Rowe Ltd.,
Chippenham, Wiltshire

Dedication

I dedicate this book to my parents and my sons, and to that marvellous thread of life that links the generations.

Acknowledgements

The people to whom I am indebted are far too numerous to mention by name. However, I give special thanks to the following:

- Frances Cameron, for her valuable editing assistance.
- Alison Tavendale, Writer in Residence, Insch, for her encouragement and professional advice.
- Angela Hilton, for proof-reading assistance.
- My husband, Alan Milne, for his endless patience in putting up with my late night sessions.
- My son, Stuart Milne, for Cover Design.
- My son, Bruce Milne, for contributing the beautiful poem in the final chapter.

I also acknowledge reference information gleaned from *The Shetland Times* describing events at the time of the *Braer* incident, and the book *Innocent Passage* by Dr Jonathan Wills and Karen Warner. Also *Genome* by Matt Ridley.

I am grateful to the folk of Shetland and of Oyne for inspiring me. However, this is a work of fiction and ***any resemblance to real characters is strictly co-incidental.***

Comments

"Well paced and absorbing, with authentic characters.

The observations of the natural environment are made with a scientist's eye but the compassion is that of an artist. Like all the best novelists, Jessie Watt challenges and unsettles yet leaves us with the right to hope.

The novel is firmly rooted in the reality of the Scottish Landscape, the cutting edge of scientific thought, yet twists and turns like the most satisfactory of fantasies. ***A great read***!"

Alison Tavendale,
Writer in Residence, Insch.

...

"Bang up to date, with a credible heroine and beautiful local description."

Frances Cameron,
M.A. English and Modern History.

Chapter 1- Bonding

Shetland is a little scattering of islands, flung a couple of hundred kilometres into the north Atlantic. It is Britain's most northerly outpost. Shetland is home to around 24,000 souls, a plethora of birds and wildlife, and 240,000 sheep. It is a stronghold for the otter.

Islanders are different from other people. They have a curious inner strength. In days past, Islanders conquered the globe with their knowledge of the sea. They were sought by the Press Gangs as the very best seamen in the world. They were the hard resourceful folk who colonised far distant lands and survived in harsh climates - the success of the Hudson Bay company hinged on their sheer determination. They have a unique ability to accept what they find as the norm and turn their hand to it. Islanders can adapt to new environments.

It is significant that Rose Anderson was an Islander, born and bred of humble stock.

There can be a perfect harmony between man and a creature of the wild. It can happen when chance circumstances permit the young of a wild animal to grow up with a human child so that their formative years coincide and they are united by the innocence of childhood. They develop a mutual trust, like siblings.

It is a rare thing and a great privilege to witness.
Rose Anderson was only nine years old when she bonded with the otter.

Heather Jacobson discarded the dishes and peered out the kitchen window at her granddaughter, Rose. She shouted to her husband who was busy with the croft paperwork and glad of any diversion.

"Just look at them, Jim! It's fascinating to see. Have you got that camera ready?"

The girl and the otter were tumbling on the grassy bank behind the croft house as if it were the most natural thing in the world. It was difficult to distinguish where the squeaks and the "tooker...ooker...ook" noises were coming from since they seemed to be communicating fairly fluently in otter language. They were both on their backs, four little webbed feet and two red rubber boots thrashing the air in sheer delight. Olli nipped the woollen bonnet off Rose's head and shook it playfully. Rose stood up and Olli hung with his needle teeth from her coat sleeve and swirled his furry body round and round, as if practising killing his prey. Rose lost her balance with the sheer weight of him.

"Oh, Jim! Is she all right? Otters have very sharp teeth! I don't want any more harm coming to the lass. She's had such a rough time already with her illness."

"She's fine, woman! Stop your fussing. She's in the peak of health right now. He'll never touch her. Look there! He's as gentle as a kitten with her. He's just playing, not biting hard at all."

"Well, he bit you once, didn't he?"

" Yes, but only because I was working with fish at the time and he was hungry. He just mistook my finger for food and he never drew blood even then. Relax woman! He's just a baby and this is playtime. They're like brother and sister, those two. They're in tune with each other, moving to each other's rhythm. I'm keeping a close eye on them. I'll be off to feed the sheep in a minute and then we'll go down to the shore. That'll tire the little devils out!"

Jim didn't take long to fill the troughs with the ration of ewe nuts, supplemented with the vegetable peelings from Heather's kitchen. Olli was quick to pinch a lump of raw turnip, which he devoured with apparent enjoyment.

"Well, well, Rosie! I always thought that otters were carnivores! I never knew they ate neeps!"

"Och, Grandda, he loves neeps... and grapes... and cucumbers ... and all sorts of vegetables. He eats seaweed as well. I've seen him chewing it up. He likes anything with a lot of juice in it!"

As they walked the half-mile over the bare hill to the deserted banks at the west shore, Jim Jacobson smiled at his granddaughter. Olli ran at her feet, detouring to bumble about in the waterlogged ditches, sifting the peaty sediment with his nose in search of the odd crunchy frog or other edible morsel.

Knowing a few words of French, gleaned from one of the guests that had stayed with her grandparents for Bed and Breakfast that summer, and showing off a little, Rose exclaimed, "He's having his hors d'oeuvres now, Granddad!"

Jim smiled. They walked on, leaving Olli engrossed in the delicacy of an enormous black slug that he'd found on the sloping bank. They were not surprised to hear his plaintive little alarm call from behind them, conveying the message, "Where are you? I'm here and I'm lost!"

Rose called over her shoulder, "Took a took...Come on boy."

His nose was soon making contact with the familiar red wellies once more. They had reached the steeper part of the final slope down to the rocky shoreline and Rosie started to run. Awkward in the longer grass, Olli tried padding after her, but settled for a pattern of short runs interspersed with long slides down the wet grass bank. Spread-eagled to the ground, with his hind legs trailing flat out behind him, it was a peculiar sight to see him sledging the grass. He was hardly elegant.

Reaching the sea, he showed not the slightest hesitation in entering the water. It was as if he did not notice the interface at all. He simply transformed into the most graceful of nymphs, gliding under the clear water, streamlined, perfectly adapted to his underwater kingdom, suddenly at home.

He stayed submerged for a prolonged period, but it was easy to follow his progress. Even when he went below the tangles into deeper parts where he was no longer visible, a steady stream of telltale bubbles rose from his luxurious pelt as the trapped air was forced out. Jim and Rosie walked along the shore, keeping pace with their aquatic friend, Rosie answering his frequent position report whistles. Every now and then he emerged triumphant with a small fish or a crab wrapped around his blunt snout and proceeded to take his prize into the shallows to eat. He was keen to play with anything interesting that he encountered, a cork or an orange fishing float. He lay on his back in the water, turning the intriguing balls around in his front paws, trying to submerge with them before they bobbed back to the surface. Rosie picked up an empty can that was wedged between the rocks and threw it to him. He immediately started nosing it around in circles as if trying to access its contents.

"Look, Grandda, he's drinking beer!" It was a bright red McEwan's Export can.

"Yes, there are too many red cans lying around these days. The other day, I heard somebody call them Shetland Roses."

"Why?"

"Well, you know that roses do not grow well in Shetland because of our cold salt winds. We have the harshest climate in Britain here. They can survive in a few sheltered gardens, or in Granny's greenhouse of course, but not in exposed places like this. However, unfortunately, beer tins are found everywhere these days: on beaches, in ditches and by roadsides. It's a sad reflection on modern society and probably only caused by a minority of litter louts. Because of their bright colouring and the sheer numbers of these cans, it looks as if they've just ***grown*** in the countryside like wild roses. Shetland Rose is an appropriate nickname, I suppose."

Olli had disappeared behind a rocky outcrop.

"Let's sneak away and leave him while he's occupied with his can, Rosie. We must encourage him to spend more time in the wild. He must learn to fend for himself and to mix with other otters."

Rosie nodded, and with some reluctance, followed her granddad's silent shadow as it moved away from the shore and turned back towards the homestead.

Meanwhile, totally engrossed in the wonder of an underwater forest of waving seaweeds and darting silver fish, the hours passed quickly for the abandoned youngster. He came ashore at intervals to sniff the scented messages in the spraints of other wild otters that marked this marine territory. Unsure of himself, he did not leave his mark here yet. The smells were exciting and he was tempted to answer the questions they asked and to ask a few of his own. He felt the call of the wilderness, but after a few hours of perfect freedom, he became troubled and confused. He encountered two of his furry kindred, but they hissed warnings at him from a distance and were not welcoming. He missed the one with the red wellies.

Eventually, he left the shore and instinctively headed east, panting hard with the effort as he scaled the summit of the hill and began to pick out the familiar landmarks with his nocturnal vision. He stopped briefly to cool himself in the burn, before tackling the last few hundred metres of hard-going land environment.

It was not until he reached the outer dyke of the Jacobson croft that he paused to leave his own distinctive aromatic signal of ownership. Every boundary was marked in this way, on all sides of the croft. Should any of his kind chance to pass, there would be no doubt that he was King of this Castle.

The red welly boots were tucked up in bed and the peaceful silence of the night had descended over the croft house, but he knew the window at which to squeak. A sleepy-eyed Rosie popped her head out and spoke words of comfort to him. He was still hungry, hardly able to catch enough to sustain him. She ran to the fridge in the kitchen for a herring and threw it out the window. Grandda kept a supply of fresh fish, willingly donated from the local catch. The neighbouring fishermen were regular visitors to the Jacobson house, to check the progress of the young orphaned otter. Jim had found him in the barn, during the big snow in January.

At first, Jim had mistaken his distress calls for some kind of a bird, but after two days, he had managed to catch the baby. He was very close to starvation. He must have crawled into the barn for shelter after being abandoned or separated from his mother. Survival was touch and go until the youngster was weaned on to little bits of solid fish.

During that time, Rosie herself had been poorly, convalescing from another episode of her strange autoimmune illness. However, she always seemed to recover faster with her grandparents. The baby otter and Rosie had bonded quickly as they each regained strength. She had named him Olli and hand fed him. She trained him to use a cat litter tray. It was so unusual to have such a tame otter that he attracted the attention of the media. He became a star of BBC and Grampian news. Film crews from three different countries had rushed to see the little miracle. Rosie gained some unsolicited fame when she appeared on a children's television programme alongside Olli.

However, she agreed with Granddad that Olli must be encouraged back to the wild and taught to fend for himself, so they took him on daily walks to the shore over the following months. Granny insisted that he must no longer reside in the house since it was too warm for him and his manners were inappropriate. He loved to rattle around in the kitchen cupboards and threw himself into water whenever he saw it - the shower, the bath... even the toilet! They had tried to install him in a cave beside the shore, but he kept coming home. He had now chosen his own place to sleep.

Olli caught the herring in mid-air like an acrobat, his sleek body shining in the moonlight and then quickly retired to eat his supper in his man-made holt. He was not locked in. The cellar door opened to the yard outside and Jim had cut a hole in it to make an otter-flap. He came and went as he pleased. He had made his own bed from the insulated jacket off an old hot water boiler.

Olli could sense his human sibling sleeping just above his head, separated only by a few floorboards. He felt secure as he curled into the foetal position in the womb of the house.

Chapter 2 - Self Sufficiency

As her Medical Notes described in great detail, Rose Anderson had been a sickly child for the entire ten years of her life, but she always seemed to thrive better in the country while staying with her grandparents. Therefore, her mother sent her there frequently to recuperate.

When confined indoors following a bout of illness, Rose liked nothing better than to explore the contents of the big oak dresser that sat in the corner of her grandmother's front room. It had remained unchanged for decades, a time capsule of handy objects. The cluttered drawers were full of wonder for Rose. She read old postcards and stared at sepia-coloured photographs of strange folk who looked familiar. She laid out the treasures in an orderly fashion: needles, thread, tangled wool, fishing line, hooks, lead sinkers, tilley lamp wicks, neep seeds... before putting them all back again. Each time, the drawer revealed another secret: a book of matches with a picture of a beautiful city, a mother of pearl brooch with a broken clasp. It was like Aladdin's cave. It was a great source of comfort to Rose.

Throughout her childhood in Lerwick, she had experienced a constant stream of allergies and illnesses like colds, flu, viral infections, including a very serious bout of glandular fever. She was three years old and sick of probing needles before they diagnosed *Idiopathic Thrombocytopoenic Purpura*, a long name to remember, but ITP for short. She had suffered recurring episodes of ITP all her life, missing about one week in every month from primary school. Yet she had been exceptionally healthy during 1991, with almost perfect attendance at school. Jim called it "the year of the otter."

The bonding with the creature seemed to do the child good.

She was a strange intense little child, fiercely independent. She had an uncanny ability to "just know" what was in folk's minds. It was like a sort of sixth sense. People with nothing to hide found her charming. Yet, some found her company uncomfortable, in the same way that certain individuals are not at ease when the family dog growls at them, sensing their untrustworthy nature. Dogs and other animals related easily to Rose.

With the passing of another eighteen months, Olli learned to be more self-sufficient and stayed near the sea for longer periods of time. Several days, even a week might pass before he was heard whistling at the window. He often came at the weekend to coincide with Rosie's visits. She was back in Lerwick staying with her mother during the week but spent every weekend at the Westside. Olli had even learnt to speak to Rosie while she was having a bath. She had first heard his "*tooker -ooker- ook*" greeting carry up from the cellar through the bathroom water pipes and they had now established the plumbing as a means of communicating, like a primitive walkie-talkie system.

They still spent time together and walked together, even swam together on the few rare warm summer days, but it was satisfying to Jim Jacobson that Olli was seen more and more frequently with his own species, where he had at last established a rapport. He now sprainted on a section of shoreline to mark his extended territory.

The experts still did not know what caused Rose's disorder, but it was always triggered by a common viral infection. The doctors said that stress in the home environment was thought likely to be another significant factor. There had certainly been plenty of stress before her father died. Rose was only six years old when he passed away. "Cardiac Failure" and some other fancy words had graced the death certificate, but he had been a chronic alcoholic for years. Her mother had always had to work to support them, since he drank away anything he might have earned, so it was little different when he died, leaving Mary Anderson to bring up Rosie and her younger brother alone.

The Consultant from the Mainland had told Mary Anderson that ITP was a very rare disorder, characterised by an overactive immune system that reacted to every foreign virus under the sun and destroyed the patient's own platelets into the bargain. He explained that platelets played a vital role in the blood clotting mechanism, so lack of platelet function resulted in widespread haemorrhaging and bruising, rather like seen in the condition known as Haemophilia. ITP usually occurred in childhood as a single severe attack, but the strange pattern of acute recurring episodes that typified Rose's condition was "almost" unique, with only a few similar cases reported worldwide.

Before the final diagnosis was made, Rosie had looked like a battered baby sometimes. Consequently, at one stage, her parents were suspected of abusing her! Her father's alcohol problem lent weight to this suspicion, and probably delayed the true diagnosis being made, although he would never have harmed a hair on her head.

Rosie was aware that she might always suffer from it. She had read about it and knew that there was a danger of bleeding in her head when her blood did not clot properly and when she was covered in the purple rash. She knew that other children had died of such problems when the platelet count fell very low. Even at the tender age of ten, she had grown used to her strange illness and was vigilant, always checking for the first signs of purpura on her wrists and ankles. She remained optimistic that she might grow out of the most severe attacks since some improvement at puberty had been recorded in another patient.

By early December 1992, Olli had truly colonised the wild again. He had not even been seen for over a fortnight, although Jim had received a couple of reports of a male otter about two miles away. That creature had apparently taken an offering of food from a fisherman's hand, so it sounded likely that Olli had moved his territory and was in another Voe now. Furthermore, that particular otter had been spotted with a mate.

It was Christmas Eve and Rosie's whole family was spending the Festive Season at the croft. Rosie and her brother were in bed, but not asleep. Mary and Jim were out in the barn filling the children's stockings before bringing them in, when Olli came calling again. Rosie heard him and was out the window into the frosty night in a flash. He was *tookering* full of excitement and news... and a lady friend was with him! Rosie spoke to him and he approached to greet her, standing erect on his hind legs like a man... and what a magnificent male he was! He looked to be almost a metre long from his nose to the tip of his heavy tail and broad too, shining with health.

The female otter squealed in alarm and shot off across the park into the night, uncomprehending of his boldness and sensing great danger. In her eyes, Olli's alliance with Man was still a dangerous and fragile one. Man appeared to hold out the hand of friendship, but it was not so long ago that he lured otters into traps and bludgeoned them to death for their pelts. The deserted stone trapping houses along the shore bore witness to the cruelty of Man. Man had struck fear into the souls of otters for centuries.

Olli did not stay long, but lingered to say a final goodbye to Rosie. She noticed that he did not go to the safety of the deserted west shore, but went east after his mate... across the main road to the sea at the other side.

He followed her exquisite scent faithfully, through caverns and crevices, over rock and under water. She taught him better fishing techniques and when their bonding rituals were complete, she accepted him as her mate.

His whelps now stirred in her belly.
They were mated for life.
Shetland was a stronghold for their species.

Chapter 3 – The Storm

It was the 4th of January 1993, the Festive Season was in full swing with neighbours visiting neighbours, and drams being drunk with friends and family as is typical of the Shetland rural community for at least a full fortnight following Hogmanay! Gale force winds swept the islands and Radio Shetland warned of worse weather to come with the imminent approach of a menacing depression in the Faroe-Iceland gap.

Jim Jacobson donned oilskins and rubber boots and ventured forth to secure every mobile object upon his windswept croft. His little boat was already upturned and tied down in its noost for the winter, but ropes were checked and an extra line and stone weights were added for good measure. The sheep feeding troughs were gathered for storage, along with planks of wood, pallets, wheelbarrows and a pile of corrugated iron. All were put in the shed. It was difficult to move against the increasing wind and he was having to drag in the last of the loose debris, leaning hard into the howling wind and battling to make his way around the corner of the byre. All the gates between the four fields that comprised his 40 hectare croft were tied wide open to allow the sheep free range so that they could instinctively wander to the most sheltered spot and move around unhindered as the wind inevitably changed direction. Meanwhile, windows were secured and doors of outbuildings padlocked.

Rosie was glad to be safely indoors with the cats at the peat fire. She had done as she was bidden and the oil and modern gas lamps were ready for use if there was a power cut. Heather was busy baking bannocks and tattie soup, enough to last a couple of days. The house creaked and groaned like a ship at sea and the kitchen door was now misaligned and unable to shut because the whole fabric of the wall appeared to have flexed a few millimetres with the severe force of the storm. Two neighbours arrived at a crawling pace, the slighter one on his hands and knees. The lights flickered and went off shortly afterwards. Thus, the lamps were lit and the whisky poured, both casting their mellow glow over the adults in the house. A radio set was linked up to a car battery and fiddle music mingled with the storm.

The roof tiles on the old house rattled like machine gun fire as the wind swept up the Beaufort scale to a frightening howl.

One neighbour simply remarked, " Hit's a richt night o' distress, fok!" He took another sip of the amber nectar.

His forecast was accurate. The real distress had yet to come.

...

The weather was atrocious, but Olli and his new ladylove found the best of the shelter in rocky taverns by the shore and took it in turns to make short trips into the raging sea in search of food. She was swelling with their cubs but still sleek and agile and much better than Olli at catching fish. She had been mothered naturally and had benefited from being taught the skills for survival. He did his best to learn from her expertise.

He had cut his webbed foot on barnacles as the uncanny force of waves like he had never encountered before dashed him up over the rocks. She tenderly licked the wound.

...

At that moment, an American managed tanker, the "Braer," built in Japan, registered in Liberia, and owned in Bermuda was making her way between continents, sailing close to the southern tip of the Shetland islands. She was a flag of convenience vessel with a mixed nationality crew, mostly Filipino seamen and Polish engineers. She had a Greek master. She was *en route* from Norway to Quebec, travelling on a well-used International waterway. Mindful of deadlines and in worsening weather, her master took a gamble. He set a shortcut course through the turbulent channel between Fair Isle and the Shetland mainland, passing close to Sumburgh Head, some 90 kilometres due south of Jim Jacobson's croft.

...

Olli had learned that the occasional fat salmon could be caught relatively easily if he ventured near the salmon farm. There were usually escapees to be found under and around the netted area. Unlike his wild kindred, he had no fear of the men who worked at the offshore floating salmon cages. One of the workers even threw a misshapen or diseased fish to him now and then. Rich in oil and vitamins, such a prize was always well received by his pregnant mate. A romping session of sheer frivolity and delight was almost sure to follow the meal. He gathered playthings for her:

the cork from a herring net...
a plastic fairy liquid bottle...
a Shetland rose...

...

Sullom Voe base had been built some fifteen years previously, and was now Europe's biggest oil terminal. It had a safety record among the best in the world. Still, Shetlanders lived with the constant awareness that a spill was possible. The ship of convenience that now strayed from its course was not bound by the stringent local safety protocols that were adhered to rigorously by all ships calling at Sullom. In the true spirit of Chaos Theory, a completely unexpected threat now came from outwith the islands and in waters well beyond local jurisdiction.

...

In the hellish weather, a salmon farm was a dangerous place for both men and otters. The floating structure strained and creaked with the terrible force of the storms. Nets were riven asunder. Salmon spewed from the enclosure. There was suddenly a relative abundance of food in the shallow waters of the Voe. These farmed fish lacked wild instincts to tell them where to go. Disorientated, with an overwhelming sense of natural disaster, some even beached themselves in their ignorance of the wild environment.

Their world was no longer defined.
They had earthquake panic reactions.

Olli could hardly believe his good fortune. Unable to venture far from shore, the otters should have been near to starvation, but food was suddenly landing at the very door of their holt.
Life surely could not get much better!

...

The "Braer" was a mono-skinned tanker. No one knows why her master did not raise the alarm at the first few signs of trouble. It is probable that the Company's financial cost of calling out a tug came into the equation. Whatever the reason, five long hours passed before Mayday signals were eventually sent out. Furthermore, her Radio Operator had a poor command of basic navigational English. His belated call for help was difficult to understand.

The ship's engine finally spluttered to a dead halt.
She was adrift without power.

She had no worthy anchor.
There were no functional wires to facilitate tug assistance from another vessel!

As the news hit the media, Rosie and her family listened intently to the radio bulletins. The entire population of Shetland were united by a cold fear. The stricken tanker drifted helplessly in the atrocious storm, dangerously close to the jagged rocky shore of their islands.

...

Full of top quality nutrients and snug in their holt, Olli curled himself like a comma around the plump body of his mate, nose to thick tail. In the words of the Bard, "*The storm withoot might rare and rustle, he did'na mind the storm a whistle...*"

A discarded red tin can adorned the corner of their sanctuary, along with broken crab shells and a well-chewed salmon head. Their front door was heavily sprainted to warn even the fiercest of intruders that this was their exclusive domain.

...

Deep in the hold of the injured ship lay the valuable cargo: 84,500 tonnes of Norwegian oil, 1,700 tonnes of heavy fuel oil and 125 tonnes of diesel.

Chapter 4 – Black Nightmare

Rose discovered at an early stage of her life that through reading one could keep the ghosts of one's own life in abeyance. She became an avid reader, especially when she was ill. She particularly liked fiction writers who drew upon the spectacular geography of Shetland as background to their novels. Robert Louis Stevenson had spent some of his boyhood on Shetland, while his family had worked at various lighthouses. Rose was intrigued and proud that the map of "Treasure Island" bore a remarkable resemblance to the island of Unst. It was in Sir Walter Scott's novel "The Pirate" that an evil witch was featured. She was called "Norma" and was reputed to live high on the cliffs at Fitful Head, luring ships to the rocks below.

On Tuesday, 5 January 1993, the injured tanker ran aground in Norma's dark domain. Rose wondered if the witch was something more than mere fiction. Within the hour, oil began to spill from the Braer's fractured hull. Her multinational crew were rescued by helicopter. In the grey mid-winter day that followed, the fleeting twilight revealed an oil slick several miles long, spreading like a web from the body of the monster.

Islanders gathered on the cliffs to view the invader with her black innards spewing into their clean waters, casting a toxic shadow over their island. Local traders were soon sold out of waterproof clothing as media personnel flocked to the site. Hotels and guesthouses were quickly filled to capacity. Within a couple of days there were no more guest beds available and absolutely no chance of a roadworthy car for hire. Then, pleas went out on local radio for extra bed spaces.

Booms proved useless in the weather conditions that prevailed. The oil went over and under the barriers. It seemed to be unstoppable.

It advanced up the western coastline and by Day Two the oil could be smelt in the air at Jim Jacobson's croft. It was the third day before the slick physically reached his shores. Around the same time, the croft house windows glistened with microscopic droplets of oil and sinister rainbow sheens spread across the glass.

Pollution experts predicted contamination of land and sea at an unprecedented level. The spill was destined to double that of the "Exxon Valdez."

A wildlife holocaust seemed unavoidable.

The International lure of mega-disaster generated a plethora of reporters, many desperate for lurid headlines. Ignorance among the film crews was rife. They even seized upon the native black sheep as an example of visible oil contamination!

However, genuine casualties were quickly obvious. Immediate victims were black guillemots, eider ducks, shags and gulls. Great Northern divers were reduced to sorry black carcasses, sharing their beach morgue with the tiny bodies of Shetland wrens, sandpipers and turnstones. It was fortunate that it was the sub-arctic winter, which meant that many of the large and famous seabird breeding colonies were not yet occupied.

Dozens of common and grey seals were trapped on the tiny island of Lady Holm, surrounded by a black moat. Freshwater lochs in the vicinity were affected. Their wintering colonies of ducks and whooper swans were contaminated.

Beaches that featured as glorious white sandy strips in the glossy magazines that attracted the scores of Europe's green tourists became a wasteland of black gunge.

The catastrophe factor that kick starts human beings to pull together in mercy mission quickly became evident. Unsolicited assistance came from every direction.

Greenpeace's campaign ship "Solo" arrived.

Teams of Environmentalists stood side by side with local folk armed with shovels, spades, rubber gloves or... whatever they had. Boy Scouts helped to collect and clean the innocents. More often than not, despatch of the crippled and poisoned birds was the kindest solution. All the time, volunteers worked with heavy hearts.

Then, the spraying began. On the advice of the pollution experts, a cocktail of dangerous carcinogenic dispersants was added to the existing toxic mess - 95 tonnes of dispolene LTSW; 15 tonnes of dasic 34S; and 10 tonnes of BP enersperse.

This deadly Fairy Liquid was obtained from old Government Stock. Some was unlicensed and unfit for the purpose. It contained benzene, butadiene and naphthalene. It arrived in rusty barrels and these leaked on to the ground at the Airport, adding to the massive pollution problem. It even burnt the lips and tongues of sheep and caused mouth ulcers and liver damage.

Greenpeace protested.
Jim Wallace, MP, was furious.
Children living in the area were issued with face masks.
There was talk of evacuation.
As a final desperate measure, volunteers formed a human barrier across the runway to stop the DC3 sprayer planes taking off.

A black petticoat spread unseen over the ocean floor killing or maiming all in its path like a sinister Lord of the underworld. After one week, the seabed was deadly sterile in the area of the wreck. Decomposing fish were floating on the surface, their gills inflamed. Shellfish miles from the incident still sucked in toxic liquids.

A ban was imposed on harvesting fish over an area of 400 square miles. Fishermen and workers on sixteen fish farms, in the Burra and Scalloway area, were threatened with financial ruin. Vital markets in the south rejected Shetland's produce and cancelled their orders: Tesco, Sainsbury, Marks and Spencer...

Jim Jacobson's land was contaminated, along with the whole western side of Shetland. Sheep were moved from shoreline fields so that they did not have to eat the sickened grass.

Crops were ruined. Emergency supplies of winter fodder were taken into the island.

The International Oil Pollution Compensation Fund opened a local office. Stringent bureaucracy was added to the chaos as claim forms were issued. Legitimate claims jostled for space alongside a few chancers, who were keen to cash in on the disaster by spinning an ambiguous tale of property damaged by the oil.

Trusting their God implicitly, armed only with blind faith, the island's Evangelical Christians prayed for a miracle.

Chapter 5 – The Miracle

Following the big feast of escapee salmon, and since the elements were so severely against venturing out again, Olli and his ladylove slept for twenty-four hours. They woke up only once during that time, to relieve themselves at the boundary line. It was driving sleet outside against a grey striped sky and two sets of webbed footprints fleetingly decorated the rocky slab by their entrance before rapidly melting into oblivion. A mutual preening session followed their brief encounter with the howling fury of the outside, preparing their coats for the next fishing trip in the calm that they instinctively knew would follow the storm, just as day follows night. The red can was briefly nosed around and juggled with, but they would conserve their energy. Hunger did not yet gnaw sufficiently to lure them out into the wrath of Neptune.

They snuggled close together in a silent pact to weather the storm. He was not afraid. She was there. Her wonderful smell pervaded the cave and the warmth of her body touched the brown skin on the sole of his sore foot, easing the mild itchy irritation. His wound was healing. He stretched his wide flat chin on her shoulder, made a quick comforting *tookerook* noise, yawned to reveal gleaming white teeth and a pink roof to his mouth and slept again, perfectly contented.

...

The severe depression in the Faroe-Iceland gap bottomed out at 916 millibars, the lowest ever recorded in the NE Atlantic. Over the next two weeks, the Evangelicals thanked their God, who had indeed performed a miracle as the worst January storms in over a century battered Shetland. Hurricane force was recorded on half of these days.

Pollution experts watched in awe as the wrath of the natural elements brought their artificial efforts to a standstill.
The sprayer planes could not take off and were permanently grounded. Colossal waves churned the oil and sea mixture into a toxic emulsion and carried it away!

Thus, against all the odds, the islands were saved from the worst of the peril. Dead and oiled birds numbered a few thousand... not the seven hundred thousand as seen in Alaska following the "Exxon Valdez." The oiled shoreline stretched only twenty miles... but not thousands of miles as was first predicted.

...

A calm eventually followed the storm and a few brave starlings sang. A lone wren emerged from a hole in a dyke-end and flitted lightly across the holt entrance. Hungered hill sheep wandered to the shore to eat the seaweed, uprooted from its watery depths and now piled high and dry. It was even draped from fences well above the usual high tide mark.

...

Olli did not leave her side when she came ashore with her thick luxurious fur matted with grease. She had done her best to clean herself, rolling in the seaweed and on the grassy bank, licking till her tongue was blistered. He gladly joined in the massive preening task.

Soon he vomited for the first of many times.

He brought salmon with festering gills that tasted strange and acrid but she would not eat. He did not leave his sweetheart until she was cold and still.

Only then did he head for his other sanctuary...

Rosie heard her otter before she saw him and was shocked by the sight of him. He was ragged and very thin. She offered him fish. He ate it quickly, but immediately regurgitated it.
He stood on his hind legs and spoke his otter greetings. He rested his heavy head in her outstretched hand and she felt the weight of his burden. He did not wish to stay long and soon he headed back towards the shore.

Rosie went after him and saw him enter the holt. The entrance was small and she could not see inside. He would not come to her call but answered with his most plaintive *tookerook* noise.

Later that day she returned with her grandfather and they called again at his front door. There was no response. Jim managed to move a massive capping stone from the roof of the holt. They saw a pitiful sight.

The female was stiff with rigor mortis.
She had hardly any hair left.
The protruding skin was raw and covered in sores.
The holt smelt of oil and vomit.

He had wrapped himself round his dead mate like a cocoon...and was gone.

Rosie stroked the thick fur of her pseudo-sibling for the last time and recalled the words of the so-called otter expert from the BBC who had been afraid to touch Olli when he reported on camera that, "Otters have incredibly thick fur, with over 2000 hairs per square centimetre."

Her granddad helped her bury them, still united, near the holt.
Jim made a makeshift little cross from driftwood.

There were no flowers blooming at this time of year and this vexed the child. Jim made her two beautiful red Shetland roses from the discarded beer tin in the holt, one as a floral tribute to her friend...and one for herself to keep.

They were very regal, very beautiful, much appreciated.
It was the gift she would remember most clearly for the rest of life.

There was no consoling the girl. She walked the shoreline that day and the next, unaware of the sleet falling on her bare head, alone with her grief, anger bubbling through her as she agonised on how many otters had crawled into their holts to die a slow sickening death.

By the evening of the day after the funeral, she had developed a cough, severe headache and sore throat. Within twenty-four hours, her platelets fell to a dangerously low level and did not respond to a fairly high dose of steroids. Her gums bled. She screamed in her sleep, demented by nightmares as thousands of tiny haemorrhages erupted on the surface of her brain.

In the thankful light of morning, she was peppered with purple bruises.

She peed red urine

Her mother accompanied her on the emergency Ambulance plane to Aberdeen Royal Infirmary. Granddad's Shetland rose was firmly clutched in her hand. She would not let it out of her sight, as if her life depended on it.

Chapter 6 - Debris

Rose slammed the door and stomped upstairs.
At fifteen, she was full of teenage rebellion.

Anti-mother thoughts pounded in her head. *She's so bloody infuriating! Yes, I love her and miss her when we're apart but I could cheerfully throttle her after living under the same roof for a week.*

She tried to have logical thoughts on why they argued so much. *Yes, the clash of teenage and menopausal hormones probably **does** have a lot to do with it... but mostly the latter.*

If the truth be told, she would do anything for her mother - but resented the constant criticism of everything she did. She knew her mother had not had an easy life, but expressions like, *"I've worked my fingers to the bone!" are so stupid!*
*I'm **not** "running around with too little clothes on" - everybody dresses this way!*
*I'm **not** "lazy" - I just don't like mornings, especially in the winter when it's dark all the time anyway.*

She easily persuaded herself that there was no foundation for her mother's nagging.

*None of her problems is **my** fault!* Rosie thought indignantly, stamping out the words with her feet on the bedroom floor to ease her frustration.

She wished her mother would just stop hovering on the edge of maternal reprimand all the time and living in the past - "*Rosie put a coat on - Rosie wear a toorie bonnet - Rosie get up - Rosie go to bed and stop being a midnight Mary, whatever that is? - Rosie tidy your room up... and get off that bloody Internet **now** - the phone bills are crippling me." She never stops!*

She resolved that she would pay her own phone calls anyway now that she had got a weekend job in Safeway. She switched on her CD player and turned up the music, listening to the words of Portishead.

She decided that she would sneak off to the country for the summer. Granddad was much more tolerant and did not nag so much and Granny's new batch of roses would be in bloom shortly. She wondered what shades the new grafts would be... and the floral thoughts mingled with the music and calmed her.

She lay down amidst the chaos of her typically teenage bedroom, thinking she might really have to tidy up a bit as she cast her eyes over two empty glasses, a plate on the floor, several chocolate biscuit wrappers, a discarded piece of toast with a bite out of it, a pile of shrivelled orange peel and a ripe yoghurt carton. There was a dark sticky stain on the desk in front of her computer and her mouse mat was contaminated by... fruit juice she decided.

She had suffered only one minor ITP attack in the past year and felt a growing sense of optimism that it might yet disappear forever. She had formed a fanciful idea of her illness and thought of it like the exact opposite of AIDS, describing it in this rather romantic and important way to her friends. She felt sure that some of her serum injected into an AIDS patient would really give them a boost in fighting their infection. However, it was a right pain being allergic to so many foodstuffs - especially the artificial preservatives and additives with E numbers. Since starting work in the Supermarket, she had been studying the labels and there seemed to be surprisingly few foods that were entirely natural any more. She was unaffected by fresh fruits, vegetables, fish, eggs and cheese, so she had settled on a largely vegetarian diet.

The fumes from traffic and the slightest trace of cigarette smoke made her wheeze uncontrollably. This was a problem with some of her friends who chose to smoke, but Rosie was a bit of a loner anyway and did not really hang around with her peer group. After all, she was different. Yet, she did not suffer from hay fever and had no adverse reaction to pollen. In fact, anything natural, plants or animals, including cats, were fine. No problem with any of them.

Friday was exciting for a school day since Rosie and three classmates were going out to the beach at Nesbister to work on a school project. They were also helping with Shetland's annual spring cleaning operation, "Da Voar Redd-Up," organised locally, when parties of volunteers attempted to tidy up the islands. It was an event that had already won several national Environmental Awards. Hundreds of willing folk turned up every year to collect the rubbish from beaches, roadsides and ditches. Much of it came as a result of the sea, compounded by winter storms. However, some was domestic: silage wrappings and animal feed bags, and other miscellaneous rubbish, blown from houses and cars, by the gale force winds that battered Shetland.

The school project was designed to take advantage of the timing of the "Redd-Up" and involved the collection and categorising of International plastic debris from the beach, to see how many different countries were represented and what the likely source of the rubbish might be. Mrs Gray was the supervisory teacher who accompanied them.

They were armed with thick plastic gloves and strong black bags and had about half a mile to walk to the bay, since the vehicular road came to a dead end well before the beach.

It was a bright Spring day but with the usual stiff breeze blowing. Sheep were on the stony beach, picking among the seaweed at the high tide mark. Shetland sheep eat seaweed to supplement the poor grazing. The shore was piled high with rubbish of all descriptions and there was a strong smell of rotting waar mingled with putrid flesh. This was quickly traced to the carcass of a dead porpoise. Arctic terns called overhead in alarm, fearing invasion of their nesting territory.

The volunteers scoured the heaps of coloured fishing net, ropes, floats, branches of trees from distant shores, old rubber boots and soles off trainers, milk boxes and car tyres. There was a kaleidoscope of coloured plastic bottles: shampoo from Norway; oil cans from the Soviet Union; detergent from France and an orange juice container from America. Had it come clean across the Atlantic? Rosie wondered, or was it another result of illegal dumping at sea? By the end of two hours, they had sourced plastic from seven different countries and made appropriate lists.

The rubbish was piled for burning and the first bonfire started before mid day. There were several responsible adults on the beach in charge of the fires.

By this time, John and Bruce were bored and playing cricket with the stave of a broken barrel, using a rusty can of foreign sardines as a ball, it burst, spraying rancid fish oil all over the two boisterous boys. They shrieked their displeasure and Rosie and Lyla looked up from their latest find and laughed.

Lyla had found an old canvas case, sodden wet and torn. It was a first aid box of some kind and contained small bottles of yellow liquid, with foreign writing, possibly Spanish, they decided. The innards of the box revealed brown stained bandages, plastic dressings and several needles and syringes, still wrapped but waterlogged. The teacher shouted a warning and forbade further investigation of the medical find. It was placed on the bonfire.

Rosie found several rolls of grey sticky parcel tape and she started threading them on to a piece of thick blue nylon rope, counting aloud as she did so, "13, 14, 15... these must have washed overboard from a cargo. The inside of the rolls might still be salvageable?"

Mrs Gray thought not and ordered them to be burnt with the rest.

The next treasure to be unearthed was a red cylinder with a warning sign ***"Achtung!"*** in bold white letters and a contact telephone number in case of the object being found.

"It's a bomb!" Exclaimed Bruce, poking it with a stick.

"Please do not touch anything out of the ordinary!" Shouted the distraught teacher. "If it looks unusual, it might be dangerous! I don't want any accidents!"

She agreed that it might be an explosive flare of some sort and suggested that they give it a wide berth and note down the number for phoning on their return to Lerwick.

Two of the adults placed a fish box over it and wrote "Danger - do not handle," on the upturned box.

Bruce had just sat down on a tar-encrusted rock and had a large brown stain on his rear end. John was poking fun at him suggesting that he might have waited till he got to the toilet and such like, when it started to rain: a fine soaking drizzle.

The sea shuddered as the squalls of wind rushed across its surface making strange steely cold patterns. The head of an otter was highlighted in the ripples a few metres offshore, making for the sanctuary of a skerry, then disappeared as a black shadow rushed across the sky. Rosie was filled with poignant memories. She shivered, wishing she had heeded her mother and put on a waterproof jacket.

"We'll just shelter a few minutes in the Bӧd there and have a short debriefing session," said Mrs Gray.

The Bӧd was an old fishing station, still used as basic camping accommodation for backpackers, but there were few visitors this early in the season. They scurried into the bare stone building at the end of the beach. It was nearly surrounded by water and could be cut off from shore with a very high tide, although that was unusual. The interior had stone ledges for sleeping bags to lie on and a makeshift hammock dangled from the roof. There were ashes in the open fireplace and a pile of driftwood gathered in the hearth.

All around in window sills and on shelves were treasures collected by transient visitors: pebbles, shells, sea urchins, bird and fish skeletons and contorted bits of heather roots, knarled by nature and weathered by salt water. A pencil sketch of herring gulls hung off the wall above the fireplace, held by one corner and looking faded and sad. There was a table and chairs so they sat down to discuss their morning's experience, but it was cold and damp and the four pupils were now lacking in enthusiasm.

"I think the rain is going to be on for the rest of the afternoon, so perhaps we'll call it a day now," said Mrs Gray. "Let's get back up to the car. The others will check the fire before they leave. You seem to have got some good lists and notes. I've taken a few photos of the most interesting plastic debris, so you can select some copies for your projects. Any Questions?"

There was nobody at home when Rose got back. Her feet were wet so she peeled off the sodden socks and went to the utility room in search of clean ones. Now that all of the three pairs of household feet were near enough the same size, Mary had introduced the concept of the *sox-box*. All clean socks were thrown in there after braving the washing machine. Odd socks seemed to multiply. The rule was first come first served for matching pairs. She found two that nearly matched.

She switched on the radio in the kitchen for company and listened to the news headlines while she made herself a sandwich. *The Irish cease-fire had not lasted long, another bomb had gone off at the Olympic games, with several fatalities and hundreds injured. John Major was holding the Conservative party by a hair or two and the EC ban on British beef was steadfast. Siamese twins had been born in Glasgow, sharing a heart and lungs... there was little hope of a long future for both of them, although one may be salvaged at the expense of the other. Another hurricane was sweeping through the Caribbean. AIDS research promised another possible drug to prolong the life of affected patients. Scientists were predicting the hole in the Ozone layer was getting steadily bigger and world weather patterns were changing as a result... hotter and dryer towards the Equator and wetter and windier towards the Poles...* It certainly was wetter and windier tonight, Rosie thought, shivering involuntarily.

She felt soiled by the dregs of humanity from combing the beach and looked forward to a bath but there was no hot water when she got home. Her mother was still at work. It was that inconsiderate brother of hers - he stood in the shower for hours and drained the tank every day. Rather than a luke-warm shower, she packed her bathing suit and a towel and went off to the Clickimin Centre for a quick swim.

There, the chemicals in the pool made her eyes water, but it was bearable. She loved the strong current in the rapids and when her eyes got bad, she swam through the curtain to the outdoor section of the pool and was relieved by the fresh air. What a marvellous facility the Leisure Centre was - it was sheer heaven to sit under the waterfall with the warm current flowing over her head and to breath the sweet outside air at the same time. She thought again of Olli and how he would have loved this waterfall.

It was clean, sanitised; there was no plastic rubbish here.

Saturday morning started with another screaming match as her mother tried to aid Rosie's alarm clock to get her out of bed in time for work. She did not feel well but forced herself up in the end to get rid of the decibel factor ringing in her ears. Her throat was sore and she had a headache.

She noticed the first signs while pulling on her socks - small pinhead sized flecks on her ankles. She rubbed them to make sure but there was no mistaking these symptoms.

"Mum, I think I've got purpura. Sorry."

"Oh, no, Rosie, don't tell me that! You've been so well for months now. Let me see?"

Quickly her mother checked all the stress points. The telltale purple rash was there on the neck... on the ankles... inside the mouth... on the tongue...

" Back to bed, Rosie. I've got an emergency supply of steroids so I'll give you 80 mg and call Dr Hill. He'll probably want to see you today. Have you got a cough or sore throat or anything? Is your neck stiff?"

"I'm fine, Mother, just a bit tired! Will you phone the Supermarket for me?" She was grateful to put her head back on the pillow.

Her platelets fell rapidly and by that evening Rosie had widespread purpura and was running a fever. She slept fitfully and hallucinated badly through the night. The green men appeared on her wallpaper and the snake came out of the wardrobe. Her mother slept on her floor on the spare mattress just in case she went walkabout as she was inclined to do when running a high temperature. She was given paracetamol and juice every four hours.

It was a long night.

In the morning she was bleeding from the mucus membranes inside her mouth and had a small red patch on the white of one eye. Her mother's fingerprints were on the flesh of her slim shoulders where she had held her to coax her back into bed through the night, away from the gremlins on the wall - even the gentlest of touches could leave fingerprints like this.

Dr Hill decided that she better be sent back to the Infirmary for monitoring and to allow the new Haematologist to see her.

Chapter 7 - Infertile

Mr Andrew Marsden, the newly appointed Consultant Haematologist at Aberdeen Royal Infirmary, scratched his head as he read the laboratory reports on the Shetland girl. He discussed the situation with his Senior Registrar, Dr Bruce King.

"Bruce, we are both aware that ***Idiopathic Thrombocytopoenic Purpura*** (ITP) is itself a rare condition, affecting only around one in twenty five thousand children, but I have never seen a case quite like this."

"I agree, Mike. In this girl, there has been sporadic recurring episodes of severe thrombocytopoenia spanning practically all of her childhood years. The great majority of the other cases we have encountered consist of a single acute attack with sudden spectacular onset and recovery within a few months at most. The remaining few cases are older patients with a chronic and more insidious form of the disorder. It is a very puzzling case."

"So, you would agree with me that this recurring acute pattern is entirely unique?"

"In my experience, yes, I've never seen a case quite like it before."

Later, Mr Marsden proceeded to dictate his medical notes, speaking slowly into the tiny hand-held tape recorder. "As on previous occasions, Rose Anderson presented with widespread bruising and petechia, oral purpura and conjunctivital haemorrhage. Haematuria developed a few hours before admission. Her platelet count was so low on arrival that it was off the scale and registered zero. There is clearly a significant risk of cerebral bleeding. I do not like the hallucinations that the girl has through the night. She has a fever and probably an underlying viral infection. I wonder if we are missing something else?"

He stopped the machine to ponder the case. The diagnosis of ITP had essentially been made by his predecessor, since retired, by exclusion of the more sinister conditions. Being new, enthusiastic and very thorough, Mr Marsden decided to run all the tests again.

He continued to dictate instructions for the ward staff, " Please take blood samples for full Haematology analyses and organise another bone marrow biopsy, from the iliac crest. I wish to rule out leukaemia, aplastic anaemia, marrow hypoplasia and consumptive coagulopathy. This time, I would also like to sent a sample to Genetics, to have a look at the chromosomes and DNA profile – tell them to look for anything unusual."

Later, with the diagnosis of ITP confirmed, Mr Marsden immediately put Rose on an 80mg daily dose of prednisolone and was considering a platelet transfusion, but the condition responded to the steroids, as it had in the past. Now, only five days later, her platelets had risen rapidly to overshoot the normal range and registered today seven hundred and fifty times ten to the power of nine per litre! He would have been happy with a more stable count nearer two hundred times ten to the power of nine per litre. He wrote up a few notes, recommending that the dose of prednisolone be reduced by halving it each day over the next week or so, and that daily blood samples be taken to monitor the stability of the platelet count.

Speaking again to Dr Bruce King a week later, Mr Marsden summarised the findings.

"There is a previous history of huge and rapid fluctuations like a seesaw in this patient. Although there has been a remission of all her symptoms for about a year now, I think it is time to consider splenectomy. I am well aware that removal of the spleen is not without risk, particularly in children, with a danger of pneumococcal septicaemia within the three years following the operation. It is not a move that I consider lightly. What do you think, Bruce?"

"I think that splenectomy is certainly justified in this patient."

"The point that really puzzles me is this unexpected report from the Cytogenetics laboratory."

"Yes, I have had trouble understanding that too. What does it say again?"

" Well, they have analysed the bone marrow and then requested a blood sample. The results on both tissues are identical."

Mr Marsden proceeded to read the report aloud to his colleague.

" *143 cells have been examined. All cells reveal an apparently balanced female mitotic karyotype with a* ***Robertsonian translocation*** *between the two homologous chromosome fifteens:*

45, XX , t(15;15)(p11;p11).

Comments.

1) The translocation appears to be present in all cells examined from blood and bone marrow, so it is considered to be a congenital anomaly, not obviously related to the patients acquired blood disorder and perfectly compatible with a normal female phenotype. A small biopsy of any other tissue e.g. skin would rule out the possibility of mosaicism.

2) Given that it is indeed present in all tissues of the body, please note that this is an ***extremely rare*** *chromosome anomaly and likely to have arisen de novo at a very early stage of development. Parental samples are requested for verification of this.*

3) While the karyotype appears to be balanced i.e. there is no obvious net gain or loss of genetic material at the chromosome level, ***this patient will be infertile.*** *The two chromosome fifteens will be unable to separate during meiosis. All egg cells will be unbalanced.*

4) We recommend that she is referred for counselling to a Genetic Clinic at the earliest opportunity."

Dr Bruce King frowned in concentration, "What a blow for a pretty young girl, to be unable to have children. Still, that will not worry her for some time yet."

"True. I think the important way forward is to stabilise the platelet count for now, and our best option is to remove the girl's spleen, since that is the organ where most of the platelets are being destroyed."

Dr King nodded his approval.

Mr Marsden resolved to speak to the patient and her mother, calling them into the Ward Office for some privacy, since this was a complicated business. He would deal with the blood disorder only and refer them to Medical Genetics for counselling on the infertility matter at a later date.

"Mrs Anderson, we've gone over the history of Rose's ITP and it seems that it may be unlikely that she will spontaneously recover from this recurring affliction. We still have no idea what is triggering these attacks. Viral infection is still the prime candidate, but she has already met most of the common childhood illnesses and should have built up immunity to these by now. She's had so many dangerous episodes over the years that I feel perhaps a splenectomy is now the right course of action."

Mary looked uncertain and asked several questions, establishing that older children could easily survive without a spleen, after all many splenectomies were done following car accidents or such like. However, if they went ahead, Rosie would have to take antibiotics every day for many years, as a prophylactic measure.

Rose listened intently, taking it all in. She chose the best time to intervene. She was a very intelligent child. She had read much about her condition, during enforced absences from school, gleaning most of her information from the Internet.

"Mr Marsden, I do not wish you to remove my spleen, since there is nothing wrong with it. You don't know what causes my ITP, but it seems to me that there is no use in correcting one problem which is poorly understood by introducing another problem."

"Well, Rosie, but we ***are*** trying to do our best to improve your quality of life. It is no fun being sick so often, missing school, being restricted in sports and spending time far from home, in a hospital, with doctors sticking needles in you all the time. There is a good chance that you would feel very much better if we removed your spleen."

" But there's nothing wrong with it, is there? And it's not a reversible action: if I did not feel better, you couldn't put it back again, could you? As I see it, Doctor, it is just juggling with statistics. At present, I have about a 1% risk of having a brain haemorrhage when my platelets are down?"

"That's exactly correct," he replied with mild surprise.

"And, if my spleen is removed, I have about a 1%, or perhaps even 2%, risk of contracting an overwhelming infection, even if I take pills for the rest of my life?"

"I wouldn't like to put an exact risk figure on that, Rosie, but there is a small finite risk."

"Then, I do not want you to take away my healthy spleen. I'd like to keep it please."

Mr Marsden was taken aback. He was not used to having his proposed treatment regimes questioned by a child, but she was a bright fifteen-year-old and he could not disagree with her simple logic.

Mary Anderson said nothing during this discussion but nodded in the direction of her daughter. There was an unmistakable flash of pride in the maternal smile, before she eventually added, "Can we think about what you've said, Mr Marsden?"

"Yes, of course you can, and I will respect your final decision, whatever it is."

There was an awkward silence. Rosie and her mother thanked him and stood up to leave the room.

"Er... However, before you leave, there is another matter that I must mention. I was going to leave it to my Genetic colleagues, but I can see that Rosie is a mature and intelligent girl, so it is perhaps better not to postpone it...."

...

Over the next three weeks, Rosie absorbed the information given to her with a quiet dignity. She took full advantage of the session with the Consultant Geneticist by asking many questions. He showed her the photographs of her strangely packaged genetic blueprint. The prints clearly showed that two of her chromosomes were fused together.

To explain the normal scenario, the consultant used Coca-Cola!
" Normal people have two cans of Coca-Cola so that when their bodies made eggs or sperm, one can goes into each egg or each sperm. Let's represent the eggs and sperm with these "shopping bags." To demonstrate, here I have a white carrier bag with "EGG" written on it, and a blue bag reading "SPERM." When the "SPERM" fertilises the "EGG," the resulting baby has two cans of Coca-Cola."

Rose nodded. "Do I ***not*** have two cans of Coca-Cola then?"

"Well, you have the same amount of Coca-Cola as everyone else, Rose, but it is in a large bottle like this, double the size of the cans. Because of the way it is packaged, it is just impossible to cut this bottle in half and to distribute its contents equally between two shopping bags. Each bag would end up unbalanced with either the big bottle of Coca-Cola or none at all."

"Thus when a SPERM comes along with its can of coke to fertilise my EGG, the baby ends up with far too much Coke - the bottle ***and*** one can, or far too little coke - ***just*** one can?"

"You've got it exactly right. Well done, Rose."

Rose found it surprisingly easy to follow this logic. Yet her heart was sore. She felt imperfect, defective and not good enough. She felt angry at the injustice of the situation and frustrated with her lack of control.

She switched off her emotions.
She distanced herself from the problem

Yet, she remained fascinated by the science involved. She resolved then and there that her career lay in this area. Genetics was surely the base science of all life.

A skin sample was cultured confirming that the same strange karyotype existed in every cell in her body. It was not inherited from her mother or father. It was a brand new mutation, affecting only one in tens of thousands of people! Molecular techniques were performed also, Rose saw her own unique DNA fingerprint - it looked like the bar codes she had seen on supermarket groceries.

This was her bar code.

She was hungry for knowledge. How did it happen? They knew ***when:*** at the single cell stage of embryonic existence - right there in the fertilised egg that produced her - but they did not know what had caused this error to occur. Mutation at the gene and chromosome level could and did occur spontaneously all the time in dividing tissue, in a very small number of instances, perhaps once in a million divisions. It could be induced by certain carcinogenic drugs or by nuclear irradiation. However, sometimes it just happened and nobody knew why.

Mr Marsden did not think the chromosome anomaly was related to her ITP, but the situation was so rare that he could not be certain.

Rose read avidly about the Genetics of Man and gleaned that it was a well-accepted fact that 1% of the population have a chromosome abnormality. Furthermore, about one in every thousand had the particular type of abnormality called a ***Robertsonian translocation***, where two chromosomes were fused together, giving them only 45 chromosomes instead of 46. Such people looked entirely normal and would not know that they had any abnormality, until they tried to reproduce. The majority of cases came to light following investigations due to reproductive failure of some sort.

She read books on Animal Genetics too, learning how each different species of plant and animal is defined by their chromosome number:

"Man is closely related to the great apes in evolutionary terms and it is generally accepted that men and monkeys share common ancestry.

Perhaps our closest living relative is Gorilla gorilla , a great ape with 48 chromosomes, or 24 pairs. It is important to appreciate that when two fairly similar organisms have different numbers of chromosomes, they are normally no longer able to interbreed and are thus considered as separate species. Occasionally interspecies breeding is successful, but the offspring are usually sterile e.g. A horse may be crossed with a donkey, resulting in an infertile ass. It is intriguing that microscopically, Homo sapiens differs from Gorilla gorilla by only two ***Robersonian*** *fusions. Although, of course, there are many differences at the sub-microscopic gene level."*

Rose had run the gauntlet of another episode of the ITP and her platelets had eventually settled at a healthy level. She felt better and stronger within herself. She felt ***different,*** but then she had always known in her heart that she was ***different***. She had never really related to her peer group on a best friend basis. Associations had been shallow, with just a thin veneer of friendship.

The best relationships she had ever had were with animals.

Like the ass, she was a barren creature, separated by her chromosomes from the rest of Mankind. She may look normal, but she differed from *Homo sapiens* almost as much as a gorilla did.

Chapter 8 - The Mart

It was hard surviving as a teenager in Lerwick when you just did not fit the mould! Rose did not share the typical interests of her peer group. She had no desire to make girly talk about fashion clothes, make-up – or boyfriends! She felt excluded. She was isolated by her stigma and desperately lonely, but she would never admit to that.

At first, she tried going along with the gang to local discos, or standing around in the doorways of Lerwick's shops on a Saturday afternoon. She even went to the Market Cross and swigged beer with the rest – once! She wheezed from the cigarette smoke and one young lady in their midst puked in Church Lane. Enough was enough!

Everybody wanted to make Rose fit their expectations. However, she was ***different*** and must find her own way. Meanwhile, she looked everywhere for allies.

The men from the Klondyke ships were ***different***. The crews from these Russian factory ships invaded Lerwick in the herring-fishing season. They were welcome enough, but certainly different. Foreigners, sticking together in little groups. Sometimes a particular ship was there for several weeks, undergoing essential repairs. It could even be stranded for months, if the Russian Company refused to pay the bill. Occasionally these ships had to be fumigated to control rat infestation. Yet the crews were friendly and cheerful.

Klondyke foraging parties scoured the town's rubbish tip for treasure: discarded washing machines with a good motor or fridges that might be repaired. They walked through Commercial Street with their bounty of old car tyres and expired mail order catalogues, full of consumables about which to dream. They chatted together in their foreign tongue and were united in charity shop clothing. They had nothing. Yet, they had each other and a common purpose.

Rose watched them as she pursued solitary outdoor pursuits, cycling or walking. Sometimes she hung around with Olafur, an Icelandic boy with a malformed foot, who did not walk very well. They took to looking in the town skips and setting out anything that might be of interest for the Klondyke lads to find. They were thought of as weirdos and were to be avoided.

Rose excelled in Science and Mathematics, with little apparent effort. She was labelled as aloof and snooty: a swot; a nerd. She told her family, categorically, that she would be a career woman and that her future lay in a University Education. She would ***never*** marry and ***did not want*** children of her own anyway.

Granny did not understand the whole business of being infertile, "How can they tell that in a young lass?" She had insisted, "She is perfectly able to have children when she's ready. She's a woman now already. It's all these new fangled scientists with their artificial foods and such like. They shouldn't brainwash the lass like that. Fresh air and a good wholesome diet will do wonders for Rosie. She's too skinny. She just needs feeding up."

Granddad was little better when it came to understanding, but at least he accepted the long-term diagnosis of the experts and then put the idea from his mind. It was not a current concern. The lass was well enough for the time being and new cures were being found for infertility every day. She was only a teenager still. There was plenty of time. He was glad to have her back home and spending Christmas holidays at the croft again. She spent a lot of her time with them, especially now that her mother, Mary, had taken up with an Engineer working at the Oil Terminal.

During this period, Rosie took an ever-increasing interest in plant breeding, carefully documenting the characteristics of the roses in her grandmother's greenhouse. She became quite an expert at grafting buds from one plant on to the rootstock of the wild briar. She tried various cross-pollination experiments.

For her sixteenth birthday, Jim Jacobson gave Rose 10 ewes of her own. One of them was black. This immediately kindled her curiosity. Grandda's ram was white and a good stock-getter. She carefully explained the situation to Jim.

"Eighteen lambs have been born now, Grandda, including a black male from this black mother. It looks as if the colour black is behaving as ***an autosomal dominant trait***."

Jim smiled and winked his approval at her. She continued,
"Can we keep this black ram, Grandda? I've named him Black & Decker."

Jim laughed.

In subsequent years, Black & Decker's offspring were 50% black and 50% white lambs, including several sets of twins with one white and one black. This confirmed that the black gene was dominant and not carried on a sex chromosome, since males and females were equally affected.

Rose persuaded her grandfather to have Black & Decker tested for scrapie resistance and they found him to be very suitable to breed resistance into her small flock.

She spent more time with her animals, or on her own, than with her peer group.

Jim was a regular visitor to the livestock market in Lerwick, although he was not one of the big players in the field of Shetland Agriculture. As is inevitable in small island places, the market was often dominated by the local dealers. They assumed important positions, elevated above the mere crofters, who were entirely at their mercy. Now it is a myth that everybody gets on happily together at small island markets. Some fight tooth and nail over minor disputes that get magnified with time. Ownership of animals can determine their sales potential. If a face does not fit, the price will be low. Rosie's lambs did not sell for very high prices, especially the black ones. She was amazed to find a colour prejudice in sheep! She had weighed them all before the sale and the black ones were, on average, heavier than their white counterparts. Nevertheless, the dealers did not want them.

It was no good being ***different***, even if you were just a sheep!

As well as learning about the qualities desirable in the livestock, Rosie took the opportunity of studying the curious species that ran the Mart. Each of the prominent main players reminded her of an animal.

The lion of the pack was around fifty years old, quite a handsome specimen, although his features were a bit saggy now and he had accumulated a few extra kilos with good living over the years. He often arrived late to the sales, delaying the onset. He rolled up in a fancy four-wheel-drive and was permanently glued to his other status symbol – the ubiquitous mobile phone! Whenever he arrived, office girls ran to him with messages, and timid followers paid him whispered tributes.

A small weasel hung to his coat tails, fingers stained with nicotine and breath smelling of stale whisky. Amidst the clamour of the regular wolf pack around the auction ring, a real mutt of a dog and a grizzly bear stood close-by the lion. Then there was the sly fox, who sometimes adopted the role of friend and sometimes slunk away with a cynical scowl and shifty eyes, to trigger of an undercurrent of opposition bidding. One fellow looked for all the world like a mole, with his tiny black eyes and uncanny ability to sneak around in his underground passages and pop up in strategic positions to listen and absorb useful information for his master. Rosie seldom heard him speak, but had to acknowledge his unquestioning ferreting ability.

The auctioneer was a puppet on a string, responsive to the Lion Master. Unwanted rival bidders were fixed with a vice-like stare and frequently backed down, keeping the prices artificially low. This was particularly noticeable when the stock in the ring belonged to an unfortunate small crofter who had fallen out of favour with the native wildlife of the Mart.

The Lion King had an easy charm of sorts, and was clearly a master of manipulation of the other animals. Rosie watched him bid with a studied nonchalance, using silent nods and winks. She did not like him but she admired him.

Her life's experience told her clearly that some animals are better than human beings and some men are worse than animals! With the exception of Granddad, and perhaps Olafur, the more Rosie saw of men, the more she preferred the four-legged variety of animal!

Granddad took her for fish and chips after the Mart sale. They walked past the harbour where a small group of Russians were manoeuvring an old car on to two planks that were precariously perched on the deck of a small ferryboat. Under cover of twilight, they were making a desperate effort to secure the MOT-failed vehicle and transport the prize out to the mother ship. Rose nodded to them. One waved and ventured a smile of recognition.

Rosie and Jim walked on up to the Knab, eating hot chips from the paper. Darkness was beginning to fall as they headed for home. The Klondykers were lit up in the harbour, a floating city, beautiful and sparkling, like brash costume jewellery, decorating poverty.

Chapter 9 – New Millennium

It was the start of a new millennium.

University life was a voyage of discovery for Rose. It did not matter how ***different*** you were. The kaleidoscope of human life was mesmerising. Every nationality of student was housed there. Variant personalities abounded: shy mathematicians; dominating and confident public school boys; the wild colourful dressers; black Goths - the whole heady mix of emerging youth - and all with IQs that made for the most stimulating late night discussions, even if you did not agree.

Rose loved it: the learning opportunities; the debating societies; the art and music exhibitions. There was too much stimulation and not enough time to experience it all.

Rose met Richard Martin during her first year at Aberdeen University. She literally bumped into him at an Art Exhibition. As she stepped back to squint at an obscure piece of modern art, she collided with the slightly built young man behind her, spilling red wine down his white silk shirt. That was the start of a special friendship with a human being, of a kind she had never had before. She connected easily with Richard, in the same way that she normally bonded with animals.

Immediately she turned to make her grovelling apologies, she knew he was Gay, but it just registered fleetingly across her mind as an observation and was of no consequence. In fact, she felt, right away, that they had something in common: they were both ***different***. Having avoided boys to prevent the inevitable explanations and likely rejection she foresaw due to her freakish genetic problem, Rose felt completely unthreatened by this gentle soul. He was open, friendly and highly intelligent. There was an instant chemistry and sincere acceptance. After they had negotiated a deal, that she must wash his shirt, by hand, in *Fairy Liquid*, no less, their attention returned to the art.

The instrumental picture was one of these three dimensional affairs, formed from a myriad of tiny multi-coloured dots.

"I can see nothing but a mess of coloured speckles," Rose admitted.

"Well, it is a little bit like a carpet in a student flat."

"Why a carpet in a student flat?"

"After a chicken biryani and fifteen pints!" She laughed with him.

"Seriously though, one has to learn the technique for viewing these pictures. Don't look for a two dimensional image. Let your eyes look deeper and open up your mind. Being technical, one eye must focus on the surface and the other on an imaginary plane behind the surface." Richard crossed his eyes, that were mischievously aglint behind silver-rimmed glasses, and pulled a funny face in an attempt to demonstrate.

"Or some folk can achieve the same effect by blinking very rapidly." He fluttered his long eyelashes and placed one hand on his hip at the same time.

Rose spluttered with laughter at his unabashed self-mockery.

After trying various techniques, the hidden composition slowly appeared like magic. It congealed and solidified in the third dimension. There was a jug of flowers, plump and rounded with a handle that could almost be grasped. It was so real that she stretched out her hand and touched the delicate petals. It was a moment she would never forget. She had seen a new view of life. She would never again doubt what could materialise from apparent chaos if she looked hard enough and opened her eyes to a different way of seeing the world.

Over the following months, they met regularly twice a week at the Gallery or took in a film, or just went for a coffee and a chat. Richard quickly probed her past life with his exacting questions and clever cross-examination. He was direct and succinct - a budding lawyer. Rose had no qualms in telling her story in a way that gave it a whole new significance. Richard made her revisit her past. He was like a fresh breeze blowing through a stale attic, seeing value and excitement and meaning in every ordinary event. She realised how very special her Shetland freedom had been, and through his interest and genuine enthusiasm, she saw herself differently. Yet however many times she skimmed over her genetic problem, Richard sensed unresolved anguish, and empathised. He taught her not to think of herself as a leper and he gave her a crash course in how to survive as "just ***different***" in a hostile world. How to avoid drugs and repel the advances of ignorant dope-heads and uncultured, over-sexed men who were, frankly, boring.

“Be true to yourself, Rose. Say piss-off mate!”

Richard was extremely choosy. She felt safe with his choice of men. He introduced her to his family of supporting friends on the Gay scene. Having been completely unaware of this substantial sector of the population, since she had never encountered an openly Gay individual in her sheltered Shetland upbringing, she was amazed at their numbers. They seemed to be everywhere. Was it the case that they were increasing in number? Or were they simply able in this new Millennium, to come out into the public eye more easily with less fear of rejection - among the young generation at any rate. Rose suspected the latter. Bias still prevailed among the older people. In many cases the Gay youths had been rejected by their own parents. They survived in their alternative family groups.

Rose excelled in the University environment, putting just enough of her energies into her work. She studied Genetics, as she had vowed to do. Although his course in the Law Department was very different, Richard shared many of Rose's interests and they both participated in political and ethical debates.

Richard taught her that it was possible to have a caring relationship without any thought of marriage or other promise of commitment. There were many people around who had made a conscious decision ***not*** to have children. She was just like them in essence. There were too many children in the world already anyway.

At the same time, Rose lost her virginity in that Millennium year, to a member of another minority group. Narish Jaffrey was a sweet young Indian student, a brilliant engineer who topped his classes in all subjects. He was her bedfellow for the next eighteen months, along with his books.

"I didn't realise you worked so much, Narish, Everybody thinks you do no studying." She ventured to comment.

"Rosie, you don't open dat book, how da hell you know what's in dat book?" Was his brief response.

Narish did not waste his words and was very down to earth. Dark and handsome, with the hairiest chest she had ever seen, he had no inhibitions. He was a lover of exceptional talent. Thus they supported one another during the peak stress periods of their respective studies. The relationship was of mutual benefit in the artificial University environment, but true love was never in the equation, just physical and mental satisfaction.

Between Richard and Narish, Rose had all she needed during those critical early years away from home. She lost all fear of loneliness. She was no longer an immature girl, but a woman and she liked herself.

When his degree was finished, Narish went back to India, to an arranged marriage with one of his own cast.

Chapter 10 – Albert Ross

Rose had chosen to study in Aberdeen simply because of the relative ease of travelling home to Shetland now and then. She found that she needed sanctuary occasionally, when her studies floundered or personal stress weighed her down. She always returned at Christmas and summer holidays. She enjoyed the stark contrast. During term time, when she needed a bolt hole to escape the artificial world of University, Shetland beckoned.

So it was that when the romance of convenience with Narish ended, Rose felt at a low ebb and went North to be revitalised

She had a much better relationship with her mother now that they lived apart, and everyday familiarity did not breed contempt, yet it was always with her grandfather that she felt most at home.

Jim Jacobson was now eighty-eight, a tall stately old man, lean and wiry, with a stoop accentuated in recent years. He was wrinkled with laughter lines and exercised every crease in his skin whenever Rose came home. His hair was thinning at the temples now and he was a little deaf. His big hands still felt like sandpaper, but the skin on the back of them was paper thin and covered with liver spots.

He greeted her in his usual way, saying in a very loud voice, "My goodness, my Guinness... Wha is dis young wife? Let me look at dee Rosie!" After big hugs and much squeezing, he would hold her from him and say, "And what does du tink o' me noo?"

Rose replied as she had done countless times before, switching automatically into her Shetland dialect, "Weel, du's just da cat's quiskers, Grandda!"

Then he'd rub his whiskers on her cheek and say "An' hoo wid du lik ta be mairried tae me?"

"Oh, dat wid be da bee's knees Grandda!" He'd guffaw with laughter, eyes shining with pleasure.

Heather shook her head at the childish antics of the pair of them.

"His du fun nae cure for auld age at yun college yit, Rose?"

"Du'll never be old, Grandda, du'll always be twenty-one!"

Yet she could see that the old man was failing.

It was during that tonic trip to Shetland in the aftermath of her affair with Narish that the thought first came to her. She was walking on a remote part of the bare hill, the old sheepdog at her feet. She had been reading the "Shetland Times" earlier and had noted with interest that Albert Ross had returned to the islands again. Albert Ross was an albatross, who had been coming to the Hermaness gannet colony for several years. Poor Albert, there was something wrong with his navigation mechanism. He was in the wrong hemisphere, searching in vain every year for a mate among the gannets!

There was a stiff breeze blowing. Freed of distraction, Rose had a clarity of mind that allowed lateral thinking. She was empathising with Albert's loneliness. She felt very strong. Recent advice from Richard entered her head, "Be as eccentric as you like Rose... but stick with an outcast community... there's safety in numbers." The Gay community had certainly organised themselves for maximum mutual support and they had given her friendship and sanctuary... but she was like Albert among the gannets...

She had a rare chromosome abnormality.
She was ***different***, but was she the only one in the world?
Could there be others out there exactly like her?
She had access to Bio-banks and Genetic Registers.
She could run a search.

...

The attack on the World Trade Centre on the 11th September 2001, when two passenger planes were hijacked by the terrorists and deliberately flown into the two high rise buildings was almost unbelievable. Rose and her friends were shocked and horrified. What drove such a deadly act of destruction? How could anyone be so desperate as to become a suicide pilot with no respect for other lives whatsoever? She had no television set, but spent many hours in Richard's flat watching the story unfold. As they watched Fox News

Live on 23rd September, there was stunned silence between them. Hundreds were confirmed dead. Over six thousand remained missing and an equivalent number were injured. A third plane had crashed into the Pentagon and one hundred and eighteen bodies had been recovered from that site.

All evidence pointed to the known terrorist Usama Bin Laden and his "Al Quida" network. They disappeared. President Bush declared war against Terrorism. Tony Blair pledged his support. 89% of the population favoured military action. Other nations united to form a remarkable coalition with the common aim of fighting the apparatus of Terrorism on a variety of fronts: political, financial, legal, economic and military. A large task force was in place within nineteen days.

Slovakia opened its airspace to the US and Saudi bases were manned in preparation for a war against Afghanistan, despite protests from the Pope and fear of civilian casualties. Economic sanctions on Pakistan were lifted and Venezuelan bank accounts were frozen.

It was discovered that the terrorist organisations had large investments in legitimate businesses, many in the UK, involving property and stocks and shares.

Commercial Airlines were crippled overnight, laying off one hundred and twenty-one thousand workers. Bush signed over a £15 billion airline relief fund and another fund for victims and their families, many of whom were firemen caught in the debris, when the buildings collapsed.

Yet the coalition with certain countries was a very fragile one, particularly where the Islamic faith had a stronghold. Terrorism knows no bounds in terms of political unity and has no religion in common.

Rose recognised it as an extremely dangerous destabilising force. Worldwide.

Her thoughts of searching Genetic Registers for those like herself were put on the back boiler, fading into insignificance in the light of World Affairs.

Ongoing terrorist attacks plagued Israel and the USA. Suicide bombers killed thousands. The anthrax letters killed only dozens, but scared millions. It was psychological warfare rather than true Bio-warfare. Yet the potential of the microbe as an agent for mass destruction was evident to Rose and she discussed this with Richard many times.

They did not always agree completely on matters of war. Richard's viewpoint was strong, "Terrorism of this kind can cut through the fabric of our society like a hot knife through butter, Rose, mocking the laws of civilised nations, who have to fight back with a handicap of conscience, with one hand tied behind their back."

"Does that imply that all terrorists have no conscience and all civilised nations do?"

"Not really. In fact, I think that civilised nations can behave like terrorists. Israel for example."

"Exactly - and yesterday's terrorist can be today's world leader – look at Nelson Mandela?"

Yet, for the most part, their minor arguments served merely to stimulate each other's minds and they remained the very closest of friends.

Islamic clerics warned of a Holy War like no other that had ever been before.

Chapter 11 - David

The ***Human Immunodeficiency Virus*** (HIV) which causes AIDS silently seeped from the rainforests in the heart of Africa during the 1970s. David MacKay was born in the middle of that same decade, far away from the danger of such infection, in Edinburgh. David's childhood years coincided with the time that HIV began its mass infiltration of human hosts. Africans were already culturing vast quantities of this virus before it began hitch-hiking along the transcontinental Kinshasa highway, advancing westwards, like a haar, travelling via the intimate-contact taxi service.

By the late twentieth century, AIDS was on the increase even in heterosexual circles. It was rife globally, and certainly common in Edinburgh.

Anybody with a promiscuous lifestyle or a casual drug habit was at risk. David was no exception. He was wild and carefree. He had played the field, perhaps more than most of his peer group.

David gave the outer appearance of being brash and insensitive. It was a good disguise. He had been a quiet and sensitive child, frequently ill due to his rare autoimmune condition. His younger brother Mark had been the perfect one in the family, never ill, hyperactive in fact. Mark was rowdy and disruptive, frequently disobedient and often the cause of trouble. Yet Mark had been the apple of his mother's eye. Their mother Kate had been the boss in the family, a hard-working and forceful woman. Their father, Peter, was shy but much more refined. David had been gently educated by his father, who had taken on the role of the househusband as Kate became the main breadwinner. They had spent a lot of his childhood days reading when he was too sick for school. He had missed around one week in every month. During that time, David had acquired a basic appreciation of the Arts and Literature.

Tragedy struck during a family seaside holiday when David was ten and his brother eight years old. They had rented a self-catering cottage in Gardenstown, on the East Coast of Scotland. Kate had gone to fetch supplies from the village and to send a fax; she seldom got far away from work. Mark had insisted on making a raft with driftwood and string. David and Peter had gone along with the idea, as they did with many of Mark's whims, especially when he whined until he got his own way. David had even pushed him off from the shore, in the home made contraption, knowing that Mark was a good enough swimmer.

The weather conditions were dull but calm.

Mark was only a few critical yards from the shore when the raft started to sink. David and Peter had laughed at him, delighted to see him getting a soaking. The little upstart deserved it. The unstable floating platform tipped sideways and then turned upside down. David laughed even louder. However, Mark was hit on the head by his makeshift mast. At the same time, his foot got caught in the loops of knotted string and he could not break free.

Both Peter and David had gone to the rescue then, but it was too late to save the boy. They had pulled a lifeless body from the wreck, minus one trainer. They had tried for an hour or more to resuscitate Mark. Peter had frantically performed cardiac massage. That freak accident killed Mark but it injured David and his father permanently. Kate went mad for a while and blamed Peter for his lack of responsible supervision. David resented that. David was never accused in words, but he felt the burden of guilt in every look from his mother and, from that time on, it was lodged deep within himself.

For a while after the terrible accident, David became withdrawn and morose. However, he changed with the surge of testosterone at puberty and it was then that he displayed all his pent-up anger. This was aided by the fact that his health showed a dramatic improvement when Kate eventually agreed with the consultant Haematologist that David's spleen should be removed to stop the recurring infections.

David developed a determination never to be hen-pecked by a woman, as he believed his father to be. The teenage David had rebelled violently against parental authority. With no strong paternal influence, he had quickly become troublesome and unruly. Subconsciously he tried to mimic how Mark might have behaved. His student days had been one long party, with wine, women and drugs. Miraculously, he had managed to complete a degree in Business Studies, despite the minimum of study, but, after graduating, he was loath to take a real job and to actually work for a living.

He was confident with women, who seemed to find him charming, although he treated them all with a certain underlying contempt. He had been very close to his brother Mark, despite their different characters, but he never sought to get close to anybody again, especially not a woman. He preferred his girlfriends to be from rich and cultured backgrounds, spoilt by their parents, but with a wild streak like his brother. ***Rich bitches***, he called them to his male friends, daddy's girls. He delighted in using and abusing gullible young ***rich bitches***. He became hard and uncaring. He pretended to hate his mother, while at the same time, he strove to be more like her. He put on a good act, nobody would ever guess it was a veneer. Even at that time of his life, when he was off the rails completely, David had a secret soft centre.

He was not tall, his growth having been stunted by the steroids used to keep his ITP at bay, but he was slim, muscular, and had a rugged natural look, if a little unkempt. He had shaved his head in his late teens, to make him look more macho, but later he let his wavy brown hair grow and it softened his appearance.

It was only when his life was touched personally by further tragedy that the immature and dangerous nature of his trendy lifestyle registered. His latest girlfriend, Lisa, was diagnosed HIV positive in 1998. His father had a heart attack and passed away in that same year. A week after his father's funeral, Lisa died of opportunistic pneumonia.

Despite the odds, all David's tests for HIV were negative. He considered himself to be a lucky guy. He vowed then to sober up and get his life together. He kicked his social drug habit. He made amends with his mother and moved back home for a while, because he could see that she had been hit very hard by the death of his father. He liked the fact that she needed him at last. Besides, there were only the two of them left now. Kate welcomed David's unexpected support and they grew closer than they had been for years.

It was during that time of mutual grief that David met and befriended Brenda. She was the part–time Administrative Assistant for Equinox Limited, the family business that had been run by his parents, mainly his mother. Brenda was several years older than David, not a rich bitch, but a sophisticated and intelligent woman, with a kind and giving nature. Kate had become good friends with Brenda, and her flat-mate Betty, over the past few years. They had gone regularly to a Salsa dancing class together, although that activity ceased after Peter's untimely death. Brenda remained a regular visitor to the McKay house, and she was easily seduced by a young man trying to impress and reform. Brenda was smitten and desperate to encourage both David's reformation, and his attentions.

A few months later, Brenda was pregnant. Kate was not best pleased with her son's role in the affair, especially since most of the courting had gone on under her nose and under her roof. The pressure was put upon David to take responsibility for his actions and marry Brenda. She was mature enough to handle David's wildness and would make an excellent mother for Kate's first grandchild.

Such pressure from any women would never have worked on David, but the bribery did. Kate cleverly offered him a 50% share in Equinox Ltd., providing he settled down with Brenda, and went to work full time in the company. As David had a mountain of debts and a genuine fondness for Brenda, he agreed to his mother's proposal and rose to the challenge.

David and Brenda were married in November and moved to a flat of their own in the Dean Village. He became less rebellious, but never entirely predictable and certainly not domesticated. He had given up hard drugs, but still grew cannabis in the wardrobe using a daylight bulb. Brenda disapproved, silently. He found himself looking forward to fatherhood.

Brenda miscarried and lost their baby in December.

Driven by a mixture of disappointment, guilt and anger, David suddenly had a sense of true purpose. He became determined to make a real success of the company, to prove to his mother and to himself that he was not a worthless failure. He concentrated his ruthless streak entirely on running the company. As a result, he became a great success in the cut-throat world of business. He felt in total control of his life. His future was secure.

...

David sat in front of the monitor as the spreadsheet he had tailored to meet the company's needs gave him the latest end of month sales trends. Equinox Ltd. was a small manufacturer of animal feedstuffs. It had been growing in success over the past two years largely due to his marketing efforts and the quality of its products, particularly the herbal remedies for horses. David's parents had started the company almost twenty years ago. His father, Peter, had been the Accountant, setting up the financial records and dealing with VAT and tax matters. He also had a little knowledge of how to source and purchase the raw ingredients. However, it was Kate who possessed the knowledge about the nutritional components and the herbs. Kate was a graduate in Biochemistry, who had worked for a few years as an Animal Dietician before they started Equinox Ltd.

Following Peter's death, Kate had scaled down her personal activities within the company, allowing David to expand the business and effectively triple its worth from £2 million to £6 million. Kate simply did not care so much once her husband died. It had been an unconventional marriage, where dominance and compliance were never quite what they seemed to outsiders, but Kate had loved her husband. She was relieved to see her son clean up his lifestyle and take a genuine interest in the family business. She retired to rural Aberdeenshire, where her mother still lived.

When she had the reins, Kate had insisted that the company invest in nutritional research right from the very start. Their steady sponsorship of projects at the Royal School of Veterinary Studies in Edinburgh had paid off since they benefited from awareness of new products, allowing the rapid inclusion of these state of the art ingredients into their own range of feeds. They were also privileged to receive early warnings of new findings at the cutting edge of nutritional science from Kentucky Equine Research, USA. The company policy had been to source the very best raw materials, even if it meant paying a little bit more. As a result of their emphasis on quality, they had been rewarded with a growing list of loyal retail outlets and satisfied customers. Equinox Ltd. had fared particularly well during the saga of BSE because they did not use any protein from recycled animal offal. It was said in the business that what Equinox rejected went down the road to the Kellogg's factory!

David was a little less scrupulous in his sourcing of materials. Price was his most important factor. Buy low and sell high was the way to triple the profits in the business! He drove a top of the range red Saab. He encouraged Brenda to give up full time work and concentrate more on starting a family. He employed a new Administrative Assistant in the form of a full time Personal Secretary and also an aggressive Salesman to push the company's products further afield.

A graphic analysis automatically appeared as David had programmed it to do. At a glance, he absorbed the salient information. He picked up the Dictaphone: "Hi, Diane, it's late. I'm back from the course and it was a bloody waste of time, so now I've got to catch up an all the things I didn't get done today! He left three clear instructions for Diane, his efficient and very patient Personal Secretary.

Turning to the memos, there were four. One was from the graphic artist who was working on the packaging for the latest drug for arthritis sufferers, a spin-off from their equine nutrition work, now destined for the human market. A couple of draft designs were ready to look at. He gave Diane the go ahead to call a meeting within the next few days, but to avoid Friday afternoon. He needed John Angus to be there as well. The second message was from Ms Slaney-Jones, probably another eager student ***rich bitch*** on some far-fetched, impractical, time-wasting mission. He threw it on the pending file. Where did all these bloody Mizzes come from? A third message was from his mother who had just enquired generally how things were going. Finally, there was the ubiquitous "Call Brenda" note.

Poor Brenda, she suffered from depression and nondescript malaise. She was finding it hard to cope with their married life as well now. No David for twenty-four hours a day, and no family nearby, even Kate had cleared off to Aberdeenshire. Her surging hormones exacerbated this. She was recovering from her third miscarriage in eighteen months. She longed for a child but something must be wrong with her. David did not ring her, but phoned the late florist on the corner and asked for a dozen long stemmed red roses to be left in the pub next door. He would collect them on the way home, before closing time. The florist knew his credit card number.

He listened to the news headlines as he drove home through the streets of Edinburgh to their penthouse flat in the old converted mill in the Dean Village. It was all bad. *A child had been murdered when delivering newspapers; a family home had burned down; a teenager in America had shot fourteen of his classmates and then himself...*

Brenda was asleep when he got home, slumped in the sofa with a pile of tissues and a half-empty bottle of Southern Comfort. He wondered whether to wake her, but decided instead to chuck a blanket over her and go to the kitchen in search of food. As he opened the fridge door, he recalled the joke he'd heard on the Time Management Course:

" Why are married men fat and single men thin? "

" Because single men look in the fridge and go to bed, while married men look in the bed and go to the fridge! "

There were no meat products. Brenda had forced vegetarianism on the household since the BSE scare. He had tried to explain the negligible risks, but she had no faith in probability statistics after twice believing her Gynaecologist that spontaneous abortion was just one of these things and that the chances of the next baby going to term were good.

David ran his hand over his slim chest, waste and groin as if checking that he was still thin and sat down with oatcakes, cheese and olives. No bloody butter either! Just the latest brand of low-calorie, plastic margarine! Ugh! Still, he had felt better since cutting the meat out of his diet altogether and his allergic reactions had been much less of a problem since his splenectomy. Later, he placed the hand-tied bouquet of roses in the sink, still gift wrapped, and ran enough fresh water to cover the lower stems.

The late overload of cheese caused David to sleep fitfully that night. His patchy dreams were full of vivid colours, smells and textures. Brenda woke him just after 2 a.m. as she came into their bed. She was cold. The icy shadow touching his back made him flinch.

"Sorry," she whispered. He feigned sleep.

Falling easily back to the land of illusion, a nightmare claimed all his senses. *He was running from some evil, his asthmatic wheezing slowing him down. He had a great sense of urgency and was searching for something. His strange quest was vital for his very existence, yet he couldn't quite determine what it was. There were crowds of strangers wandering aimlessly with an air of hopelessness. Brenda and his mother, Kate, were clinging together in a corner, both weeping. His brother, Mark, smiled from the embrace of an identical replica of himself. The skies gathered as if a great storm were brewing.*

He woke, with a start. Sweating. Uneasy.

He lay perfectly still, glad of the reality of a bright new morning, listening to Brenda's quiet breathing and the tick of the clock. It was 5.57 a.m. He felt unclean somehow. He had a sense of great foreboding.

Nevertheless that day went smoothly. In fact, it was a satisfying day.

The business lunch had clinched the deal with the American firm and the afternoon meeting had resulted in a unanimous decision on the new design packaging. Although he grudged the inconvenience of interrupting his work schedule, David was on time for the Hospital Clinic appointment at 4.30 p.m.

He met Brenda in the Car Park and took her arm into the foyer. They had been married for almost two years now. They had tied the knot in a Registry Office and John Angus, a friend of the family who was also a priest, had blessed the union in a short private ceremony at home. This had satisfied Kate.

Brenda had changed dramatically since the marriage. She looked so thin and washed out lately. Her eyes had lost their former sparkle. She missed her work. Her grief for the lost babies had gone inwards. The carefree frivolity that they had shared briefly had evaporated from their relationship. She sometimes doubted if it would ever be the same, even if she did conceive a child. His work absorbed him so he was not quite so bothered about their childlessness. Perhaps they could adopt? David would ***not*** discuss that.

"You OK?" he asked, softly, embracing her shoulders.

She nodded and sniffed.

"I'm trying, David. It's just not easy for me. Maybe you should get rid of this old MOT failure and look for a replacement model?"

"Don't be silly, I want YOU. We'll sort it out. Perhaps we'll get some sensible advice today."

The Receptionist at Outpatients directed them up the corridor to the appropriate waiting room. David hated the clinical smell of the hospital, polished plastic odours mingling with chlorine and an artificial floral essence: attempts at fooling the senses that all was well here. The terror he had felt as a child on his frequent visits to the Paediatric Haematology Clinic came flooding back. He had hated those needles. Hospital clinics were alien yet strangely familiar places. The anxious faces of other waiting couples, linked together in quiet isolation or speaking in hushed whispers, did nothing to lift his spirits.

Dr Frank Edwards went over their history and jotted down dates – *It was eight weeks since the last miscarriage - eleven weeks gestation this time, similar to the previous two incidents. So, the pregnancies never got beyond the first trimester. The laboratory had examined the products of conception (POC) but had not managed to culture anything*. Mr Edwards explained that they needed to do some further tests and would require blood samples.

"We'll need samples from both of you this time, Mr McKay," he said, bringing out the appropriate tubes and labelling them in preparation for venepuncture.

"But why blood from me?" David queried. "You've already checked out a semen sample and my sperm count was in the normal range."

"Yes, that's correct, Mr McKay, but your wife has now had three consecutive first trimester miscarriages and that raises the possibility that we are dealing with a genetic disorder of some sort. It is normal practice to check the chromosomes of both partners. It is just a routine screening test at this stage and it may tell us nothing, but it may reassure you that all is present and correct at the cellular level and that you need only to keep on trying to have a family."

David rolled his sleeve up. He could not help noticing Brenda's arm, bruised and yellowed from previous invasion. He had escaped lightly. He resolved to try harder. He would take her out to eat that evening. He could try to take a weekend off work soon.

"The results will take around three weeks, so I'll make an appointment to see you this time next month if that is alright, Mr and Mrs McKay? In the meantime, try to put these worries out of your mind. You are both young and healthy and anatomically fine. Many couples have trouble starting a family."

Brenda was particularly clinging throughout the evening and made a big effort to be cheerful, aided by the bottle of Valpolicella that accompanied a pleasant meal of Tomato and Basil salad with sliced black olives, and Tagliattelli Pavarotti, followed by Zabaglione and Boudoir biscuits.

The Italian waiter brought them two complimentary glasses of Marsala. Something familiar about the way he moved made David wonder if he was Gay. He lent across the table and whispered to Brenda, " Another bloody woofter, eh?" He nodded in the direction of the waiter. It was clear that he did not have a lot of time for homosexuals.

"Don't be so unkind, David. He's very friendly and efficient. You really should have more time for people. We are all different you know. We all have our problems."

She looked sad and forlorn, like her drained coffee cup.

He held her as she slept, but did not attempt to make love. She would come to him when she was ready. When he drifted off to sleep, the disturbing dreams came again...

Chapter 12 – David's Diagnosis

The letter from the clinic advised that the results of the tests were ready. It was difficult for David to find time to attend a mid-afternoon appointment, but he delegated all his duties for that afternoon. It *was* important.

The clinic was running late.
Mr Edwards kept them waiting over an hour.
David became increasingly irritated.
He had work to do.
He was a busy executive!

Eventually, the Consultant ushered them into his office and told them that the problem had been diagnosed. Brenda wrung her hands and looked at the floor.

"I'm afraid that you have a very rare chromosome disorder, Mr McKay."

Brenda stared at him in disbelief, not sure that she had heard properly. David asked him to repeat what he had just said.

"There is no problem with Mrs McKay. She has an apparently normal, 46,XX female mitotic karyotype... but you, Mr McKay, are carrying a very rare chromosome rearrangement. This is the reason for your wife's recurring pregnancy losses."

David gave a nervous little laugh, "I see. Can you explain exactly what the problem is?"

"If you don't mind, Mr McKay, I'll call in my colleague from the laboratory to explain the technical stuff. He'll bring some photographs of your chromosomes to have a look at and then we'll discuss the situation in more detail."

David nodded approval.
Brenda, colour flooding into her pale face, took his hand.
He felt her own personal relief in the touch.

Dr Steven from Cytogenetics was summoned and came armed with a small bundle of high quality photographs. He introduced himself and spread the glossy prints on the table.

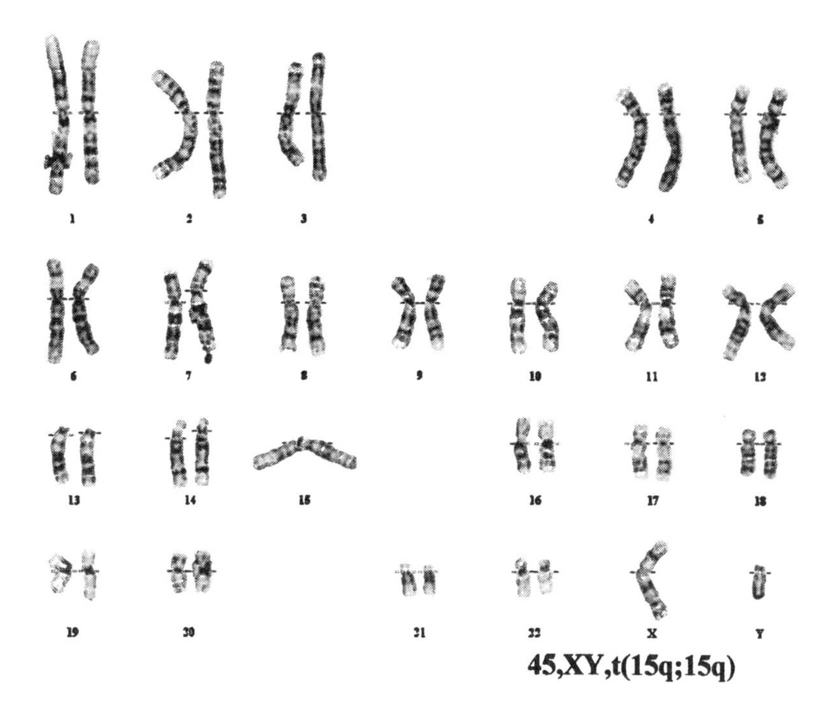

"These are dividing nuclei from white blood cells, taken with a photo-microscope, at the limits of light microscopy. The size is magnified many thousands of times. There are normally 46 of these chromosomes, 22 matching pairs and the 2 sex chromosomes, X and Y." He pointed as he spoke.

"In your case, Mr McKay, there is a ***Robertsonian translocation***. You see, here, these two chromosomes are fused together. Instead of 46, you have only 45 chromosomes."

" I see that, but what exactly is the significance of this...this Robertsonian thing? I am perfectly healthy and normal."

" Well, there is no obvious gain or loss of genetic material. It's all there, just packaged differently. However, when your cells undergo meiosis… Sorry, when you make sperm, these chromosome pairs must separate. 23 would normally go into each sperm. Another 23 are contributed by the female egg, so combining to make 46 again in the baby. In your case, there is one pair of like chromosomes, ***number 15***... Here see... these are fused together. They cannot be pulled apart when your cells divide and therefore all your sperm are abnormal containing either two fused 15s or no number 15 at all.

Robertsonian translocations are purely chance events, but it is very rare to have fusion of two homologous chromosomes… it is usually two non-alike that are fused, for example one number 13 and one number 14."

"This is all very complex," Dr Steven, "but what exactly can be done about it?"

" Absolutely nothing, Mr McKay," intervened Mr Edwards, "I am very sorry to have to tell you that you cannot father a child. All conceptions will have either monosomy 15, that is one 15 missing, or trisomy 15, that is one 15 extra. Both of these conditions are incompatible with life and will end in early abortion. This particular rearrangement is a very rare problem and one that I have never personally encountered before. I do not advise that you attempt again to have a child. When you've had some time to digest this, you may wish to consider artificial insemination from our donor bank... or perhaps you have a brother who may be prepared to donate a sample? There is nothing physically wrong with Mrs McKay. She should have no trouble conceiving a child if given normal sperm."

“You must be mistaken! There’s nothing wrong with me! I’d like a second opinion!”

“That can be arranged. However, you will get the same answer.”

“Can I go to a private consultant? Pay a higher fee perhaps?”

“You cannot ***buy*** your way out of this problem, Mr McKay. However, here is a leaflet on a private Genetic Services Clinic who are based in Harley Street, London.”

Brenda was quietly crying, rubbing her eyes with a tissue. Thoughts raced through David’s mind.

He stared at the pictures. He saw red.
There was a long heavy silence.

"Shit! I just don't believe this! Why me? Sod's law, I suppose! I guess I need time to come to terms with this lot. Look, we really must go. I've wasted my entire day with this place! Can I keep hold of these photographs?"

Over the next few days, he read everything he could find about ***Robertsonian translocations.*** His training was in Business Studies and Economics. He had only very limited knowledge of what human chromosomes looked like under a microscope. However, through the Internet, he had access to the relevant scientific literature and quickly traced the salient reviews.

These abnormalities appeared sporadically with no known cause. The incidence of the particular variety that he carried was unknown, but estimated at only one in several hundred thousand. None of the patients referred to in the documented cases had ever had children!

He was surprised to learn that the human karyotype differed only slightly from that of the great apes. In fact, the gorilla appeared to be the closest with 48 chromosomes as opposed to the 46 of man. Two *Robertsonian* fusions separated *Gorilla gorilla* and *Homo sapiens.*

So, ***Robertsonian translocations*** were enough to prevent species interbreeding. Totally.

Slowly and sadly he realised that another of these peculiar *Robertsonian* fusions separated him from the rest of Mankind. He was not the perfect guy he had thought himself to be.

His broad shoulders slumped as his great ego took a nosedive. He was a freak of nature, a mutant that could not reproduce.

Chapter 13 - Searching

Viruses are ancient, primitive, yet highly successful life forms.
Viruses can be frozen in ice and remain alive for decades.
Viruses can happily live in the casings of nuclear reactors.
One hundred million crystallised virus particles can sit on this full stop.

Rose specialising in Molecular Virology for her Honours Degree thesis. She chose to do a project involving gene insertion into cultured human cells using a safe virus. Although she was not working on a dangerous pathogenic organism, the stringent Health and Safety Regulations dictated that she must be trained to handle all cultures as if they were highly pathogenic. She became an expert at the aseptic techniques involved in human tissue culture and her knowledge of viral genetics steadily grew.

Viruses became her life.

She was fascinated by their potential to attack and infect their host. At times ambiguously alive, these sub-microscopic particles could lie around in dust for years before springing into parasitic action when conditions were right. Their versatility was astounding. Mere single strands of deoxyribonucleic acid (DNA) or ribonucleic acid (RNA), encased with a few structural proteins, minute capsules full of coded instructions. A few were beneficial to their host, but many were deadly when switched on by favourable environmental conditions... and one never saw them coming.

The medical ethics surrounding Rose's research into viral modification, as well as the related Departmental projects on gene therapy, early prenatal diagnosis, in vitro fertilisation, stem cell culture and animal cloning were always of major interest and concern to Richard. He was an excellent ally when it came to finding lawful means of progressing many of these new techniques. As a postgraduate now, with a junior position in a local Law firm, he helped Rose and her colleagues lay out the necessary applications for ethical approval to both local ethical committees and national bodies like the Voluntary Licensing Authority.

Richard and Rose had both developed a great interest in the subject of genetic modification (GM). Throughout their years at University, the global war over genetically modified crops grumbled on. Frankenstein foods, as the products for consumption became known, aroused passionate reactions among a significant proportion of the population. Monsanto, the leading commercial company who pioneering GM seeds, undertook the promotion of GM maize, soya-beans and, later, wheat products. While soya-beans and maize were headed mainly for animal feed, wheat was destined for the human plate. Monsanto underestimated the strong public opposition when marketing these biotech foods. The very term "genetically-modified" filled the lay public with fear.

Opposition groups, particularly throughout Europe, but also closer to hand in Aberdeenshire, set fire to research facilities; tore up the test fields and tried their damnedest to disrupt the production.

Rose had no problems accepting the concept of GM, in principal. She endorsed the idea that these modified plant crops were beneficially altered to fight crop pests and therefore needed much less in the way of herbicide control. She could see the economic advantages to the growers particularly in situations where pests like the European Corn Borer could cause millions of dollars worth of damage. She would much rather eat a ton of modified DNA than a ton of toxic chemicals.

Richard kept her abreast with the bulletins from the National Centre for Food and Agricultural Policy (NCFAP) in Washington. In the year 2002, the average saving for farmers using roundup-ready GM soybeans was £10 per acre. This was simply because growers had to apply Roundup only once to control all the weeds, instead of the usual three or four applications in a season. It was easy to see why 63% of the US soya-bean crop, or twenty million hectares, consisted of GM beans of this type. GM crops would always remain popular for one simple reason - money!

Rose could sympathise greatly with the potential to feed the world's growing population with cheaper foods. They were necessary if developing countries were to conquer poverty and hunger. Even drought resistance could be bred into them.

However, the world was not ready for GM foods.

Rose was a passionate supporter of the view that GM foods should be segregated and labelled as such, allowing the public free choice. Yet this was not a simple matter. The Canadian Wheat Board, which ranks third highest exporter of wheat in the world, insisted that separating GM wheat from non-GM wheat would make costs excessively high. There was also the problem of unsolicited contamination. Starlink, a GM corn with a history of causing allergic reactions in man, showed up in Taco chips! Million dollar lawsuits raged as farmers reported unwanted contamination among their non-GM crops. It proved impossible to keep GM grains separate from their wild counterparts.

Rose firmly believed that very stringent controls were necessary, to ensure that all scientific trials were complete with reference to impact on health and the environment, and that corners were not cut in the interests of boosting the profits of large commercial companies. Both Richard and herself played active roles in local safety debates on GM crops. They attended demonstrations in an attempt to keep an element of balance among the extremists. Their names were listed on the Internet by various GM interest groups, keen on the promotion of clear labelling. They both became forceful and fair speakers on the subject.

They also played a leading role in the setting up of the Internet site *eco-warrior.com*, whose opening statement read "*The life support systems of our planet are hurtling towards exhaustion. We must tread carefully. When we visit the land, we must take only photographs and leave only footprints.*"

It was during one of many late night sessions glued to her computer screen, in contact with other visitors to the *eco-warrior.com* site, visitors from countries all over the world that the thought came back to her. Here she was, easily communicating with minority groups in China and America - brought together by a common cause. She really should try to search the Genetic Registers and Bio-banks to see if there were other human beings out there with the same rare chromosome anomaly as herself! That night, her detailed strategy was pieced together during sleep, when the sub-conscious does its handiwork. She had access now to the Grampian Area Records as a starting point and it ***was*** several years ago since her diagnosis - perhaps they had diagnosed somebody else?

A search of Grampian Records revealed no match. Yet she consoled herself with the fact that there were only half a million people in Grampian and her kind of abnormality was very rare. Over the next couple of weeks, she proceeded to check the listings for all forty-two Genetic Centres in Britain. As a bone-fide research student, it was an easy matter to access the Registers. They provided only statistical data, with absolutely no details of the patients themselves. She was beginning to despair when the computer registered a match during the second week of searching - and it was a ***male*** match! Rose's heart raced and she stared unbelievably at the skimpy detail on the screen.
92/00417: 45, XY, rob t(15q:15q)

Encouraged by this success, she proceeded to search the records on the incidence of ***Robersonian translocation*** from sister Registers throughout the world. Over the next few weeks, armed with the codes to enter the Bio-banks information world-wide, she sat for hours reading screen after screen of data... Laboratory numbers.... Unit numbers... Karyotypes documented in the strange language of ISCN (International System of Chromosome Nomenclature).

Driven by an inner demon, she neglected her studies, temporarily. Her desktop and floor became littered with piles of printout, hemming her in like a playpen, forcing the search forward.

She did not stop to eat.
She kept going on strong coffee.

At the end of a marathon search effort, Rose had identified ***six*** matching karyotypes with the t(15q:15q) anomaly. Two were females like herself.

There were ***four precious males***:
one in records derived from a laboratory in Houston, Texas;
one in Brisbane, Australia;
one in Johannesburg, South Africa;
and the one she had already located in the UK, from the Central Scotland Bio-bank, subcategory Edinburgh Genetic Register.

She went out for a well-earned bite to eat, settling for a carry-out vegetable bhuna, and slumped down on the chair in her tiny room to eat it. She started to plan a further campaign of action, wondering what these four precious males would be like. Old? Young? Ugly? Handsome? She had a real burning ambition to meet them.

She may have to work on, or even bribe, a few key people to acquire the names and addresses she needed, but they would never guess her true purpose. Come to think of it, what was her true purpose? She felt a little unsure. She wanted to ***meet*** these few similar souls. Did she want a potential partner? Could she be fertile with another like herself? It was merely an academic question. She needed to discuss this with Mr Marsden. She decided to make an appointment to see him.

She woke up some hours later, with a fork sticking in the side of her face and a strong smell of curry pervading her nostrils! She had not realised how tired she had been.

Chapter 14 – First Impressions

Do not be indecisive. Go for it! Better to have tried and failed than to sit on your arse and grow old. That summarised Richard's advice to Rose when she told him of her personal quest.

It did not concur with the advice from her Consultant though!

She had gleaned from the arranged meeting with Mr Marsden that she was entirely correct in her basic assumptions. ***If*** another human being, of the opposite sex, could be found, carrying ***exactly the same*** rare chromosome anomaly as herself, it was theoretically possible that they could breed. The gametes that they produced would be complementary and they could cancel out each other's imbalance.

However, he warned Rose of the virtually impossible nature of such a quest for an ideal biological partner. The abnormality was far too rare for a chance meeting. The probability of encountering somebody with the same problem was near to zero, in his opinion. There was no worldwide Register of such things. National Registers were patchy and incomplete. There were ethical considerations too, of course. He was unwilling to help in such a search.

Rose did not tell him that she had already searched all the registers... and located ***four males!***

He went on to say, " The outcome of any pregnancy could not be guaranteed since this sort of thing has never been done. It would in fact be selective breeding, the creation of... a sort of ***sub-species***. I do not think I would wish to assist you in this matter, Rose, even if I could!"

He underestimated the sheer determination that suddenly drove Rose. She could be very persistent when she had a clear goal. Furthermore, she did not need his help. He had already verified the medical possibility and she had her own agenda now.

"It was merely an academic question, Mr Marsden, It's a natural thing to want to ***meet*** people like myself, surely, but I see it could be difficult. Thanks for your time anyway."

All she had to do now was to make contact. The Edinburgh patient was closest and she intended to start there, but events overtook her.

Two days later, Professor Jones, her Head of Department, invited her to present a scientific paper in Johannesburg in August. Only a month away! The World Summit on the Environment was to be the largest International Conference in the entire history of the world, with 65,000 delegates! She was terrified, excited and flattered all at the same time! She agreed.

The Conference would concentrate on so many subjects dear to her heart: sustainable development, green issues, climate change, pollution, waste recycling. Besides, it was in South Africa, an ideal opportunity to track down potential mate number two!

She could not wait to tell Richard. She was even more pleased to learn that Richard was also going to the Conference. He was representing a Scottish Ecology Group.

Richard then persuaded her to take one further step in her quest. “It’s not far to Australia when you’re half way around the world anyway, Rose. Why not extend the trip and meet your Ossy lookalike as well?”

“Can’t afford it, Sweeto."

“Look, Rose, don’t be thick. All you have to do is seek a three-month exchange sabbatical with a student in an Ossy Virology Department. They do exchanges all the time. You’ve got skills that they would die for! You’d probably learn something too and it would be good for your career.”

Assisted by Professor Jones, and his professional contacts, Rose had little difficulty in securing a short exchange with a postgraduate virologist from Melbourne. Jones thought it was an excellent idea to gain first hand experience of an Australian Service Laboratory. Filled with purpose and excitement, she wrote her paper, prepared her slides and planned her trip carefully.

Richard agreed to come with her as far as meeting the South African gentleman was concerned, but only if she accompanied him on the Gay Pride march in Edinburgh the following week. He had bought her a T-shirt for the occasion and would drive her down and she could stop over with his friends there. She could not refuse. She said she would be proud to march with him.

Since it transpired that she was going to Edinburgh anyway, she decided to have a sneak preview of ***02/00417***. She had several close contacts in the Edinburgh Laboratory and she managed to get a name and address. She innocently claimed that she was doing a viral follow up on adult patients with translocations involving chromosome 15. She needed to send a non-invasive questionnaire about childhood infections.

The printout gave her hopeful information: ***Name: David McKay; D.O.B.: 1974.*** Well, he's not a child, a bit old maybe. Marital Status? Shit, he was married... but no harm in looking at the guy. Address: Penthouse Flat, Dean Village, Edinburgh. There was a telephone number and an e-mail address. She focused on the e-mail, "***DavidEquinox.@ virgin.net.***" Equinox? That rang a bell. It was a company name. She had come across it recently in her dealings with ***ecowarrior.com.*** She quickly found the salient web page and checked her memory.

Yes... there it was, Equinox Ltd, an animal feed company, having a rather unscrupulous recent track record with reference to the use of GM ingredients without adequate labelling! Perhaps that gave her a plausible contact reason?

She carefully worded an e-mail and sent it off.

"Hi, DavidEquinox, my name is Rose. I am 21 years old and live in Aberdeen. I believe we may have something in common and I would like to meet you. I am coming to Edinburgh next week and would be happy to meet you in a public place. Please respond."

David had no idea why a strange woman might want to meet him. Was it because of her work? Probably another overambitious ***rich bitch*** student.

He e-mailed back: "*If this is connected to work, please highlight your interest. If it is a personal contact, please state the source. I am not amused by this kind of unsolicited mail!*"

She replied quickly, "*Sorry for causing confusion and offence. It is a personal matter but not one for the e-mail. Please will you meet with me at a place and time convenient to yourself and all will be made clear. I mean you no harm and it may be beneficial to you.*"

David was greatly intrigued by the message and could see no harm in a quick public meeting. Rose suggested that they meet in the Red Dragon on Broughton Street. She had heard Richard mention the place as one of their intended venues. She didn't realise that it was a well known Gay pub.

David replied : "*OK stranger, I'll meet you in Edinburgh next Saturday in Red Dragon?! This had better be worth my time! How will I recognise you?*"

" *I'll have pink and purple streaks in my hair! How about you?*"

"*Can't boast such flamboyance! I'll wear a rose in my buttonhole... to match your name.*"

David was apprehensive before he even entered the Gay bar, and when he saw the girl with the multi-coloured hair sitting with two Gay men and a butch-looking woman, he jumped to all the wrong conclusions. Conflicting thoughts juggled for space in his mind - *She was oddly striking... not unattractive... but so young... so immature looking... and a woofter?*

Rose spotted him right away, out of place in this environment, business suit, complete with the agreed buttonhole. Old. A bit married looking. With a small rush of panic, she realised he was heading for her table. She chickened out. She decided to take the easy route forward by side-stepping the whole issue of looking for a potential mate.

As he walked towards her, with a distinctly hesitant step, he looked like a lone stranger who had just ridden into town in a Spaghetti Western.

He felt uncomfortable among the clientele, wishing like crazy that he could be somewhere else. He had felt like an outcast ever since the diagnosis of his infertility, but this place was not for him. The odd crowd seemed to close in around him. The noise and heat were oppressive. He was already angry at the waste of his valuable time and the effort he had made. Why on earth had he agreed to meet this weirdo?

The meeting was further strained by the noisy public surroundings. Rose introduced herself and friends whose names were instantly forgotten by David. He was invited to join them.

By force of habit, he offered to buy a round of drinks. This was most gratefully accepted in true student fashion. He was relieved when Rose suggested they move to at a quieter table.

"So, what's all the mystery about, then?" he prompted.

" I.... er... No way would she tell him the true reason for wanting to meet him. She searched for an alternative. Well, I understand you are something of an expert on genetically modified crops?"

"Well, not really. I do have an interest in them, but I'm no expert. My company uses some GM ingredients. That's about it really."

"Er...Yes, that's where I saw your name. It was on a list of contacts distributed by the Anti-GM lobby. I should explain that I have an interest in allowing free choice..."

He cut her short, "Christ, so you're a GM activist then?" He made to stand up to leave.

"Not at all! I thought, perhaps, that I could be of use to you in achieving the acceptable status for your company and avoiding blacklisting. I don't know much about animal nutrition, Mr McKay, but I hold very balanced views about GM products, and I like to see a good standard of labelling. I've been contracted to assist with several labelling projects. It would do your sales no end of good if you could be earmarked as a conforming company, rather than blacklisted as an offender. No doubt you are aware that lists are posted on the Internet and updated regularly? My services need not be expensive."

"So, you're looking for a job, young lady? Why didn't you just say so?" He relaxed a little and Rose smiled at him. He was instantly infected with her smile. The ice developed a hairline crack.

"Let's start again! Hello, David, I'm Rose and I'm pleased to meet you." She held out her hand and he took it. He felt a tiny electric jolt, like static. He wanted to stay and listen to the strange girl with the coloured hair.

"Now, David, why don't you tell me a bit about your company? "

"Well, Equinox Ltd. is a small manufacturing business, producing a range of cool mixes and chaffs, but also additives and medicines for horses."

"I read somewhere that most ailments in horses are man-made and caused by bad feeding."

He laughed. "That may be true, but it is an oversimplification. We are experts in this area of nutrition. We produce all the common additives - biotin, garlic, cod-liver oil... We use a lot of wheat and soya bean extracts. The Board of Management want to aim for a GM-free product, but personally, I think this is not necessary."

"It may be difficult to get GM-free wheat and soya - cross pollination is widespread now, but I think your Board are right to try and to label accordingly. That is the most important thing. So that the public are aware of what they are buying."

"Yes, the Board are keen to get the right form of wording on the product labels. So, you suggest that I might commission ***you*** to assist with this?"

"Well, I might be able to. If it's worth my while of course." She winked. She'd had a little too much wine.

He frowned. "I may well seek assistance in the design of our new labels, but what are your credentials? I'm a bit puzzled by you, young lady, I still don't understand. Why on earth did we have to meet for you to ask me that? There's nothing underhand in it, is there?"

" No, it's a genuine offer. I'm heavily involved in ***ecowarrior.com*** and I have a small portfolio of work in this area. I certainly would ***not*** be prepared to compromise my reputation by covering up any scam or other, mind, for an unscrupulous cut-throat business tycoon."

David frowned again at her. The bloody cheek of this... child!

There was a wild commotion from the table of her "friends" in the corner. A creature of indeterminate sex had come out of the door of the toilet and was doing a fashion parade up and down the aisle to hoots of laughter.

Rose was summoned to join in the frivolity.

Glad of the excuse to curtail the meeting and keen to exit this place, David handed her his card and said, "Look, I suppose I just might need some advice on legitimate packaging. Give me a ring at this number and we can discuss terms. This is not the best place to talk, is it?"

Rose nodded and gave the courtesy, "Nice to have met you" farewell handshake. Again, David felt the twang of static electricity.

Relieved to be free of the rather arrogant middle aged specimen, Rose struck his name off her wish list and prepared to march with her friends.

As David left, he focused on an older man with a sad face. He was sitting alone at the next table clutching a drink. He wore a T-shirt that read, "***Gay son - and proud of him!***"

He looked around, observing, considering... *There was a similarity about these woofters, like male worker bees are distinct from drones in a beehive. They had another purpose altogether, a non-breeding remit. They were a sort of third gender.*

Rose was a pretty specimen. What a waste.

Chapter 15 – Blyde River Canyon

It was not safe to walk around alone at night in many parts of Johannesburg.

It was a restless, energetic, exciting city, with bubbling street life, and a very high crime rate: a murder was apparently committed every half hour, not to mention armed robbery and rape being commonplace. The atmosphere was troubled, violent and optimistic. Years of segregation between white and black citizens had resulted in grand mansions rubbing shoulders with cardboard shanties and BMWs with bicycles.

The Environmental Conference was both stimulating and disappointing. Rose's paper had gone down well. Richard had proved to be a powerful probing force during the question sessions on various Green issues, but there had been a lot of talk and very little action agreed. In some cases, only lip-service had been paid to the urgent need to change domestic and industrial practices with reference to waste recycling and pollution. The talks had come frustratingly close and then circled around the obvious proposals and then petered out through lack of time.

The poor public transport system in Johannesburg had led to a massive taxi industry. Fourteen-seater mini-buses had mushroomed out of the apartheid situation. Therefore, throughout the fortnight of their visit, Rose and Richard used *Z J Muzonda's reliable and safe taxi service* to tour the suburbs of the sprawling city: the rich Sandton area in the north; Sowetto in the east. In addition to the known population, there were an estimated two million squatters, many of them proud street artists and talented musicians living in hideously grafittied ghettos.

Pretoria, some 40 km away was a much more beautiful and peaceful city, on the Apies (Little Monkey's) river. It had magnificent sandstone buildings dating back to the early twentieth century and four Universities. It was affectionately called the Jacaranda city as these flowering trees frame its Union Buildings. Rose was disappointed not to see the Jacarandas in full bloom, since they apparently coated the city purple with blossom in October. She was fascinated by the fact the very first two Jacaranda trees had been planted in 1888, and there were now 70,000 trees lining the streets of this beautiful city, providing much welcome shade and greenery.

After ferreting around the various sources of information, Rose had been given a contact, who would be willing to lead her to potential male number two, providing he was paid a small fee for the service. Dr Mosis Van Zyl was an ex-employee of a Harley Street laboratory in London, who was now carrying out lucrative paternity testing for the rich white South Africans.

Dr Van Zyl met Richard and Rose in Pretoria, at the Tourist Rendezvous coffee bar, at the corner of Vermeulen and Prinsloo street, just off Sammy Marks Square. He was a sly, greasy creature, with nicotine fingers and a gold-capped front tooth. There was a dusting of dandruff on his collar and gold rings on three of his fingers. He had been briefed by the private laboratory grapevine to do Dr Anderson a small favour by tracking down ***940336/BF,*** the man she needed to meet.

They learned that potential mate number two, had lived, for some time, in Sowetto, while being paid to "volunteer" to take part in some obscure drugs trial, but he was now in Mpumalanga, the place of the rising sun. His chromosome anomaly had been picked up as a purely incidental finding. His name was Lenny, but Goldtooth had no other relevant information about the man, not even a surname. If they wanted Lenny, they would have to travel to the Northern Province, to the village of the Rain Queen. They were given the name of a contact, Mrs Molumba, who would be able to help them locate Lenny when they got there.

Rose felt like a client in a lonely-hearts club, but was determined to make the journey and meet Lenny, especially after travelling so far already. She was keen to see the Northern Province anyway, since one of her favourite authors, John Buchan had set his novel "Prester John" in that region. Richard agreed to go with her, with some reluctance, since The Bush was simply not his scene. Goldtooth, who had a very poorly conceived idea of why she wanted Lenny, assured her that everything was "no problem" and offered to go with them to "arrange things," so that Lenny could be taken back to the UK if they wanted him.

"I don't think that will be necessary, Dr Van Zyl," Rose had explained, "I think you've possibly got the wrong idea here. We just want to ***meet*** Lenny. We've taken up enough of your valuable time. I am sure we will be able to get a guide through our University contacts, and Mrs Molumba will assist us in tracing this Lenny once we get there."

Mr Goldtooth was not amused. He spat black tobacco dregs at their feet and held his hand out. Richard slipped him a generous backhander, and in his cultured solicitor's voice said, "Thank you so much for your time, Sir. You have been very helpful."

After preliminary enquiries with Pretoria University, they were able to accompany a student, called Sypho, who was studying Cycad ferns, in an area quite close to the village they wished to visit. He was not very talkative, but efficient and useful. He took them by jeep through part of the Krugar National Park, past Sapekoe Tea Plantations and then on foot through the Venda Bushlands where huge, hardy, horned cattle roamed freely, tended by equally hardy children. Both man and beast in this region had survived harsh climate, impenetrable mountains and the cattle-hostile tsetse fly that had plagued the early settlers with fever.

When they were within sight of their destination, Sypho went on his way to collect his specimens. Rose entered the village of the Rain Queen, with some trepidation. She knew that Lenny would most likely be a black man. Her mind was full of the strange sights and smells of the past two weeks. The adventure had a dream-like quality, events seemed almost unreal. She tried to focus on the facts of the situation, to remind herself exactly where she was and why she was here. She, an island lass, was deep in the Modjadji forest, in the Northern Province of South Africa!

Cycad ferns, as old as dinosaurs, guarded the Rain Queen's village. Wooden staves carved with figures and grotesque faces surrounded the settlement itself. The Rain Queen was reputed to have secret rainmaking powers that were passed throughout the ages. When old, she committed suicide after handing her secrets to the next generation. It was easy to understand why the mysterious Rain

Queen had been the inspiration for Rider Haggard's immortal Queen, "She."

They were expected at the village. A small party of colourfully dressed members of the Karanga Roswi people met them beside the equivalent of the village square: an ancient Baobab tree, with a massive fleshy trunk. It was an odd-looking tree. Local legend had it that the Baobab had offended God, so God had uprooted it and replanted it upside down.

After preliminary greetings, they were ushered by Mrs Molumba into a thatched-roofed shack, where a skinny child was captive, accompanied by an evil looking old woman, who grinned toothlessly and ran her hand over the boy's chest.

Lenny ***was*** black, and may have been all of twelve years old!

The child looked terrified. He clutched a ragged sports bag, presumably filled with belongings, as if he expected to be whisked away. His thin wrists were bruised. Rose had wondered what purpura looked like on dark skin. The boy's cheeks were stained with tears.

Rose had a strained conversation with the child, who spoke English, but did not have a lot to say, mostly just, "Yes Missy," and, " No Missy," to her. He responded differently to comments from the sun-wrinkled woman known as Mrs Molumba, "Yebo N'gami," he said, nodding furiously in agreement with every single word she said.

Mrs Molumba spoke quite good English and explained that she was a Government Health Worker. She told them that Lenny had been a weak and sickly child.

"His mother died of AIDS and his father is also infected. Two brothers and a sister are HIV positive, but Lenny is clean." She assured them. *He had unexplained immunity.* Rose was fascinated by this and asked if she could have a blood sample for her research. The crone wanted to know if they would be paid.

Rose handed the child a few notes from her purse, telling him that she just wanted a small blood sample. She tried to explain that he was a very rare young man, like herself. There was some vague inkling of understanding, but clearly he had no grasp of the complexities of what Rose meant. He smiled revealing a missing front tooth. She took the blood sample and also noted details of Mrs Molumba's official address where she could write to Lenny later.

Rose was glad to escape the poverty and indignity of it all. As they trudged back through the Bushland, guided by Lenny and another youth, who had volunteered to accompany them to the rendezvous place where they had agreed to meet Sypho, Rose felt disappointed. She could not conceive of this child as a mate. She also felt an overwhelming sadness for the boy. The image of this slight black youth who somehow shared her strange genetic affliction would be with her for a long time. She silently pledged to herself that she would send him a little financial assistance on a regular basis once she was working full time.

As they approached Sypho's jeep, on the outskirts of the nearest town, the chirp of the crickets was just starting to herald the dusk. There was a distant call of guinea fowl and the rustle of wind in the savannah grasses. She hugged Lenny when they parted and she felt tears spring to her eyes. He did not understand why she made a fuss of him, but relished the attention all the same. Lenny had been admiring her bracelet, a Celtic design in silver, so she took it off and slipped it over his thin wrist. A haunting cry from a distant hyena punctuated the still night air. She shuddered.

Before they left South Africa, Richard and Rose made one last trip together, to see one of the most spectacular sights in the area: the Blyde River Canyon and the Three Rondavels. These were three strange-looking columns, like mountain-sized standing stones, gouged from the earth's crust by the Blyde River, the River of Happiness, over sixty million years. Rose was intrigued by the name since it reminded her of Shetland. She remembered her grandfather's voice from the past "Oh Rosie, Aa'm dat blyde tae see dee coming hom."

It was an unforgettable place, ancient and regal, almost sacred. It seemed the right place to make a wish. *She wished happiness for Richard, a better life for Lenny, and that the next leg of her journey to inspect potential mate number three, would reveal her Mr Right.*

...

Rose felt unclean when she left Egoli International Airport, *en route* to Australia. She was vexed that Richard would not be with her in this next phase of her quest into the unknown.

She did not mind the misting of insect spray that filled the aeroplane cabin before landing in Melbourne. It seemed appropriate.

Chapter 16 – Smokehouse Kippers

Rose liked Melbourne City, with its parks full of possums that came out at dusk and foraged tourist bins... and pockets. They could bite as well! There was a huge, multi-storey, glittering store called Daimaru in the main shopping mall. It was like Harrods in London and boasted large departments selling absolutely everything. She was amazed to find that the fish counter had kippers from the Shetland Smokehouse. From sheer curiosity, she had to check the sell-by dates. She smiled and told the assistant proudly that she came from Shetland. She bought a kilo of huge tiger prawns and ate them for three days. They were the best she had ever tasted!

Within a week she was well settled in her host department and had been introduced to several new temporary work mates. It was a very modern Virology Department with Level Four facilities. There were six qualified professionals together with four technical assistants. They specialised in tropical viruses. Rose was accommodated in a student house and instructed to shadow Dr Slater, a senior Virologist. He was quite short and around forty-seven years of age, although he looked older, having pale freckled skin that had not stood up well to the southern sun. He was a pleasant and patient man though, and Rose soon found that she could contribute to the diagnostic procedures and offer small ways to improve one or two of the technical processes.

She was allowed weekends off. Melbourne was a green and pleasant place, reminding her of any big British city, having many suburbs and built up in all directions. There was no "Bush" to be seen though and she felt a little cheated since the only Kangaroos to be found were in the Melbourne Zoo! It was there that she had the worst fish and chips in her life! The fish was grey and rancid, like a pseudo-herring. She had no idea what it was, but even the seagulls would not eat it!

Australia held the promise of her third possibility of a biological mate. She had been given no contact here, since the web of private services did not seem to stretch that far.

Rose was not credited with any vacation until her last seven days in Australia. Thus it was three months before she had sufficient time to visit Queensland and continue her search for Mr Right. During those months, she became a useful and valued member of the virology team and had full access to the computer records for the whole Australasian Area.

She was able to obtain the missing name and address details for case ***AA/17077*** from the Brisbane Genetic Centre by correctly posing as a Research Fellow from the UK. She claimed that she was doing an obscure project, necessitating follow-up of the long-term health status of human patients with a ***Robertsonian translocation,*** involving chromosome 15. This also had a strong element of truth. She already had a printout of the Australian Genetic Register with laboratory numbers, and she was employed by a respectable Melbourne practice. All she needed were addresses.

The head of the Brisbane laboratory was away on the day Rose called, so the secretary sought permission from his deputy, who was under some stress of work and could not really be bothered with an unsolicited additional task. He listened to what Rose had to say, glanced at her ID and the letter heading from the Melbourne Department. He knew Jeff Slater by reputation. It all sounded quite harmless.

Rose assured them that she was just on a fact-finding exercise at this stage and that there would be no drug trials or invasive procedures without the necessary ethical approvals. In her briefcase, she carried several impressive glossy publications, and three published articles in her own name that she presented as a gift to the deputy.

The secretary was given clearance to furnish Rose with the basic information. She was provided with the vital names and addresses of seventeen patients. Sixteen of them had chromosome 15 attached to another acrocentric chromosome. Four patients had t(13;15). Nine had t(15;21) and three had t(15; 22). As Rose already knew, only one of them had the vital t(15:15).

He lived north of Brisbane, on the sunshine coast.
His name was Benjamin Cunningham.

It had a nice ring to it!

...

Rose hired a car for the drive up the Sunshine Coast. She was fearful of the heavy traffic in the strange city of Brisbane, but soon settled to the quieter roads. On the outskirts of Brisbane, she screeched to a halt. There was a sign saying "Shetland Ponies." Time did not allow her to be distracted to investigate. The small size of the world registered with her then. If Shetland ponies and Smokehouse kippers were to be found at the other side of the world...who knows what else she might find?

...

She drove past miles of golden sandy beach at Agnes Water, sub-consciously noting the presence of what appeared to be the two commonest types of small town enterprise in Australia - the Estate Agent selling plots of land and the General Store, selling the ubiquitous chips but no liquor. You had to go to a special wine shop for that! She stopped briefly to stretch her legs and noted in the Estate Agent's window that one could buy 100 acres of prime real estate on the outskirts of Agnes for a mere $58,000. It had its own dam and was partly fenced too. It was all very beautiful and she mused that if this man was any good, she could be persuaded to stay here. Thus daydreaming, with a certain forced optimism mixed with apprehension, Rose continued her journey.

Glancing at the map that was now sticking to the passenger seat, welded in place by a melted bar of chocolate, she headed towards a sheltered bay of shallows at the other side of a prominent headland. A roadside sign displayed a tempting view of a blue lagoon and advertised catamaran trips to Lady Musgrove Island, just over an hour away.

Eventually, the sleepy little fishing town of 1770 was reached via 58kms of dust track road, littered at every bend with the carcasses of squashed cane toads. The hired car slithered dangerously on loose gravel where the slope became very steep and she wondered if she had misread the map. She was thankful that there was no sign of any oncoming traffic. The sun beat down relentlessly. Despite a stiff breeze blowing, her forearm that was sticking proud of the open window was stinging with the promise of the blisters to come. She had a headache.

As she rattled down the last section of dusty track towards 1770, Rose was full of apprehension. She felt an empathy with Captain Cook who had landed in this remote place in the year that gave it its name. They were both folks with missions, trying to conquer something new. She wondered if Cook had also had a headache.

Rose felt the isolation and the thrill of the explorer on the brink of discovery.

She stopped the car at the jetty where a few small boats were berthed and a couple of bare foot children were fishing with a small circular weighted net. She was glad to be out of the car. Her trousers were sticking to her legs and she was tempted to strip off and walk into the water. It was very rough with strong wind whipping the surf into white crests and she could feel the pain of sharp sand peppering her roasted right arm.

Then came the sand flies, and all other sensations faded into insignificance as they bit and sucked their way into the unsuspecting flesh of a new victim. "Little bastards!" She muttered, running back towards the car. Their onslaught eased with fast motion so she walked quickly on towards a ramshackle wooden shed at the end of the jetty, where a Hire Company had a "Tourist Information" board. It contained nothing but a cancellation notice, and warned that all trips to the reef were meantime postponed due to adverse weather. The door was open, so Rose tentatively entered into the welcome shade of a cooler interior. A middle-aged man in shorts, with weathered mahogany skin, looked up from mending a net.

"Hello, mate, ow's it goin? Trips to the reef're all off 'til she blows over!"

Rose explained that she wasn't looking for a tourist trip, at least not at this time, but trying to contact a local man, Benjamin Cunningham.

"Oh yea, I know Ben fine. He helps me out sometimes with my book-work in the peak tourist season, but he's mostly involved with his animals. What a man for wildlife! Are you a relative?"

"We-el, not really... but we do have a lot in common, you could say. We... sort of... share an interest. My name's Rose Anderson, by the way. I've travelled a long distance to see Mr Cunningham."

"Well, Rose, you're almost there now - just carry on along the coast road, past the shop and the Cunningham place is next on the right. You'll see the name on the mail box. Ben may not be home, always out in the bush studying critters and the like. Always scribbling in that notebook of his. He writes a wildlife column in the local rag, you know? Chances are he'll be out till supper time, but you'll find his Pa, old Joe Cunningham round there somewhere. He grows vegetables and keeps chucks - supplies most of the shops in these parts. He may not take kindly to a stranger though!"

" Is there a hotel in the village?"

"Hell, no miss!" Laughed the bronzed man; "This here's only a one-horse town - no hotel! There is a caravan park just outside town, and Mrs Flynn, the caretaker woman, might find you a spare bed in one of her statics this time of year."

A caravan! Rose did not relish the thought. Still, she could see that she would get no five-star treatment here in this outpost. Besides, it was only for one night.

Anxious to refresh herself after the dust and heat and sand flies, and before springing herself on the unsuspecting Ben, or being driven off by his father, Rose drove first to the shop for a can of something cold and a sandwich. It was a typical outback shop with a limited selection - no fresh meat, no fresh bread, overpriced... She felt as if she had come to the ends of the earth! She managed to purchase a Pepsi, some potato chips, a carton of yoghurt, a strange looking fruit called a custard apple and a fresh unmelted bar of chocolate, before continuing on her way to see Mrs Flynn. She would plan her approach to Ben in the early evening. First she needed soap and water and fresh clothes, and the security of a bed for the night.

As she drove into the rather scruffy looking caravan yard, a pick-up was loading up to leave. Two young male hippie leftovers with goatee beards were lifting a bashed-up foam mattress into the ute. They had filthy T-shirts on, full of holes. A couple of mangy dogs sprawled in the back. Three females appeared from the caravan, all with golden hair, olive tans and tight tight shorts on trim backsides. These women did not seem to match the men. Two of the ladies were of medium height, but one was tall and stately, with legs up to her ears. She ran one of her fingers down the spine of one of the scruffy guys and Rose wondered how on earth he had managed to hook that! She hoped that Benjamin Cunningham was a cut above the scruffs.

Mrs Flynn was welcoming and allocated a four-berth caravan for Rose's exclusive use. She was relieved to find that it was clean. There were few tourists around now and Mrs Flynn was glad of the custom. Her two small boys were curious to the point of irritation. Daniel and Alex, the terrors were called. Alex, the younger, was about seven years old, tough, very cute, and very grubby, with the most amazing mop of totally unkempt hair. Alex followed Rose around like a shadow from the moment she arrived until his mother prised him away to be fed.

Later, washed and changed, Rose took a walk to get used to her surroundings and to escape the two terrors. At the far side of the sandy bay was a point up which she scrambled. The waves were battering the rocks but it was relatively sheltered at the lea side. A few arthritic trees were growing in the most inhospitable places, arial roots dangling in the hot dry air, ever optimistic of finding safe anchorage and a drop of fresh moisture, but mostly embedded in bare rock, nourished only by bird shit! Higher up the cliff, strange tropical plants grew in abundance: bougainvillaea in red, orange, purple, peaches and pinks; avocados and tulip trees. There were kookaburras and wagtails darting around in the denser areas of vegetation. Magpies whistled their distinctive Australian songs.

Rose was still wheezing a little from her car journey the previous day. She had travelled through a sugar plantation road, with canes over 2m high on either side and the atmosphere was so full of alien dust and exotic pollens that the air conditioning in the car simply could not cope.

The fresh sea breeze was blissfully soothing.

Returning to her van, she took a seat outdoors to eat her meagre meal. Alex promptly re-appeared to help with the chocolate and was about to start on her yoghurt, when Daniel cautioned him sternly and told him not to eat that "monkey puke!" They had a language all of their own and it was with much interest and amusement that she watched their afternoon antics. First they converted a metal coat-hanger and an orange string bag into a catching net and proceeded to stalk a mother duck, catching her babies one by one and examining them, while the distraught parent squawked and fluttered in terror. The boys were interested in the beaks, the webbed feet and the tail end or "shabbitat area" of the duckling, which Alex called the "vent" in a very important voice, before they dissolved into hysterics and released the fluffy chick back to its mother. They seemed quite obsessed with vents, moving their attentions to an unsuspecting tree frog with green suckered feet and "a very large vent. Giggle giggle." They had no luck with the pelican that they tried to lure to the shore for similar examination.

"Alex thinks that a vent specialist is called a ventriloquist!" Daniel informed Rose, with a knowing, superior smile on his face, "and go on, ask him what boat sounds like his favourite pudding?"

"Catameringue Pie" piped up the little one, without being asked, and laughed at his own joke.

"Is that what you had for your dinner, then?" Rose ventured to ask. She was not very at ease with children.

"No, we had Ked-ger-eee, ugh! It's horrible - worse than monkey puke!"

They brought Rose two of their favourite pet "gribblies"- that roughly equated to a very large brown hairy "spider-type gribblie" and a red striped "shit-of-a-thing-gribblie, with spines" swimming in a bucket. Daniel had hooked the strange creature while fishing and torn his hand getting the hook off! Their final offering to her was a sea snake, thankfully pickled in a large jar! Daniel claimed that it had been caught right here on this beach. That put all thoughts of an afternoon swim out of her mind, since sea snakes are among the most venomous creatures on earth and she had no wish to run into one.

...

It was around seven when Rose drove up the lane leading to the Cunningham house. She had not rehearsed what to say. She was a great believer in spontaneity and figured that things would go well if they were honest understanding folks. No amount of fancy words would change the outcome if Benjamin was unreasonable. She was met by Ben's rather gruff father, but quickly rescued by the gentleman himself.

Ben shouted to his father from a rocking chair on the porch, "Don't you be mean now, Pa! Give the lady a chance to speak her business!"

Ben was finishing off a meal and bits of food were scattered around the veranda, rapidly being devoured by a flock of small birds. A possum scuttled across the table and grabbed a morsel from his outstretched hand before retreating into the rafters with its prize.

A large short-bodied lizard slithered out from under his chair to observe the intruder and shot a pure blue tongue out to taste his airspace.

"It's all right, miss, Ben laughed, Blue's harmless, he's just after my fish bones! So, what can you do for me now?"

The flock of little birds scarpered in a great twitter and flutter of wings as Rose approached the steps.

Ben was one of the most reasonable people she'd met in a long time... but not at all what she expected! He was well over fifty years old and looked every bit of it, wrinkled prematurely from his outdoor pursuits and long hours in the southern sun. He was a tiny, slim man, skinny really, with rough hands and a scar on his nose from the surgical removal of skin cancer. A motley assortment of the most unfashionable garments she had ever seen hung on his bony frame. Rose was aware that she was staring rudely at the man. Ben paid absolutely no attention to her scrutiny. Such material things as clothes did not even register with him. He was clearly a biologist and an artist of exceptional talent. The place was full of painting, sketches and skeletal specimens of birds and reptiles. A computer screen flashed its saver design in the corner of the room as he left his work to entertain his unexpected visitor.

Rose introduced herself simply as a Research Fellow from the UK, on sabbatical and following up some of the more unusual hospital laboratory records from the Brisbane area, particularly with reference to long term health and predisposition to viral infection.

Ben had the clear strong voice of authority, a complete contradiction to his appearance. His smile was radiant. It was helpful that he fully knew and understood his chromosome disorder and no longer had any difficulty accepting the *status quo*. It was a long time ago since the diagnosis, he explained, and he had long since learned to live with his infertility. He had parted with his young wife some twenty-five years ago, following a history of recurrent miscarriage and knowing the problem could never be cured. He was angry, unreasonable and bitter at that time. No wonder the relationship had failed. He had never re-married, but was wed to his work now... and content.

Rose could detect some sadness in Ben as he spoke of his past.

She did not tell Ben of her identical chromosome rearrangement, fearing that he would then guess her ulterior motive and sense her concomitant rejection of him as a potential mate. Instead, she opened a notebook, and Ben brought coffee. This was accompanied by a tame magpie that sat on his shoulder and then hopped on to the arm of her chair, examining every word that she wrote and making melodic whistling comments now and then. Rose wondered if the bird could read and was relaying some form of coded message to his master. Ben answered all her questions. She was surprised to find that, just like herself, Ben too had been a sickly child, asthmatic and allergic to a lot of different foodstuffs.

"Yet Queensland is the asthma capital of the world," he explained, "so these allergies were not thought to be related to the chromosome change, more to the dust and pollens blowing out of the red centre of Australia."

"How about viral infections?"

"Yes, I have had several very bad viral infections, with bleeding a common side effect, but mostly my father kept me at home, away from the dirt and germs of hospital wards. Dad had his own cures."

They touched on the delicate nature of the conflict in the East. *Another suicide bomber had just killed seventeen Israelis. In retaliation, Israeli troops had attacked the Palistinian Headquarters in the West Bank town of Ramalla. There seemed no hope of peace.*

Rose's ankles were alive with uncontrollable itch and she could not help scratching them. The skin was inflamed and raw and the irritation was driving her crazy. Ben noticed, and without a word, rose and fetched a small jar of strange-smelling, green cream.

"The sand flies have had their fill of you, I see. Take your socks off. This'll fix the itch."

Rose automatically did as she was bidden. Somehow, one could not challenge this small authoritative voice. The cream felt soothing and very cold. Ben said it was a herbal remedy of his own making and had always worked very well for his own allergies. There were many startling similarities between his childhood and her own. She began to suspect that the ***Robersonian translocation*** was indeed linked to a hypersensitive immune system in all cases.

A couple of hours fled past quickly in Ben's excellent easy-going company.

Rose vowed that she would stay in touch with this strange, sad and highly gifted member of her species. She liked Ben very much, but could not conceive of him as a mate! They exchanged contact numbers and Rose left Ben to return to the warmth of his computer.

Far from tired and with a calm twilight now descendent on the Caravan Park, she decided to walk along the sandy shore. The wind had died down and silver tipped, gentle waves lapped the beach. It was a beautiful peaceful place now that the boys were out of sight! *Kids* she thought, smiling, with water in her eyes, *do I really want them anyway?* The sky had turning a beautiful shade of red, tinged purple, and the silhouettes of giant pelicans were on the water.

There were two, a pair, of them.

Her sunburnt arm throbbed with red-hot pain and Rose felt very alone in this alien country.

Chapter 17 - Labels

Rose was downhearted on her return from Australia. It had all been a rather disappointing attempt at matchmaking, although she had met two like souls and she had enjoyed the sabbatical work. There was only one more possibility of a biological match and he resided in Houston Texas. She would have to put him on the back boiler for now. She resolved to get on with her research work and her ordinary life and forget her more fanciful ideas.

She was brought into contact with David McKay again by a strange plethora of coincidences.

She was in Edinburgh six weeks after her return to Britain, attending a Scientific Conference in the Rosalind Institute – the place made famous because of *Dolly,* the first cloned sheep. The Conference over, she had decided to pay a visit to the Government Drug-Testing unit at Inveresk, to ascertain exactly which methods of testing were in current use. She took a taxi and paid the fare at the outer gate. She ran into chaos in the car park. An Animal Rights group had stormed the grounds of the building and an angry mob waved placards protesting the use of innocent creatures in the testing of beauty products. Rose knew that the centre only tested pharmacological drugs, not cosmetics. She suspected too that protocols in current use would mainly be through the use of cultured cell lines, not live animals. However, in view of the circumstances, she thought it prudent not to hang around. She approached the rather distressed woman at Reception and picked up a couple of leaflets that would probably tell her most of what she wanted.

On the way out, she stopped to speak briefly to one of the protesters, a shaven-headed fellow with a painted T-shirt and baggy jeans and a great display of body-piercing and tattoos. He quickly lost interest in her when he discovered that she was not a member of staff, just a passing visitor.

She was still standing there, on the outskirts of the mob, when David McKay slipped out the side door of the building and made towards his car. David had been at the Test Centre to seek information on the legal requirements of having Equinox's new Flexion Gold Liquid tested, prior to marketing it as a human alternative medicine product. The preparation contained a new anti-inflammatory substance extracted from ***biopharmed*** potatoes. ***Biopharming*** had been pioneered by the New Zealand government and was increasing in popularity. Potatoes were being used to make specific proteins to help body repair after heart surgery. The humble and immobile spud was considered much safer than using transformed bacteria. There was a good yield of product and it was relatively cheaply produced. Equinox Ltd. had purchased a ***biopharmed*** protein, called ***flex9*** reputed to ease joint inflammation. Their routine equestrian feed trials had subsequently shown that ***flex9*** was of little value on its own. However, when mixed with an existing remedy, *chondroitin sulphate*, the combined preparation worked better than any previous formula. David thought that it was now time to enter the lucrative world of Human Health care.

He immediately took Rose to be a member of the militant group. He tried to manoeuvre his way towards the car without crossing her path, but the dynamics of the crowd forced them into juxtaposition. There was no hiding place.

"Hi, there. We meet again," he ventured, feeling distinctly uncomfortable.

"I... I was just leaving!" Rose stammered, all too aware that the manner of his greeting, while friendly enough, was something less than that. Along with the smile, he had projected the faintest hint of accusation, as if he considered her and her kind to be a total pain in the arse.

Perhaps it was paranoia? In her mind, Rose branded him as *an intolerant*.

"Can I offer you a lift, then? I'm heading back to the city centre." David asked, expecting instant refusal.

"Actually, I would appreciate that. I was wondering how to escape this potentially violent situation and I don't have transport of my own this trip." Rose replied. *Intolerant...but useful*, said the voice in her head.

"Isn't that a bit like running out on your friends at a critical time?" he said, surprised that she had accepted his half-hearted offer.

"Oh, No! They're not my friends. I don't know them at all!" she replied indignantly. *Jumps to conclusions,* she mused, giving him another negative score.

David opened the passenger door for her, with a mildly puzzled expression.

By the time he deposited her at Waverley Railway Station, he understood better that the situation they had left behind at Inveresk was purely co-incidental to both of them being there. He also became aware that Rose really did have quite a bit of knowledge about GM foods and ***biopharming***. He had not seriously meant to contact her again regarding the labelling project, but he did still need to sort out the wording for the new packages if only to satisfy the Board of Directors.

He needed to know more about the pros and cons of using GM and ***biopharmed*** ingredients in the feeds manufactured by Equinox Ltd. since the inclusion of GM soya and cereals could significantly decrease costs. Still, it may be no good using these things if the market forces were against it. Perhaps there was a way of hiding their use by clever wording?

"Do you have to leave Edinburgh today?" he asked.

"'Fraid so. I've got a lot of work to catch up on. No peace for the wicked... and all that."

" Pity! I would've bought you dinner... in exchange for picking your brains."

"Let me guess... Frankenstein food?"

"Subject for discussion? Yes. Dinner? Certainly not!"

"That's a relief, anyway." She smiled, "but all the same, no can do. Perhaps another time?"

In the cloistered confines of the car with only a few irrelevant words exchanged, still the mysterious, invisible chemistry was there. It was not the love at first sight crap, not even a sharp stab from Cupid's arrow, but a comfortable feeling of ease in each other's company, spiced with a need to be closer, to know more about the fresh new intriguing human being. That thing without an adequate name that makes a little bit of your heart leap into living with the realisation that you are not alone in this great vast void of a world after all.

Rose guessed that she was just in need of company after her frustrating trip abroad.

David thought her less flamboyant than before, more business-like. She did not look like a Dyke today. And what if she was? She could still be paid for assisting him with the labelling.

"Well now, as coincidence would have it, my mother and my grandmother live in your neck of the woods, just North of Aberdeen. They're due a visit. Poor old gran is a bit senile now. Maybe I could give you a shout when I'm next up your way?"

"Where does your granny live?" She said, with more than a hint of disbelief.

"It's perfectly true. My mother stays in Inverurie, and Gran is nearby at a wee place called Oyne, at the foot of Bennachie. I like it there. It's a beautiful wild place, with plenty long walks... Just the ticket to reduce stress and wear off these business lunches that are beginning to stick to my middle." He patted his seatbelt strap and immediately felt ridiculous and wished he hadn't.

She eyed his middle and grinned. There was dappled sunshine streaming through the side window of the car, catching his eye and causing him to squint at her. The soft music that was playing on the car radio was interrupted with a news bulletin... *A young Palestinian had killed 19 civilians and injured 55 others on a Jerusalem bus loaded with schoolchildren and office workers. It was the city's deadliest attack in many years. 7 high school pupils were killed. The suicide bomber was a 22-year-old University student..."*

"That's terrible!" Rose exclaimed "And it is surely likely to delay the release of a major Middle East policy statement by the US President!"

"What's the world coming to? Do you understand all this suicide phenomena among young educated people, Rose?"

"No. I find it hard to understand a student, with everything to live for, blowing himself and others up. Something powerful seems to be able to stir these young men into a frenzy, like religious zealots. Life under Israeli occupation, with no rights and being stuck in refugee camps without prospects must be worse than I can imagine. I'm sure that Yasser Arafat has a lot to do with it."

"I believe their families, in some places anyway, are well rewarded financially for their Supreme Sacrifice, and the youngsters themselves believe that they will receive their rewards in Heaven."

"I don't know where it will end. I'm no politician, just a mere scientist, but surely no political grievance or circumstance can justify the wilful targeting of civilians for political gain? Those who glorify and encourage such atrocities, teaching and preaching hatred and violence cannot be absolved of their responsibilities either!"

"Wow! I'd better change the subject and let you catch your train before you get too serious, young lady! Returning to the labelling project. Perhaps we can communicate on the e-mail and discuss an arrangement for a short term contract to assist with the wording on the feeds and on our new Flexion Gold additive?"

Rose was a little snubbed at his comment. He ***was*** arrogant and flash. He thought far too much of himself, and yet he had a vulnerable look this time, not the predatory stare she remembered from that strange first meeting in the pub. He was older and a little staid and... definitely married looking, but so what? He was the best of a poor choice, so far. It could do no harm to do a paid job for him.

"Sure, I'd be glad to consider your requirements and quote a price for my services. We can do most of the negotiating on the phone, I expect, but if you are up in Aberdeen, look me up. I'll see you sometime then. Thanks again for the lift."

He was much more pushy on the telephone, a right bossy-boots! He wanted her to use wording to disguise the fact that they were using GM ingredients. She steadfastly refused.
She strongly advised against the deliberate use of genetically modified ingredients in the Equinox Ltd. range of Equine feeds, but agreed that it should be less of a problem to include these cheaper ingredients in the Agricultural feedstuffs, given accurate labelling of course! She figured that most of the horsey fraternity would be well educated in the subject and would look for exclusion clauses, even be prepared to pay a little more for the security of mind that the products were GM free. On the other hand, farmers' top priority would be price so that a cheaper range of feeds could probably be marketed there as long as no attempt was made to cover up the sources of ingredients. She would not sanction this at any cost.

However, when the source materials for the horse feeds were scrutinised, it proved difficult to rule out GM ingredients entirely because of the widespread cross contamination of crops in the areas concerned. Therefore, the wording that she eventually suggested for the Equine feeds was, "*Equinox Ltd. use identity preserved ingredients to ensure that every reasonable attempt is made to exclude any possible genetically modified material.*"

This appeared on all the new packaging and had an instant appeal to horse owners.
Sales rose immediately.
Profits rose 15% over the next three months
David was well pleased.

Chapter 18 – Cider for Molly

It had been a hell of a week for David McKay! Sales had taken a downturn, largely due to price increases to cover excessive haulage costs. Bloody government! They didn't give a toss about small businesses! Brenda was having a liaison with somebody else and was hinting at divorce! His Grandmother had died and his mother needed him to help with the funeral arrangements. Then, to cap it all, Bob, the bloody cat had been in a fight with a neighbourhood Tom and needed stitches in his hind leg - costing him £169 for the vet's fee!

He rubbed the scent glands at the side of Bob's cheeks and the cat nuzzled closer. "I wish life was as easy as understanding you, Pusso. I just have to feed you and give you a stroke in the right place and you're content... and pay the bloody vet's bill of course!" He tweaked Bob's ear a little harder than necessary and the cat made a short sharp noise of disapproval, but stayed for more. "Still, we are in perfect harmony, you sweet boy!"

The cat purred louder and turned upside down, legs in the air, his soft belly parts exposed in purrfect trust of the strong gentle hands that caressed him.

The two of them silently surveyed the empty armchair opposite.

As he stroked the cat, he analysed the past year. Following the diagnosis of his chromosome disorder, Brenda had been very supportive for six months or so. A load of guilt had been taken from her shoulders and she became more like her old self. She resumed her painting classes and went out with her former flat-mate, Betty, every Monday, the way she used to do. However, there was a great rift in the relationship and the gap was destined to widen. Total immersion in work was the best relief from loneliness. He was good at that. He valued the uncomplicated company of the cat more and more.

Brenda had first suggested a trial separation. He had not really tried to prevent it. Then, she had met someone else. She was desperate for a family and thirty-five years old. Her biological clock was ticking away rapidly. Her reproductive window was closing. She was sorry, but they had drifted apart and work had always come first with him. He accepted the inevitable. They had decided to live apart until divorce proceedings could take place. There was no apportioning of blame.

He rose from the warm chair and went out into the drizzle of the night. He needed to walk. The cold air might help clarify the confusion in his head. In the morning, he would drive North to the funeral. Should he drop in on Rose? When he was not wrapped up in his work, he thought of Rose occasionally, with a growing curiosity and admiration. He could just routinely say thanks for a job well done. After all, she may be away soon. She had been talking about going to the States for the final phase of her research work.

...

A sliver of new moon was etched in the orange-streaked sky as David let Tara, his grandmother's dog, out to investigate the noise. Something was disturbing the chickens. Tara sped off as fast as her old black legs would go, snarling a warning to the intruder. A large dog fox, with a white tip to his tail, shot through the railing and disappeared in undergrowth, leaving a trail of brown feathers and a remnant chorus of alarm from the henhouse.

His grandmother had passed away in Oyne, after a wearisome illness. Physically fit but mentally blown, she had lingered on for five long years in her own world of confusion. His mother had done what she could, but grandmother had no concept that her daughter lived a few miles away and visited regularly. Still, she had died in her own house. She had always dreaded being institutionalised. Kate was exhausted and grateful that her son had readily agreed to help at this time. She had decided just to stay in her own place and let David get on with it.

As the sole beneficiary of the old lady's meager estate, David felt it his duty to see to the funeral and clear up the house prior to putting it on the market. He was tentatively considering keeping the place as a weekend retreat.

The ground was brittle with frost and Tara's breath condensed in furls over the crisp meringue peaks of grass. Small puddles shattered as she crashed through them.

"Well done, lass. These hens are going to a new home today anyway. I don't know what we'll do with you though?" Tara wagged her whole plump body and nosed David's hand. He shut the door and put the kettle on. There would be no more sleep now. He was wide awake with the medicinal dose of chilled fresh air.

The mantle shelf was covered in photographs, mostly of Mark and himself at various stages in their life... babies, primary school, holidays, graduation, his marriage to Brenda. Mark was absent from the later photographs. All of them, except Mark, were there in the grandparents golden wedding portrait. He stared at the familiar smiling face of his grandmother, feeling the sharp pang of realisation that she too was gone forever. In the photograph, taken before she deteriorated mentally, she was surrounded by two generations of her family. Her smile was proud and regal.

Another snapshot showed David at the age of twelve, with seven little brown piglets! He let his mind wonder back to happy summers at this house, when Willie his grandfather had been alive. David had always been fond of animals and was allowed to help tend the few pigs and geese that were kept on their smallholding. He was also encouraged to ride their Highland pony, Morag. David had somehow understood the basic psychology of animals from a very early age, just as some folk can sing well and some can paint pictures. He had a natural ability with animals. He was always practical about diagnosing what was wrong with them and treating the ailment. He remembered the day that Willie had bought two maiden Tamworth pigs. David was recruited to help him to take them to the boar to be served.

At that tender age, David was, of course, very interested in the procedure.

The boar had been an impressive beast. With little in the way of introductory courtship, he had chased and mounted one of the young ladies, performing the deed with great grunting and efficiency. The other maiden, Molly, had been a skittish creature. She had squealed and flown about, throwing up her heels and kicking the boar in the teeth. He had soon lost interest in her. Grandfather had been stumped. David had stroked Molly's neck. She had been shivering.

"She's just nervous, Granddad. She needs to relax."

"Easier said than done, young man. Have you got any suggestions?"

"Yes, I think she's just like Grandma... a glass of cider or two should do it."

Willie smiled at his grandson. "You might just be right there, David."

Cupboards were raided and Molly was given a can of cider and a double Glenlivet. David would never forget the long ginger eyelashes fluttering at the boar after that. Molly stood for service and fair enjoyed it. After the event, she acquired a knowing look of sheer bliss. She smiled her piggy smile at them.

The seven piglets that had resulted from this drunken orgy were all called after whisky brands ...Glenmorangie, Glenlivit, Lafroaig...

It seemed like only yesterday!

Chapter 19 - Bennachie

After the funeral, David needed to break free of nostalgia. He was yearning for company. The television had been depressingly awful… *The death toll in the East continued to rise. In the past year, 700 had been killed on the Israeli side and almost 3000 Palestinians. The US President was being pressed towards a proposal for Palestinian Statehood. There had been another planned raid on Iraq...*

David decided to give Rose Anderson a quick call.

...

Rose was living in a twenty-three foot residential caravan in a small private site on the banks of the river Don. By going on the three-month exchange sabbatical in Australia, she had lost her student flat in Johnston Hall. Anyway, it was high time she moved out and made way for the Freshers coming in. Private flats in Aberdeen were expensive and scarce and she did not like the potential flat mates that she had seen so far, having replied to several "Press and Journal" adverts. As a last resort, she had borrowed some money and bought her own little mobile home, a bijou little place, complete with double bedroom, shower room and open plan lounge/kitchen.

Living in a caravan in Scotland was a completely different experience from her short Australian exposure! The necessary gas fire had generated considerable condensation over the winter. This had been a real problem, causing walls and furnishings to be permanently damp.

It was Friday morning. She was at home writing up her proposals for spending the final year of her studies in the States. Professor Jones had given her the possibility of two USA Centres of Excellence from which to choose. She had chosen Houston, Texas: home to her last and final possibility of a male match.

The telephone rang. "Hi, there, remember me? David McKay. I've turned up again, like a bad penny."

"Yes, I remember the nice guy who gave me the welcome lift to the station... and the very difficult executive who employed me to do the labelling project. Which one is calling?"

David laughed. "Well, I guess I'm in humble mode, just looking for company. I'm in Aberdeenshire. My grandmother died last week and I've been arranging the funeral. It's past now. We cremated her yesterday. I'm here for the weekend to clear up a few of her personal belongings. I thought that I would do as I promised and look you up. Do you fancy a trip out to sunny Oyne, a walk maybe... and perhaps that dinner I didn't manage to give you last time, cooked by my own fair hand?"

"We-ell, I'm quite busy with my writing, actually, and I shouldn't really have a day off at this stage. Besides, your wife may not approve of you entertaining young ladies."

"Brenda and I are getting divorced, but that's immaterial... I only phoned for a bit of company since I'm here anyway, so don't flatter yourself! Nevertheless, I would, very much, enjoy the company!"

"We-ell... I was hoping to persuade Richard or Alex to have a look at my damp problem so I wanted to catch them when they get home at about six o'clock this evening."

"Well, there's plenty of time then... so why don't I come in and pick you up?"

David wondered who Richard and Alex were.

"But hey... I'm a pretty practical guy, so I could investigate your damp for you if you like? What's damp anyway?"

"My bed is the worst."

"I'll certainly investigate that for you, anytime!"

Arrogant guy. Rose thought. Yet, thankful of a diversion from the computer screen and feeling cooped up and listless, she was glad of the chance to escape Academia for a while.

"Who could refuse such an offer. I admit that I've been surviving on indoor convenience food for weeks. So, if you can fix my damp problem, I'd love to come for a walk in genuine countryside and to eat real food. Just tell me when, Sir Knight?"

Armed with the toolbox that he always carried in his car, David arrived at Rose's humble abode around ten o'clock. She had been frantically tidying up and jumping in and out of the shower before he came. Books, discs and her laptop cluttered the kitchen table.

God, he hated damp caravans! How could anyone live like this? It was so primitive! The crepey vinyl walls were already peeling and the cheap lino looked exhausted.

Yet he noted that it had a homeliness about it. Photographs were pinned everywhere in an attempt at making this little box her own. He stared at otters, sheep, rainbows, angry seas, gentle beaches, purple rocky hills, and a grey haired old man in a boat with a girl in pigtails. In the corner of the cluttered room, there was a Fair Isle sweater being stretched on a frame. Scattered here and there, were knitted woollen cushion covers in the natural colours of sheep. There was a little cactus plant flowering happily on the apologetic windowsill, and a strange metal Rose...

After the usual strained preliminaries, she put the kettle on while he went into her bedroom to check out the damp problem. Being so small, the door between them had to be shut while he lifted the mattress and laid it up against the wall, so he had to shout through the partition.

"Aha! I see the problem. It's just a lack of circulation. The base-board is solid ...er... chipboard...so the warmth from your ***body***..." He emphasised the word as he looked at her... "is condensing on the base. I'll fix it in no time."

Rose heard drilling and ten minutes later, David emerged triumphant and invited her to inspect the workmanship. The base-board was drilled full of holes a few millimetres in diameter, to allow the free circulation of air.

"That should improve the damp. Like to try it?"

She smiled and leant forward, “Oh-oh, what about this?” She reached under the bed and withdrew a suitcase. It was drilled full of identical holes!

“Oops... well, what do you want? Perfection?”

“Yes!” They both laughed. She warmed towards him then.

They drank luke-warm tea, with a feeling of growing comradeship.

“Who are Richard and Alex, by the way?” David asked, out of curiosity.

“Just friends. Richard has been my best friend for years, but he’s pretty useless with a screwdriver! Alex is a little more practical though!"

“Do you have a serious relationship with Richard then?”

“Oh, very serious!” She laughed “But not in the way you think. Richard and Alex are ***an item*** if you see what I mean.”

“ God, ***woofters***?”

“ What a lousy, biased attitude!”

“Sorry, it just slipped out. I take it they are Gay?”

“Yes, they are Gay, and they are both wonderful guys. Richard is a solicitor and Alex is a pilot with Eastern Airways. He has a share in his own plane. There’s a little airfield out somewhere near where your Granny’s place is. It’s near Insch. It can be very handy sometimes. He flew us to Ireland for the weekend about a month ago. It was fantastic!”

...

Mutually primed for an easy-going day, they headed forth into the countryside.

They had developed a natural rhythm to their body language as they ambled up the shady footpath from the car park at the Back of Bennachie. There were intriguing willow sculptures near a grassy picnic area, looking like out-of-place wigwams. The small field was edged to the north-west by majestic blue spruce trees. It was quite warm in the shelter of the trees and birds were singing.

Tara bounded through the ferns and jumped into the burn, right up to her shoulders. David envied her, feeling the heat and his own lack of fitness as he stepped up the steep part of the path, terraced with railway sleepers to make the walking easier on older legs. He whistled to get Tara out of the water, but had to go closer to scold her. There was a large pink granite stone in the water, upon which was written, "*The running of water is the teeming of life.*" He would never have noticed it if it hadn't been for Tara. He worried briefly about the damp doggy smell that would pervade his precious car later.

"What a lovely place!" Rose said. "The water is so clear and that stone is so... unexpected... like treasure."

"Have you ever been panning for gold, Rose?"

"Nope. That's a Wild West kind of thing isn't it?"

"Well, I guess so. My parents used to take Mark and I panning for gold. It was great. I'm sure dad seeded the stream with little bits of fools gold, but we loved every minute of it. I kept the little gold specks in a box under my bed for years."

"They sound like great parents. Mine never had time for such nonsense." Rose said, sadly. "I didn't know you had a brother."

"Mark drowned in a freak accident when he was only eight."

"Oh! I'm sorry."

"It was a long time ago. My father also passed away a few years back, so it's just mother and I now. Mother has changed a lot and become more easy-going. Perhaps you'll meet her later on, although she is a bit reclusive these days and tends to hide away in her garden at home. She lives in Inverurie."

He chose the path to the top of the peak called Oxen Craig first, aiming to swing along the side of the mountain as they came down. The walks were marked with blue or red coloured arrows boldly displayed on posts. The path beneath their feet was uneven. They stood upon the giant knarled roots of ancient pine and fir that snaked across the footpath, denuded of soil by countless trainers and walking boots, covered only with a sprinkling of pine needles. Several whole trees were lying across the path, the leftovers from late winter storms, ripped prematurely from their soft beds of sphagnum moss, sprawling roots exposed, still clutching clay and boulders, destined now to die, already colonised with the first of the opportunistic lichens and fungi. A twenty-foot high totem pole suddenly appeared in the centre of the path. It was constructed from many trees bolted together in a zigzag pattern, like tongue in groove flooring going round and round and up and up. It was dead straight and whoever built it had a good spirit level. The trunk bore the statement. *"The stretching of the trunk is the lengthening of the timber"*

There was holly and broom with last year's pods still hanging brown and battered. They passed a dead tree still standing upright and its trunk had been skilfully carved with representations of giant insects, centipedes half a metre long and other huge and wondrous creepy-crawlies. Words were carved alongside "*The loss of a great heart is the gain of a small invasion.*" Rose thought it was very clever and admired the unknown artist. She ran her palm over a wooden snail the size of a soup-plate and smiled at David in silent appreciation. She looked radiant. He took the hand from the snail and felt a sudden jolt of static electricity, as before. He could tell by her involuntary movement that Rose had experienced it too. Still, he held on to her hand as they walked on. A breathless lady ran towards them trying to retrieve her retriever who was sniffing at Tara's behind.

"I hope that's not a dog!" She panted, "My bitch is in season!"

Tara answered the question by snarling a warning at the impudent intruder.

The mature forest gave way suddenly to a felled site with new planting as they went through a beautifully sculpted man-made arch, like a giant skewed distribution curve. Etched on to the side of the archway were the words " *The harvest of the trees is the rebirth of the forest* " The new sapling trees beyond were protected with opaque plastic tubes from the inevitable rabbit and deer grazing. As they walked through the arch, David felt that something in his life was changing; something new replacing the old. He felt strangely moved by the symbolic arch. Here they passed three old ladies having a picnic. Tara joined in. They did not mind. It was a carefree day.

There was an ease in the way they interrupted each other's conversation and an air of expectation of something deeper than the trivia they exchanged orally.

"How old are you, David?"

"Ancient... and I feel it today." He said breathlessly as they clambered up a steep part of the incline, "Is it a matter of any consequence, young lady?"

"No, I think age doesn't matter at all. We seem to gravitate to an ideal age and stick there. My grandfather has always been twenty-one, and my mother has always been around sixty! It's something to do with one's outlook in life. Age is so vitally important when we're young, even half a year is significant. I remember being nine ***and a half***. But when we reach the biological age of thirty, the relationship between one's age and the rest of humanity becomes blurred. It's like a critical mass. I think all people over thirty are the same age really. "

"Guess what age I am then?" He said, picking up a branch and throwing it for Tara to fetch. He pretended to throw it up the hill, but cheated and threw it over his shoulder as his grandmother's deaf and bewildered old dog charged off after thin air.

"Well, I'd say about ***twelve***!" she laughed, coaxing Tara back towards them.

Chapter 20 – Oyne Village Shop

On the way back David stopped the car at the Oyne village store. The car park was full of enormous potholes and free ranging brown chickens. There was a strange metal stick-man erected on the grass by the gate, like an outsize figure from a Lowrie painting. He was dressed in a kilt. He was leaning at an odd angle and somebody had put a grass rake in his box-metal hand. Inside, it was a quaint little place with a pleasant couple behind the counter, instantly friendly, and having good rapport with the sole elderly customer in the shop. The old chap had been there some time but did not appear to have purchased anything.

The proprietor was handsome: tall, lean and a little wind swept, with a heavy moustache, wearing paint-stained overalls and a woollen hat. The woman looked younger, at least from a distance and wore jeans and a vividly bright flowery T-shirt. She had a cotton hat on with a large bunch of very garish artificial flowers hanging to one side of it. The hat rivalled the T-shirt for attention. She had a child-like voice and laughed heartily at some incident or other.

The store was a real country emporium, and David felt instantly at home. It smelled strongly of molassed chaff and chicken mash, and he recognised the new Equinox labels on some of the products. Bags of horse carrots, compost, peanuts and sunflower seeds jostled for space with Bennachie whisky, Lazy Git fudge and pasta with an expired sell-by date. They walked cautiously around the central aisle, avoiding the semi-organised clutter, amazed at the variety of dog chews (pigs lugs!), bread, wine, jewellery, garden tools, tinned beans and eggs. A sign beside them said "*free to roam.*"

There was a very fluffy grey and white cat asleep on a pile of Press and Journals and a tortoiseshell snuggled into a hollow in a bag of pasture mix.

"What age are they then?" Rose whispered, pointing towards the shop assistants, "Do you think they're married... or father and daughter?"

"I think they're married... but not to each other! They have ***affair*** written all over them." David said, thoughtfully.

He spied a sign in the wild bird area saying, "*Tit boxes £7.99*" and pointed at it with a quizzical look and raised eyebrows.

Rose sniggered, "Well, you've just progressed to age thirteen!"

David blushed then. Among the crazy selection of products that were fit for human consumption, he was amazed to find Extra Virgin olive oil, good quality balsamic vinegar, flour, butter, cheese, fresh onions, red lentils and an excellent bottle of Australian Shiraz.

Rose picked up a packet of basmati rice... "Washed in the foothills of the Himalayas," she read, impressed that it was a cut above the boil-in-the-bag first impression of this little village shop.

"Not in the foothills of Bennachie?" he retorted, with a chuckle.

Several customers had now gathered in the store and were standing around gossiping. There was a distinguished looking, slim, balding man, with an umbrella, who seemed to be grumbling on about a footpath problem; an ex-army-major-type with a booming voice, planning reel dancing and jumping around the floor to settle a dispute by demonstrating the correct Strathspey step. David recognised the eccentric fellow as one of the many local people who had attended his grandmother's funeral service.

A younger woman burst into the shop in a nervous flap, muttering something incoherent about being bitten by a Scottish wild cat and rolling up her trouser leg to show the major. All eyes fixed on her leg. It had a large bite about the size of a man's hand. Something had clearly bitten her all right.

"Odd people around here!" Rose whispered in his ear.

"We're in good company, then." He winked.

Gingerly fighting their way through the wall of frivolity and social chat, they paid the woman at the counter, who didn't seem to mind if they paid or not, and were immediately sucked into the chit-chat conspiracy like a whirlwind. It was clear that the shopkeeper knew exactly who David was. She seemed to know everything about everybody in the village as if it was an accepted occupational hazard.

"We do not have a big customer base and things turn over slowly." She apologised for the out-of-date spaghetti, putting it in the bag free of charge. "We stock the things that we can easily eat ourselves when they expire," she explained simply.

There was a local newspaper headline poster stuck to the wall reading "*Oyne Haggis Signs... Mystery Deepens.*" Beside the notice was a small stand of Haggis Keeper's Permits costing £1.95 each, a pile of tinned Bennachie haggis, and some knitted haggi, with one leg shorter than the other so that they, "*could run around Bennachie in a clockwise direction!*"

After supper, Rose and David walked to the top of the Archaeolink hill. Archaeolink was the local pre-history park. It was called Archaeodome, by a vocal ***minority*** within the community, who felt that it was like the Millennium Dome - a white-elephant waste of taxpayer's money. Rose thought it was a brilliant place. The museum itself was built underground, covered in a mound of grass. A wider area of reconstructed archaeological ruins and excavated sites surrounded it, with several short steep walks to the top of the ancient hill. In the evenings, locals were free to enter the grounds. The walkways were planted with native species of trees, and medicinal plants, all labelled to point out their particular significance in ancient times. Hide huts, an Iron Age thatched roundhouse and wicker fencing separated various areas of interest. Stout wooden benches were found at strategic places on the route.

They paused to have a seat on the top bench. A beautiful sunset warmed the ancient ruin of Dunnydeer in the distance and they sat in silence, Tara panting at their feet. It had been a day to remember and it was not yet cold, although frost was forecast to appear during the night again.

"I wish we had sleeping bags and could just sleep here now," said Rose, "It would be so much better than going back to my damp bed... damp and ***holey*** as it is now!" She teased.

He did not answer. It sounded like an invitation but it was innocent.

She was not ready to discuss the serious business of stud services, although she thought much more of the man now and he would certainly be placed in reserve for the future. Although unspoken between them, they both knew that they would not spend the night together. He liked her well enough, but she was immature. He thought her frivolous with her streaky hair and loud clothes. It was far too soon. This one could not be treated like a ***rich bitch***. David instinctively knew she would reject him. He could tell already that she thought him old and staid and arrogant. Therefore, they promised nothing but were content with the little space they had found with each other. It was a small but comfortable space, the kind that could be encouraged to grow in the future. They knew that they would remain friends and that was important to both of them. With luck, a physical arrangement might be discussed later.

Rose explained that she was intending to go to America after the summer. She had a provisional offer to go to an Institute in Houston, Texas. Her career was of paramount importance to her. Nothing would hold her back.

A rabbit hopped out on to the path below them and seemed to have no fear. Tara pricked her ears up and whined but did not leave his side without permission. He felt strong and in control.

"Leave the rabbit, Tara!" She lay down obediently at his feet. A second rabbit joined the first.

Rose and David blended into the scene, woven there like a living tapestry.

A few stars had started to appear in the twilit sky. As they watched the heavens darken, she asked him if he believed in Destiny.

"I have no strong belief, but I guess I think there must be a higher force at work sometimes. What about you?"

"My Grandfather always speaks about *Mr Fate Esquire*, but I'm a scientist. I try to explain things in terms of factual scientific concepts, like Evolution for example. I firmly believe that natural selection is daily... even hourly... scrutinising the slightest variations found throughout the living world, rejecting those that are bad, preserving and adding to all that are good, silently working..."

"Insensibly working, you mean? As I see it, if Darwin's survival of the fittest is true, all morals in Mankind would vanish."

"What do you mean?"

"Well, real survival benefits are bestowed by cheating rather than truth. Aggression and brutality are what secures the survival of nations. Look at the current slaughter in the East, in the USA. Yet, still a moral sense in Man persists."

"Sometimes a misguided moral sense though. We discriminate against so many things on moral grounds, race, religion, and *sexuality.*" She gave him an accusing look. "Many people nowadays sense that there is something fundamentally wrong with society, but they dissipate their energy by arguing about inconsequential nonsense instead of pondering the Origin and Nature of Man."

Silence fell between them. All afternoon he had been realising that she was more mature than her appearance.

She spoke again. "Look," she smiled, "This is all too deep for me at this time of night. I think I am *morally* obliged to seek a lift back to my base?"

She looked at him with no self-consciousness. It was not the look of a stranger but had the familiarity of kin. It was the first time he was aware of the smell of her, a clean fresh outdoor smell.

Chapter 21- Grandfather's 21st

Next morning, Rose received a telephone call from her Mother. This was a rare event!

The family had organised a party for her grandfather's birthday, in only two days time! Rose knew it was his birthday and had made him a special card as usual, but she had not realised that Jim Jacobson was ninety years old. He lived in a sheltered house in Lerwick now that Granny was no longer there to look after him. His croft was sub-let to a neighbour. Rose was also not surprised to hear that he had been very depressed since being forced to move to the town. Her mother informed her that he was deteriorating fast. Rose was angry that she had not been given earlier reports of his ill health and more notice of the planned celebration. She had argued on the phone with her mother but then this was quite usual. Her mother seemed to think that mere students could just drop things at any time. Still, she did not want to miss the event, so she rang her Department and pleaded compassionate leave for a few days.

She was flustered, having had to change all her work schedules and arrange for a colleague to tend her cell cultures that needed feeding every forty eight hours. Also, her period had started that morning and she always ached for the first day. It did not help that she was a bit hung-over from a slight excess of David McKay's wine and port the previous evening.

David rang her that morning. "Hi, I'm missing your company already. Can I see you again?"

"No! Sorry, I'm off to Shetland on the six o'clock ferry. My grandfather is having a nine... a ***twenty-first*** birthday party. Mother has organised a family get-together - at very short notice!"

"Oh, I see. I thought you hadn't mentioned it yesterday. Well, I hope you have a good trip. The main reason that I phoned is that you left your purse in my car. Can I insist on dropping it back to you? I'm going to return to Edinburgh today, so I could come in on my way south. Around twelve OK?"

"I didn't even miss it! There's not much in it mind. However, I will need my student ID to get a concession ferry ticket. So, yes please, I'd be grateful if you can call in here."

She was packing her *holey* case in a haphazard fashion when David arrived, dressed only in a sleeveless top and jeans with bare feet. She was unlike his timid yet sophisticated Brenda. She was no ***rich bitch*** either. Rose was unkempt, wore skimpy clothes and skirts up to her navel. Even in those old jeans, she had a soft young body. He could detect no panty line. She moved with a sexual energy he had seldom seen before. He was infected with her sheer exuberance as she bounced up and down on the overfilled suitcase, trying to force it shut.

Before he arrived, she had made up her mind to tell David about their shared chromosome abnormality. She had felt no need to tell Lenny or Benjamin Cunningham, but David was a possibility. She really liked him. He had a right to know. After offering a cup of obligatory black coffee, she got straight to the point. She was a little too blunt perhaps.

"David, please sit down a minute. I need to talk to you."

"I'm listening."

"I need to come clean with you David. I don't know how to say this really, so I'll just come right out with it. I know about your chromosome problem."

She was not looking at him. She was still packing a final carrier bag with books and more shoes. That was a mistake. He interpreted it as dismissive body language. Such mannerisms were indicative of his mother!

"How do you know that?"

David seldom got angry, but overbearing women and also snooping of any kind had always made him mad. Rose's timing and method of delivery was terrible.

"Well, I guess I gained access to your records... but..."

"You mean to tell me that you pried into my personal medical records?"

"I'm sorry, David. There was no other way."

There was a silence after she spoke, as if he had fallen asleep. He was extremely sensitive about his abnormality. He had not told anybody about it. He stared at her. She seemed to shine with a garish and artificial light. He was full of opposing emotions. Then came the outburst, taking her by surprise.

"You have the hard neck to seek me out to see... well, am I the freak you expected? Do I fit your research requirements... like a... pair of bloody shoes? God, you really are a ***cold*** bitch, aren't you?"

She threw another pair of shoes into her hold-all with a thunderous crash. Her voice gathered momentum. His comment hit a raw nerve.

"Yes, right now you are the freak I expected!" She could have bitten her own tongue. "But listen, David, you haven't given me time to explain. I'm trying to be honest here..."

"***Honest***, that's rich! "

Rose felt taken aback. His quick temper shocked her. She had been just beginning to like him as well! She should have trusted her first impression of the man. She certainly should have kept her mouth shut. Her hard exterior was beginning to crumble. She pulled on a sweater. It was inside-out.

"Your sweater's on the wrong way." David said, feebly.

"Oh, Piss off!"

She decided not to waste time with him now. It just was not worth the effort. She felt unwell. She needed to concentrate on going home. She would just ignore him and he would leave perhaps. She crashed about in the tiny kitchenette, filling the noisiest kettle on earth, but then she did not seem to know what to do with it.

David sat still and silent, observing, considering what to do next.

"OK, why don't you make us some tea, and we can discuss this ***snooping*** like adults?"

He spoke softly, but with a distinct edge of sarcasm and superiority. She did not like that at all. He tried to take the kettle from her trembling hand. She poured the water down the sink, and banged down the empty kettle.

She held open the door and said calmly, in an ice cold tone. "Look man, I made a mistake. I won't make another. Please leave now. I have a lot to do."

He left.

...

Rose felt annoyed with herself for handling her confession so badly, but was relieved that she had caught a glimpse of his volatile temper. She had already pencilled him in her notebook as a possible biological stud, but now she put a large question mark against his name.

She put him out of her mind for the time being.

She occupied herself that afternoon buying a gift for her grandfather. She looked in an Antique shop and picked out a tiny hardwood chest of drawers, about 350mm high. It reminded her of the old Whiteness dresser that used to stand in the croft kitchen when she was a child. Grandfather had assisted her to search through its contents so many times.

She filled the tiny replica drawers with memories for him. She wrote him a poem. She knew he would get more pleasure from that than from all the chocolates and whisky and socks that he would get from the rest of the family.

The poem was in her Shetland dialect.

"Da Whiteness Dresser.

I've tocht lang tae fin dee a special gift
Tae gie dee hert a peerie lift.
Tae mind dee on happy days lang syne,
Whin Olli an dee wis graet freends o' mine.
Life wis sweet... and filled wi pleasure...
Whin we raikit ida Whiteness dresser.

Dir wis secrets galore fur peerie haands,
Postcards and stamps fae distant lands,
Boxes o matches and sheepy salt licks,
Net mending needles and tilley lamp wicks.
Dir wis buttons & kirbies & pandrops & Aa
In dat wondrous Whiteness dresser drawer.

Dir wis makin wires & raevelled oo,
Carbolic soap and pipecleaners new,
Foreign coins and binder twine,
Sinkers, hooks and fishing line!
Dir always wis anidder treasure,
When we raikit ida Whiteness dresser.

Dir wis darning needles and pirns o tread,
A muckle bag o good neep seed!
Pen knives & old photos o uncan fok,
A key... dat didna fit ony lock?
Herring corks, a lang tape measure,
Aathing wis dere... ida Whiteness Dresser."

Jim Jacobson beamed at her as she read him the poem. He took her hand in his sinewy calloused one and squeezed it. His eyes were grey and watery, but, beneath the dull film, there was the unmistakable sparkle that she knew so well. He was very frail but he still had a strong enough voice to say,

"Du's still da bees knees, Rosie."

Alas, Jim Jacobson died peacefully in his sleep two days after his birthday. Rose would miss him sorely.

Immediately after the funeral, her mother left the islands with her Oil Man. With her grandfather gone, Rose realised that there was little to draw her home now. The croft had been willed to her, but she could not justify keeping the land, because that would exclude a young local family from having it. She decided to decroft the little house and keep it so that it could be her place of escape in years to come. She passed the thirty acres of croft land to her brother Michael, who would be able to build another more modern house on it. She did not know when she would next visit Shetland, so she decided to stay a few days longer, in the perfect peace of the place.

...

She thought of David McKay a great deal during that time. She had been strangely drawn to this older man, before he showed his true colours. Yet he was still a possible biological mate, despite his temper. All right, so they had had a disagreement. She had to admit that she had done a poor job of explaining the situation. She should apologise. She decided to drop him a short e-message.

"*I've thought a lot about you. You've been niggling away in my mind. You are certainly one of the most arrogant bastards I have ever met. The trip to Bennachie was brilliant. The conversation wasn't bad either, before you became a bad-tempered* ***old*** *man! I guess I handled things badly. However, you didn't give me much of a chance to explain.*

My grandfather has just died and I suppose grief is making me think more deeply about what is important in my life. I do ***not*** *want to see you, and I'm sure that sentiment is shared. I* ***do*** *want to keep in touch. You see, the thing that I failed to tell you is that I have exactly the same chromosome abnormality as yourself. That is the reason why I tracked you down. I wanted to see others like me. However, you are really nothing like me! Our anomaly, as you will have been told, is very rare. The chances of either of us meeting another by chance alone is negligible. Nevertheless, we could, in theory, be a fertile combination.*

Don't flatter yourself that I am putting a proposal to you, I am just trying to give the facts, in true scientific fashion. However, on a purely business footing, I may wish to discuss the possibility of purchasing a sperm sample from you in the longer term future. I intend to go to America next year, where I have tracked down one more male that I hope to meet. I also want to complete my final year of postgraduate study there and ***nothing*** *will prevent me doing that.*

Please forgive my snooping, there really was no other way. Please allow me to keep in touch by e-mail and consider my long term proposal. Rose, the ***Cold Bitch****!"*

David mailed back the same day.

"Jesus wept, woman! What the hell can I say to that? I really don't know what to make of you. You are so unpredictable, so calculating, so... well, you're not ***boring*** *anyway! You have a backbone of steel, like that metal Rose on your desk! Tell me about that some time? In fact, tell me about everything? We need to speak about our shared status. I'm in shock right now – but I want to get to know you even more. Meantime, OK, you win. I will keep my distance, but I will* ***certainly*** *keep in touch!"*

Chapter 22 - Leaving

As the plane took off, heading for the USA, Rose felt as if an umbilical cord had been severed. She was leaving behind everything and everybody she knew. Grandfather was dead. Richard was settled with his Alex and she missed his comradeship. She had messed up big-style with David McKay.

She drew upon her inner strength. Opening her briefcase, she switched attention to her work She filed all other thoughts and useless emotions away to the back drawer of her mind as she had always done.

Dwelling on emotional nonsense made her restless and inefficient. She was lucky that she could switch into an all-exclusive working mode quite easily. It was sheer self-preservation. She needed no serious involvement with anyone. She had her own strength and her career. But she felt lonely and discontented when she let her mind free. She regretted the way she had parted company with David. Despite the row, their short time together had displayed a gravity that had seemed appropriate for her ultimate purpose. Other than the heat of the disagreement, which was largely her fault, she had to acknowledge that there had been no selfishness on his part. They had talked of their past lives and only the shallow part of their hopes. They had exchanged only trivial meaningless words. Yet there remained a hint, just a hint, of future promise. It was never really spoken... but she felt that an arrangement with this man ***might*** still be possible in the future.

Having found one potential mating partner, who was, for the most part, tolerable, she did not want to lose him. She did not want to scare him either. She was well aware that there had been no dignity in their parting. Still, he seemed keen to stay in touch at any rate. She needed to maintain a grip on how she handled herself, so she would play safe and minimalist.

Besides, the ***fourth*** and final possibility for a biological match still awaited her in Houston! What would he be like?

The strange lump in her throat made it difficult to swallow coffee. She consoled herself that she had no immediate desire to have children anyway. For the time being, she was only interested in her career.

Unable to concentrate on work for long, she accepted a gin and tonic from the stewardess and settled back with an in flight magazine. It was a historical review of the pre-Iraq-war period. The centre spread glossy map showed the current forbidden air zones with red cross-hatching. She was glad they were all distant from the route she was taking. The article read :-

"It has been known throughout the centuries that military power rests upon wealth. All the World's military power balances have followed productive economies. During the last century, it was merely a bipolar world, with only the USA and USSR having the means to ensure each other's destruction. However, the balance rapidly shifted.

Oil giants gathered wealth. Saudi Arabia could produce 7.5 million barrels a day, and Iraq was close behind, and growing fast. Wealth and military power gathered in the East. Russia, who also produces around 7 million barrels, was wooed as a Western ally. However, the association was a fragile one.

Even before the declaration of war on Iraq, there was compelling and overwhelming evidence that Saddam Hussein had developed weapons of mass destruction, hiding both nuclear and biological warfare centres behind the grand facades of Presidential Palaces. He did not allow the United Nation's Weapons Inspectors to search these places. Hundreds of tons of dangerous chemicals have gone missing over the past decade - believed to have been diverted to make weapons. A few were discovered by the Coalition troops, but it is believed that more significant finds have yet to come to light...

At the time of writing, the Southern cities have fallen, notably Basra. A second military strike has now been launched on Baghdad. Terrorist parasites have crawled from their underground holes and hundreds have surrendered to the Coalition forces. Others continue to dress like civilians and strike the US or UK troops when they least expect it. A stock pile of nuclear war heads has been found just inside the city boundary. Vials of unknown bio-engineered germs have been discovered at a second location.

Carl Sagan, the eminent Astronomer, may have been close to being a soothsayer at the end of the last century when he said: "Perhaps we will destroy ourselves. Perhaps the common enemy within us will be too strong to recognise and overcome," although he added, "I have hope. Is it possible that we humans are at last coming to our senses and beginning to work together on behalf of the species and the planet?"

There have been four minor attacks of terrorism in Britain but a major incident is expected at any day. Everybody needs to remain alert.

The Holy Men warned way back in 2001 that one wrong move could determine the future of the World as we know it. Have we already made the wrong move?"

Rose fell asleep despite the unsettling nature of the article.

She had barely set foot in America when the news broke that two oilfields in the North Sea had been bombed in the latest terrorist attack and one jetty at the Sullom Voe Oil base had sustained substantial damage.

No corner of the earth was immune from terrorism.

Chapter 23 - Savage

Rose was immediately overwhelmed with the hustle and bustle and ear-drum-shattering American city noises. The sheer change from the clear cool quietness of a Shetland croft, where even one sheep or a curlew seemed loud, was quite dramatic. However, she was an islander, good at adapting.

During that year David McKay kept his promise of regular contact. He was content to allow her time to get the career bug out of her system. She was very young. David had changed for the better since the diagnosis of his own chromosome abnormality. He was no longer so arrogant and sure of himself. He developed more tolerance for others. People he would not have passed the time of day with, in his youth, became friends and companions.

He had been, in effect, improved by his imperfection, truly humbled by his stigma.

He was encouraged that Rose always responded quickly to his e-mails. Gradually, he began to see beyond the cold scientist, there was something shining and new in her. As time went on, he felt frustrated that he could not see her. The video-telephone was all right, but not the same as meeting in the flesh. She still wore outlandish modern clothes. It was a sharp contrast to the deeper maturity of the individual who spoke to him on the web. He felt a growing confidence that he could woo and win this intriguing young woman, who had taken the initiative to track him down. She was unique. He liked her because she was plucky and undiluted. Yet, he was aware that he must respect her wishes and allow her the time she wanted to complete her postgraduate degree.

They got to know each other much better in that little electronic space.
A closeness of the mind developed between them and blossomed.

Although Baghdad had fallen and a system of temporary government had been established, the sporadic fighting in Iraq lingered on unresolved and global unrest intensified. Britain's motorists were the first victims of the spectre of war. Petrol prices soared as fragile economies plummeted and oil sanctions against the West were introduced.

Equinox Ltd. spiralled downwards into recession with the rest of the British Manufacturing sector.

David put all his energies into the business. Fearful of Rose's disapproval, and in a highly competitive business climate, he was now extremely vigilant about materials used in the manufacturing process and careful with the wording on packaging. He played fair and honest and this paid off in that the business remained viable, when many others fell by the wayside. He found that he liked himself better. His mother, whom he had always taken for granted, became more important to him. He dated a few women, sticking to the ***rich bitch*** category, but they were mostly one-night-stands. They lacked depth.

Besides, none of them could give him children!

...

Do you know what it's like to feel off colour after a vaccination? Well, imagine what it's like to have about a dozen of them, all within a short time period. You feel like shit. It's not surprising that you over-react and lose perspective on the personal relationship front!

Rose was destined to work with a level four virus called *Ebbinflo 7.* In preparation for handling a hot virus, she was further trained in the Hot Zone Laboratory in Houston, Texas. Over the course of the first year, she was pumped full of vaccinations: Yellow fever, Rift Valley fever, Q-fever, the VEE WEE & EEE complex, rabies, anthrax, botulism, HIV7 and Ebola-1473.

Rose liked Houston. It was not the prairie-dry dusty place she imagined. There was a lot of greenery, if you knew where to find it. It was in one such gentle cool park retreat, near to the laboratory complex, while playing with her lunchtime sandwiches, feeling sick as a parrot, that she first met Jason Savage.

She was feeding her lunch to the pigeons when he sat on the bench beside her and said, "Hi there little lady, do you mind if I join the pigeons for lunch?"

"Be my guest, I can't eat anything. I'm feeling squeamish." Rose replied, handing him the last remaining sandwich. He opened it, checked the contents and ate it with relish.

"So, do you have a name?"

"Name's Rose Anderson, I work over there. Look, I don't mean to be rude, but I really don't feel like having a conversation today."

"Jason Savage. I work there too."

"Oh, Dr Savage! I saw your name on the staff list. Pharmacogenetics Department, isn't it?"

"Spot on, Rose. Look, I can tell by your newness... and your colour... that you've probably just had the starter vaccination programme? I remember it well." He flashed his ID card and offered her a small blue pill. "Try this. I personally guarantee that it is nothing but a herbal remedy, made from kaolin infused with three extracts of mountain herbs, but it will make you feel better. It is not anything dangerous or illegal. Unfortunately, it is not a seduction drug."

Islanders are trusting in nature, naive really.

Rose looked carefully at his identification badge and then at his eyes. Everything seemed in order and she took the offering, swallowing it with a gulp of mineral water. That herbal remedy sealed their friendship. Within minutes the nausea subsided.

"Well, Rose, do you have any interests other than feeding pigeons and taking pills from strangers in the park?"

"Yes, I'm passionately interested in viruses!"

Jason Savage was a typical big, brash and handsome American guy and a fellow scientist. He was indeed an expert in the field of Pharmacogenetics. Built a little on the heavy side, but with the kind of male shape that women do not mind leaning against, he walked with a swagger, oozing confidence. His hair was auburn red and he had a ruddy complexion, despite his largely indoor environment.

Rose liked him right away, from his jovial friendly approach to his expressive hands. They started to date on a regular basis. They were alike, both with a hard core and a tenacious attitude to their work. At first, Jason was just her computer man, helping her to set up essential programmes for her research project. He was totally computer-orientated at work and at home. The many hours in contact with keyboard and VDU had apparently trained his personality. He outwardly operated like a computer. He had the ability to slot in a new floppy disc at will and become a different person. His main programme gave him a glossy efficiency, complete with a pleasant firm telephone manner and a deal-with-any-crisis function. Whilst in this mode, he was cool, calm and business-like, invoking admiration from all who came in contact, including Rose. He had a softer side also, and Rose had glanced it a little, but he had the ability to switch it on and off as he pleased and it seemed just a little artificial. Nevertheless, she accepted him as just a ***different***, eccentric kind of fellow.

To some extent, her friendship with Jason made up for the disappointment in her search for the ***fourth*** biological partner - he had died in 2002 of a brain haemorrhage, following glandular fever.

Strangely enough, he too had suffered congenitally from a low platelet disorder. There seemed to be little doubt that a faulty immune system was linked to this particular chromosome anomaly.

It was a few months into their relationship before Jason Savage switched to an intimate mode for very short periods of select time. Their sexual union was mechanical and adequate to fill a need. He never appeared quite genuine in the role as lover. He also had an assumed status as a man above that of a mere woman. Just a trace of this gender superiority came across. He liked his orders to be obeyed.

Three months after they met, Jason Savage was head hunted and appointed to a new position, as one of the leading scientists in the United Nations Drug Control Project.

At the same time, Rose grew closer to the electronic David, looking forward to his frequent messages, most of them quite shallow and frivolous, but regular contact nevertheless. She told him that she was seeing Jason Savage. She was pleased that David had changed company practices for the better. The man himself seemed more human. She felt that she could rely on him being there if she needed anybody and that was a wonderful security net. Yet, he was such a long way off and not part of her real life. David had become a daily escape from reality and the pressures of work. She hoped to meet him again... some day.

It was like losing yourself in a film or a book. She did not know where the story was going. She had made it very clear to him early on in their correspondence that ***if*** she ever decided to attempt to have his child, it would be by means of artificial insemination and she would want to keep the child. She would choose the timing to fit her career. Such unorthodox suggestions did not seem quite so out of place in America. He had not agreed to this. He had insisted that they would discuss it fully like adults when they met.

David was bemused and a little angry about the scientific and rather callous way that she treated her relationships. However, he felt a sense of power that at least he could give her something that no other man could - and vice versa of course!

He waited.

Chapter 24 - Poppies

The war in Iraq had officially ended with the toppling of Saddam Hussein's corrupt regime. However, although he was reported as dead, no confirmation of a body was possible. Large sums of money were withdrawn from the bank by his son and never recovered. His iron grip on the country was being loosened one finger at a time, but still a little finger-hold remained. Despite cautious optimism that the war had been successful, pockets of resistance persisted and skirmishes broke out frequently. Although the Coalition troops withdrew, a US Military presence remained in Iraq to deal with the sporadic outbreaks of fighting.

Terrorism incidents were on the increase, not just in the East, but in the West as well.

Rose worked very closely with Jason Savage during the early part of 2004. She was frequently coerced into doing lucrative consultancy work for top classified projects. However, she did not always agree with the direction that these were heading. Towards the end of her year in Houston, she was called to investigate the nature of a new micro-organism.

Tests showed that it was a fungus, named by the team as ***Cleospora nidulans destructum.*** Having done most of the analysis, Rose was invited to the meeting where Jason Savage gave the report of their findings to his superiors.

"American Intelligence has shown that much of the funding for certain known terrorist activities comes from the drugs trade. The fungus ***Cleospora nidulans destructum*** has been engineered by my research group and is thought to have great potential as a Bio-weapon. Our Research and Development programme has shown it to be highly infectious, aggressive and dangerous... to the ***Papavar*** family! It has no direct human effects. Now, as you know, heroin mostly starts life as a poppy in Afghanistan. This new agent against heroin could be a biological weapon of mass proportions, seriously crippling the drugs trade by hitting the terrorists where it hurts - in their pockets!"

Rose spoke up quickly, "Dr Savage, I think that more work is perhaps needed..."

Colonel Burnett intervened. He referred to the unconventional war that had now grumbled on for two long years. There were more and more desperate networks of terrorists, mass suicide incidents. Thousands of innocent civilians had been killed on both sides. There had been nine separate attacks in the USA and four now in Britain. There was irrefutable evidence that the opium trade financed much of it. He concluded by saying, "Gentlemen, we simply don't have the time to delay. This is surely a plant attacker... it is harmless to people... is that not so?

Rose responded.

"Well Sir, I have tested CND on one hundred and fifty types of other plants. It ***seems*** to be highly specific to the heroin poppy, but I cannot exclude unknown side effects. It might mutate in the wild. It could attack other plants, for example food crops. It could be extremely difficult to contain. It will, if released, go at maximum speed with minimum supervision. Slight genetic modification of this fungus could end up with an even more deadly pathogen. What if it attacked crops like potatoes, wheat, soya beans? Massive famine could, ***theoretically***, occur!"

"In view of recent events, Dr Anderson, we are prepared to take that chance. CND will be our silver bullet in this lingering war against terrorism, and indirectly, the war against drugs. It is my understanding that it takes out 99% of poppy plants in the field. It can be spread easily with crop dusters, and only the target plants will be eliminated. It's ***green*** warfare, really, if you see what I mean?"

"You know it wouldn't be the first time that innocent science backfires when it breaks free of the laboratory, with deadly consequences!" Rose replied.

Jason Savage frowned his disapproval at her.

Cleospora nidulans destructum was passed for selected action.

Later, Jason and Rose continued their disagreement in private.

"Why are you so against this action, Rose? It's a well-known fact that heroin crime costs even Great Britain around £5 billion a year. The International Drug Trade is bigger than the Oil Trade! This little beauty will surely perform a double service! You should be proud to be a part of all this."

"I don't care about the costs involved, Jason. I don't wish to become a part of what is rapidly becoming a ***Bio-terrorist*** organisation. I want out of this! You know as well as I do that there has not been enough testing done. But don't listen to me. I'm only a woman. What do we know about the global economy?"

"Well. True. Your gender spend more per ounce than pure gold on a stupid oil and water emulsion called ***makeup***!"

"OK, Mr Know-all, but you cannot win the war against drugs or terrorism in this way by unleashing a wild card effect, just as you cannot stop women... and men... wearing cosmetics!"

She stomped out, peeking back through the door to add,"Don't think I haven't noticed your dyed hair! You hypocrite! "

Chapter 25 - Catalepsis

Rose completed her doctorate in record time via the submission of seven published papers, in July 2005. Largely assisted by contacts made through Jason Savage, she had made a substantial impact in the field of viral genetics. The ambitious Jason was on a fast-track career drive. She was strongly advised to complete a postdoctoral year and was offered a Fellowship in Jason's new department, simply called, "The Institute," by the US Military. It was only to ensure her long-term career prospects that she agreed to accept this.

She had made up her mind that the time would be right after that to take a career break and investigate the possibility of having a child. With this intent, and to conclude some kind of mutually beneficial bargain, she invited David McKay over for her Graduation Ceremony. She set rules for the meeting in the same way as she set her rules for scientific experiments. Cold rules. Clinical boundaries.

He could stay at her apartment - in the spare room. He would be her guest at the ceremony, to be introduced as an old friend of the family and he must never, under any circumstances breath a word of their real relationship. The rules made it clear to David that she was perhaps a little ashamed of him... or of herself for persisting in the cold-blooded approach.

Nevertheless, David was excited about meeting Rose again. Leaving aside her strange scientific principles, in terms of her intelligence, he had long ago elevated her to a platform way above any other woman he had known. He needed her to have respect for him as well. He really wanted this relationship to work, and it need not be at the distance she dictated. However, if that was to be, then he could surely rent her uterus, pay her for surrogacy, just as easily as she could purchase his sperm! Why should she be in control and set all the bloody rules?

He arrived two days before the Graduation Ball. He felt unsure of himself. He was rather weary of the unpredictability of the relationship, not to mention the negative effects of the prolonged global unrest on the UK business economy. There had been several recent terrorist incidents in Britain. London Underground was partly closed and Heathrow Airport had lost one runway. The North Sea oilrigs had suffered two separate attacks. He wanted to settle down with a partner again. If Rose was not willing to give him a serious hearing, then he must find somebody else and forget about her, and the whole vexing subject of children. He knew she dated a few other guys, one name in particular kept cropping up: Jason Savage.

The first evening together was strained. It felt strange facing each other in the same physical space, knowing so much, yet so little. He had kissed her on the cheek when they met at the airport. She had made no attempt to retaliate and brushed the whole action aside, talking incessantly, controlled as always, although perhaps just a little nervous. He did not attempt to touch her again that day or the next. They just enjoyed each other's company. He was staying with her for a week. She would show him the sights. She planned to talk about a possible practical arrangement for the future.

During the second day, Rose showed David her workplace. It smelt of ether and absolute alcohol. She had a tame rat called Simon, who lived under her microscope cover. Simon was very fat. Her desk was littered with glass slides and lens tissue. Clinical books lined the shelves. A photograph of the team was pinned to the wall, curling at the edges with the dry heat. David noticed the red-haired muscular guy with an arm around her shoulder. They looked comfortable together. David did not feel comfortable in this alien place. It smelt of complexity. However, this was her sacred domain and although he didn't understand it at all, he honoured it and kept his thoughts to himself.

By the third day together, they had found that ease with each other that all of us crave. They lost themselves in the little private space they had shared for the past couple of years, only it became more real now. She smelt as he remembered her, familiar.

Wow! She ***had*** grown up! Dressed for the Ceremony, she was so sophisticated that she took his breath away. She wore a plain cream dress, tight as a second skin with a little silver dolphin brooch on her shoulder. Her golden hair was up in a clip of some sort, emphasising a long slender neck, with fine strands feathering downwards from the nape. She just sparkled.

Rose thought that David looked younger than she remembered and more fit. He was wearing well. She could not help but notice that he was a striking figure in his dress McKay kilt, long-haired sporran and Lovat tweed jacket. He even had a sprig of purple heather in his buttonhole. He suited this traditional Highland outfit much better than any business suit. She felt a shot of exhilaration.

She noticed that David walked with a swagger of confidence, comfortable with his appearance and his rich family heritage.

He remained hopeful that he was not the end of his line.

It is strange how we are sometimes unaware how special a moment is until it is past and we look back on it. The Graduation Ceremony was special in that way. David did not see the dozens of other graduates, only her, with her flowing robes and her parchment held high. Her radiant smile, with white teeth flashing, cut through the crowds and came straight to him. He was very proud. It was one of the few moments in his life when he was aware of perfection, at the time.

Rose was given an Award of Merit for the most outstanding work in her field and his heart soared with her as she received it. The champagne flowed that evening at the reception at the Campus. Both of them probably had a little too much, but it felt good, like a release valve. There was no pressure to pretend. They were just themselves.

In the confines of the taxi, he was enchanted with her tantalising body aroma; pungent, sweet, glorious and exciting - a fiery yet primeval odour. As their cab dropped them back to her apartment, and she fumbled for the keycard, David took both her hands in his and she fell still and silent.

"Hey! What ***are*** you doing, David? Remember the rules!"

"Look. To hell with the rules! I don't want the perfection of this day to end, Rose. I want to remember it after the night has passed. I know if I come in there with you, I will want more than you may be prepared to give me. I know you feel something for me. But please, Rose, I have observed all your rules. You know I am not a fly-by-night stranger. Don't take me through that door if you are going to reject me!"

She did not answer, because she was already kissing him, gently. He tasted salt and felt tears on her cheek.

"What's wrong?"

"Today, ***nothing*** is wrong. That's the problem. Come in David. I want you to come in."

That night also reached perfection.
It was not the champagne.
It was real.

There was a genuine need in the desire that glazed her eyes and made her pale skin shudder beneath his touch. He was as gentle as his aroused state would allow. She was straightforward, uninhibited, yet forceful. So different from any other lover he'd had. They seemed to fit like pieces in a jigsaw puzzle. He wondered how her body, that he had never seen naked before, could feel so familiar, so perfectly tailored to his own.

They were both aware that this was not merely a mechanical coupling. It was a deeper force that stirred their physical beings into a crescendo of hunger, and extended way beyond that. Their very essences blended together like a potion of powerful magic. They both knew in the firm rhythmic collision of their flesh that, whatever the future held, this time was meant to be. It was a precious time. They felt that they were returning to the sanctuary of home after a long time lost and wandering in wilderness. Material concerns were wiped off the face of the earth. They felt no need to talk, yet they communicated fluently in another dimension.

For David, the presence of this strange, clinical, iron-willed woman suddenly took on a significance that was full of wonder and deep joy. From that moment on, meaning and real purpose entered the strange equation of his life. He thought only of this woman who filled every space within him and drew him into her hot soft core so that nothing else was of the slightest consequence.

When he woke in the morning, he felt no remorse, only the secret, heart jolting remembering of blissful union. The pungent aftermath smells were all pervading, still exciting, and urging him to seek her again.

The bed was empty.

A leap of panic coursed through him. A note was left on the breakfast bar. "*Thanks for last night. I needed that. I've gone back to work this morning. There is something I've got to finish. I'm feeling a little hung-over. See you later. Don't go away! R.*"

David had taken to reading his father's books on the Arts over the past few years, in a belated attempt to improve his knowledge. He recalled the words of John Armstrong who wrote, "The Intimate Philosophy of Art." Armstrong had highlighted five phases in the perceptual contemplation of an object. The fifth phase was ***catalepsis*** or mutual absorption.... "*A state of mind or soul - one of contentment or concentration - which puts thought and feeling into harmonious accord. We are so taken up with the object of contemplation - that other more distressing thoughts are squeezed out. We gain relief from anxiety and egoism - it has an ability to liberate us from the general round of self-centredness: the multitude of desires, concerns and worries which occupy large parts of our mental space.*"

David decided that he was well into ***catalepsis***.

...

He wished that their night together would never end, as they lay entwined, ***different*** from the rest of the world, yet making the same age-old and futile attempt that all true lovers do to get deep inside each other and stay there forever.

In the morning, David was depressed at the thought of going home and leaving her behind. Rose showed no such emotion.

She laughed heartily and ate breakfast like a horse.

David asked her to return to Britain with him. She calmly told him that she was staying in America. She had been offered a Fellowship for at least one year. It was necessary for her career prospects and a great opportunity. After that she might seek work in the United Kingdom.

"Look, David, please don't think that sex, even great sex, changes everything. It's the twenty-first century. It doesn't change that much."

"Sex doesn't change anything, but trust does. I thought we had trust? What are you afraid of?"

"Nothing! But the answer's still no. Not yet. It wouldn't work out for me at this time in my life. We both have our careers and I don't want anything more than we have - at least not yet. I'm still too young to embark on a pregnancy, even if it were a possibility. I'm just not ready."

David suspected Jason Whatsisname had something to do with it. He briefly thought of exterminating him!

"I believe that I truly love you, Rose, and it's the first time I've ever said that to any woman. I'm not so young. I've wasted time. I've been a right bastard, but I ***have*** changed. I'm weary of life on my own. I'm sickened by what we human beings do to each other in this bloody world. I want to share my life with you."

"I don't want to discuss this right now. I don't wish to act on impulse. I'd prefer you to go home and let me think things through without distraction. Look, I'm coming to Britain in September to another Conference. Let's meet up and discuss things then? A nostalgic trip to Bennachie. That's what I'd like. I'm going up north to spend a weekend with Richard and Alex anyway. Why don't you come along as well? "

"Rose, if that's what you want, I can't force you to think differently, but I'm not giving up on you. I intend to come back again and again - like a Jehovah's witness!"

An ominous shadow hung over their last day together. David left on schedule, because he had commitments at home, but he was determined to win her lasting affection. He would contact her every day until September.

Rose was also determined. She would not be rushed. She was not ready to commit to David. Not yet. She would stick to her schedule and serve one more year. Always the practical scientist first and foremost, she could see the benefit of notching up a few rungs on the career ladder before taking precious time out to try for a child. It would be so much easier to slot back into the profession afterwards.

She was one of the leading experts in the field of filoviruses. There were few around with her particular blend of qualifications, practical skills and contacts. The latent but growing threat of ***Bio-warfare*** made her a much sought-after expert.

News was just through concerning the latest find in Iraq by the US Military that still remained in the country as a back-up for the fragile new government. A considerable stock-pile of nuclear weapons had been discovered, disguised behind the facade of a school. A modern laboratory complex had also been unearthed at a nearby location.There was a substantial Bio-bank of engineered germs awaiting analysis.

There was a vital role for her - in Jason's department.

Chapter 26 – Mors Janua Vitae

As arranged, Rose returned to Britain in the Autumn of 2005. The subject of the Conference she was attending in London was, "***Measures to put in place during Bio-warfare.***" It was largely a closed shop, with several prestigious International delegates and absolutely no guests allowed. There was little point in David travelling to London, so Rose hired a car and drove to Scotland on the Thursday afternoon, after her official duties were over.

She listened to the radio as she travelled north. The news bulletin was depressing..."*A bomb had exploded in Harrods Department Store in central London. Thousands of Saturday shoppers were innocent victims. A suicide pilot had hit Alton Towers Pleasure Park. Hundreds of families and groups from schools had been killed...*"

Was there no end to this bloody terrorism?

It was a tiring eight-hour journey north and she arrived late in the evening. It was great to see Richard again. He had grown very distinguished and less flamboyant. Alex had toned him down a little. He had taken up gardening and the house was full of home grown vegetables and Bonsai trees.

Despite the late hour, they drank wine and laughed like teenagers. They reminisced about the carefree days of University until almost three in the morning.

David joined them on Friday. After spending an obligatory hour with her friends, he whisked Rose away, wanting her exclusively for himself.

They had often spoken about their first peaceful trip to Bennachie and that was where Rose wanted to spend another weekend together. David could have taken her to his Grandmother's house, but he was in the process of doing major improvements and it was barely habitable yet. Besides, he wanted to impress her so he had opted for booking a room in the local hotel.

Pittodrie House Hotel was a beautiful old place, full of stone passages and character. Also, he knew the owner and had negotiated a good deal on the room in return for a few bags of a new brand of Applechaff for his fussy thoroughbred mare.

Rose and David had different expectations of each other. She wanted complete control of their time together, his unquestioning friendship and no complications. He wanted much more than that. Leaving aside his mother, he was not used to women who did not bend to his will and who did not find him irresistible. Pent up emotions were at fever pitch.

They compromised and stayed within the boundaries of that small, defined space they had shared for the past few years. He suspected that she was still consorting with that young American scientist. It was not easy to compete when Dr Jason Whatsisname was on her doorstep, or inside her house. He had a vision of that seven-foot tall rugby-playing, red, muscular God in the photograph in her laboratory. He hated him.

Rose was nauseous and shaky for the entire week she spent on British soil due to her latest batch of booster vaccinations. Thus, their weekend together was not spent entirely in the four poster bed, but in the fresh air. They walked and they talked and they simply "chilled out."

For prolonged periods, David just looked at her reading or sleeping, trying to preserve these moments by branding her image into his mind. He feared losing her, yet he knew that whatever happened now, she would remain in his bones forever. Something he had read recently intruded on his vigil... "*The one who holds the power in any relationship is the one who cares less.*" Perhaps his callous treatment of past girlfriends was coming home to roost?

They were both wearied of the different aspects of the global unrest, and here they felt far removed from it. They walked on the peaks of the mountain and beside the gentle waters of the Gadie Burn. They wandered in the extensive grounds of Pittodrie Estate, chancing upon a tiny walled cemetery on top of the hill. It was well tended and had a beautiful wrought-iron gate, with the inscription "*Mors Janua Vitae*." David explained that it signified death and life, linked together by January, the first month as one enters a new year. Inside the enclosure were the headstones of *"Sir Robert Workman Smith: 1880 –1957 and Jessie Hill: 1880-1978."* Rose found the history of the place quite fascinating.

They circled Bennachie by car, looking at it from all the different angles. On the Sunday, Alex and Richard joined them for lunch. Afterwards, Alex took the four of them in his plane, over the entire Bennachie Range, visiting the peaks of Oxen Craig, Craigshannoch and Mither Tap. They looked down on the Pittodrie Estate. David pointing out the small house, nestling in the foothills, where his grandparents had lived. He explained that he now owned it and was renovating it as his place of escape, as their sanctuary. Rose loved the wild beauty of the whole area.

Rose had brought a watercolour pad with her, and she painted five little sketches over the three days. From a distance, the peaks looked like the profile of a sleeping woman with large breasts. David explained that the name "Mither Tap" meant ***Hill of the Pap***, because it was indeed shaped like the breast of a woman.

They visited archaeological ruins and old churchyards. Ancient stones had always fascinated Rose.

It was getting late, on their last evening together, that they found themselves in the old kirkyard at Logie. It was an eerie place in the dying sun, against the backdrop of the sleeping hill-woman in the distance. The gravestones were covered in lichens and difficult to read. Many were set at leering angles, casting long shadows over the ground. Others had fallen flat and were being colonised by creeping mosses. David peered at a small flattened stone, shaped like a shield. A child had been put to rest there decades ago.

"Jeanie Deans, 11 years old," he read aloud.

The terrain was uneven, with sinister undulating green hillocks of ivy covering dilapidated tombstones. A granite cross was sticking proud of the underworld of dark ivy. A marble gravestone, with the surname "Bremner" barely discernible, was entirely wrapped in an ancient yew tree, like a heavy shroud around the shoulders of a spectre.

It had grown suddenly cold.

“I don’t like the atmosphere here, Rose. We’re surrounded by dead people.”

“They won’t harm us. They’re dead. It’s only the living that can harm us.”

“Yes, people can and do harm each other. Not just with war, but with actions of a much smaller scale. I guess man is the ultimate enemy. We’ll probably end up blowing ourselves off the face of the earth.”

“That’s a happy tune! I can see you don’t like this place... but, for the record, you’re wrong. Man is ***not*** the ultimate killer... the microbe is!”

“Surely wars caused by man have killed more people that mere bugs have? Man is his own worst enemy!”

“Nope! Man has a much more lethal enemy than himself. Through the ages, microbes have killed more men than wars. The great Justinian plague killed 40 million between 540 and 765A.D. In the 1300s, the Black Death claimed 25 million. 30 million died of a deadly flu in the period immediately after the First World War. I truly believe that viruses are the ultimate conquerors of this earth and will outlive all that’s in it!”

“A comforting thought. I see you are still passionate about your work. I don’t suppose I need ask if you have given any more thought to my proposal?”

David looked downcast, knowing her answer already.
They stood apart.

“I think of it all the time actually. I like you a lot, David, especially the new you. You’ve changed for the better in the past three years. You’ve lost your arrogance and don’t look down your nose so much at other people. I feel comfortable with you now. I guess there is even trust. I may even be a little in love with you. However, I have to return to the States this time, because I have one special piece of work to finish. I need to complete a period of notice. However, I am currently looking at positions back in Britain, lecturing at a University perhaps. I've decided that in the near future, I will consider a short career break and I would like to try for a pregnancy, because the time is right. I am so sick of the whole concept of this awful war. I don't like the direction that it is going. I want to live - in a place like this and - grow things."

David could not believe what she had just said! This was the nearest thing to a promise of commitment he had ever heard from her. The shadows seemed to lift from the dreary kirkyard as the last rays of watery evening sun dappled the blackness of the ivy. He put his arms around her. His heart sang. His mind raced. She had started looking around for jobs in Britian! Knowing this, he wanted to follow her immediately to America, but she forbade it absolutely. He could not just leave his job and his company. She was not going to ***marry*** him or anything, just live together a while and see if a pregnancy was possible. Perhaps they could even ***try*** joint parenthood. David was happy with any terms. He loved her.

They sat long into the night in their hotel room, talking of everything and nothing the way lovers do, chewing over the events that had brought them together.

"I know that I engineered our meeting in the first place, David, but I'm beginning to think that perhaps ***Mr Fate Esquire*** has also played a role."

"Like some sort of pre-determined intervention? I'm afraid I can never ponder such nebulous things. It's all too big for a mere mortal like me. I thought you didn't believe such nonsense?"

"I'm a scientist. I try hard to exclude a Greater Force, but, sometimes I have to admit that the probability of life appearing spontaneously on earth seems minute. Imagine a scrap-yard, with all the components necessary to build a nuclear-powered space shuttle, but just lying there, all jumbled up. I can't accept that such a sophisticated space ship could just appear by ignorant trial and error. It requires something else... some... complex organisation... some kind of very special knowledge."

She fell silent for a few minutes, then continued, " Jason likens it to a blind man trying to solve the Rubik cube by chance. It would take him thousands of billions of years, or five times ten to the power of twenty to be precise... and that would be the equivalent of achieving completion of only ***one*** of the thousands of proteins in our body. Yet each of our proteins is made and designed with military precision. The chances of designing the 200,000 proteins, upon which our life depends, is infinitesimally small. I guess I do believe in ***something*** - something very superior to myself."

"Me!" David said, pulling her towards him with a laugh.

She whispered in his ear, "Oh no! You're just a defective... like me!"

A niggling shadow hovered over the bliss of their lovemaking on the last night together at Pittodrie House. She was still seeing that Dr Jason Whatsisname.

Chapter 27 - Secondment

The telephone was ringing when she got back to her apartment. It was Jason. "Hi there, Rose! How was your trip back home?"

" Oh, some good and some bad. Let's just say not the way I expected!"

" You want some company? A listening ear? A romantic dinner? Passionate sex?"

"Nope... to all! Jason, look, it's a long story. I'll tell you another time. It can wait."

"I missed you, you know?"

"I missed... Houston. I missed... work... and I guess I missed you... a little!" Rose laughed, realising that the end of the sentence was particularly true.

"I need to see you as soon as you like."

"I'm knackered, Jason... can we leave it till tomorrow?"

"Sure, but can you come to the Department for a couple of hours in the morning? It's work, I'm afraid."

"Yes, but where is your new work-place? I've never been there yet."

"I know. I'll send a cab for you. Around nine all right?"

"OK, Jason, I'll see you in the morning. Bye now."

Rose was too tired to think much about the *ad hoc* meeting in the morning.

The cab took her to an underground car park in the middle of the city. She was met in the lift by Jason and taken to a high security Reception area, where she was asked to sign various papers in connection with Official Secrets and Secure Affairs. It all seemed a bit over the top, but she complied and was sworn to the strictest code of confidentiality regarding the meeting to follow.

There were twelve persons in the Conference suite, ten of them unknown to Rose. Jason introduced her to everyone, but she was too nervous to hear. She focused only on the group chairman, Colonel Andrew Burnett, Assistant Secretary of Defense, and the man seated on his right, Professor Blair Spooner, the Science Advisor to the President of the United States!

This was no ordinary meeting.

Colonel Burnett gave the opening address, "Ladies and Gentlemen, thank you for coming here at such short notice. This is a matter of the greatest National importance. You have each been chosen, after careful vetting, to represent a particular area of expertise and to assist the United States of America to shorten and win the current war decisively! You have each fulfilled all the criteria for total secondment to this project and will be removed from your everyday occupations for a period of twelve months. We have been forced to take this unusual action because of several recent security breaches from within our own most trusted ranks! Rest assured that you will be well rewarded financially."

Rose struggled to take in what this high-powered official was saying. Could this be done without her consent? She looked to Jason for reassurance. He smiled and nodded.

The man droned on...
"As you know we have been fighting on a number of fronts for the past few years and you will be well versed with our military and financial efforts. I will not go into these here. Suffice to say we have been unable to entirely quell the tiresome recurring incidents of unconventional warfare in the East. This group represents the BMW, Biological and Molecular Weapons, Branch and includes official delegations from Washington, the National Science Foundation, the Department of Defense, the President's Science Advisory Committee, the National Security Council and the National Security Agency."

At this point a few black-suited observers arrived with gold passes. Colonel Burnett nodded in their direction and continued to give the background scenario.

"You have each been seconded from society to do a particular task. You will be moved to a specialist facility at a top-secret location. It is inevitable that you will be cut off from all contact with friends and family. Most of you have few, if any, living relatives who will seek to find you, so that does not present a problem. You will have six hours from the end of this meeting to gather together a minimum of personal effects. Full scientific facilities and reference materials will be at your disposal at your new base. You are forbidden to make contact with any person outside this room from this time..." He looked at his watch as if implementing the curfew immediately.

Murmurings filled the room. A few voices were raised in protest...

"I fully understand your shock and anger, but this is a grave situation of paramount importance to the USA and perhaps even for the future of the world. You are ***ordered*** and ***honoured*** by the President to serve this country for the next critical year. Now, briefing papers will not be issued and I regret that there is no opportunity for questions at this time. Each of you will return to your homes under an armed guard and collect only essential belongings. We will reconvene in six hours. This is a top-secret mission!"

"Jesus, Jason! What the hell ***is*** all this? I want no part in this!" Rose whispered.

"Not possible, dear heart. We need you. It's only for a year and you'll enjoy the work. Besides, we'll be together on this."

...

The classified base was in the middle of the Nevada desert, ultra modern, purpose designed Laboratories and Medical Suites, built to the highest specification. Six scientists, including Jason and herself, three other men and one woman, were interred together, testing the contents of obscure vials of micro-organisms, flown in from the two known Bio-banks that had so far been discovered by the military units, one in Iraq, one in Israel.

The six scientists had slightly different areas of expertise, but all would be involved in laboratory testing, writing reports, and presenting their data to the BMW officials on a weekly basis.

...

David threw himself into work with a vengeance after Rose disappeared. He felt jilted and scorned. He was angry. He thought she had changed her mind and vanished deliberately, with Jason Whatsisname. He discussed the situation with Richard Martin, who assured him that, in his opinion, there was no way Rose would do such a thing without explanation. Richard promised to look into her disappearance.

He contacted the authorities in Houston, Rose's Department, and the police. He drew a complete blank. Reluctantly, he informed David that Jason Savage had also disappeared and that it was widely rumoured among their colleagues in Houston that they had emigrated together.

After Rose disappeared, David took sanctuary in Oyne. At first, he started using the remote place regularly as a weekend retreat, and then gradually spent more and more time there. He loved Bennachie. It was filled with memories of Rose.

He developed a deeper relationship with his mother. They went hill-walking together. David took her to the occasional Opera performance at Haddo House, a stately home nearby. He told her all about Rose. Kate advised him not to give up, "Anything can be achieved with hard work and determination, my son."

He posted messages to Rose's e-mail as before, but they came back as, "unable to be delivered."

Then in the spring of 2006, David opened a distribution branch of ***Equinox Ltd*** at Ryehill, on the outskirts of Oyne. He had quickly realised the potential of the location for sales of Equestrian products in particular. There were in fact more horses than people in this whole area. That was probably why he liked it.

Although it was slow to gain a foothold, the new enterprise grew steadily over the next six months. David moved permanently to Oyne, settling into the small community and participating in local events. He started riding again and volunteered to assist his mother with her lessons at the Riding for the Disabled Centre (RDA.)

He was occupied but so desperately lonely.
There was a hole in his life the size of St Paul's Cathedral.

Chapter 28 - Virulent

Rose sighed and checked her cell cultures wearily. She was tired and resented the isolation of her forced appointment. She was frustrated that she could not contact her family or friends to explain her disappearance. She had been working long hours and was suffering from a deepening depression. ***Bio-warfare*** was growing in popularity and she was trapped in this line of work by her own expertise.

Looking back to the fungus, ***Cleospora nidulans distructum,*** that had been released the previous year, she still harboured regrets. The Afghanistan poppies had indeed been wiped out but this had not had the desired effect. When the poppies died, the drug barons soon found other sources of raw materials. As she had feared, the fungus mutated in the wild and several food crops had also been infected. The resulting famine was ongoing, now predicted to wipe out one third of the population of Afghanistan and northern Pakistan. Furthermore, the Terrorists still struck even harder in several areas of the world. Mass suicide was commonplace. Innocent civilians were wiped out in their thousands as urban street-fighting broke out once more, after a period of relative calm, in Baghdad.

Rose wanted to leave the USA and return to Britain and she had made this known to her jailers. She had been promised release from duty at the end of the twelve-month spell and an understudy was being trained to take over her key role. Other than through their work, she no longer had anything much to do with Jason Savage. They had simply drifted apart and had different beliefs now. Rose felt she had grown older and wiser. She longed to contact David: to explain that she had not eloped with Savage; but all contact with the outside world was strictly forbidden.

All communication channels were coded and monitored.

It was while daydreaming about her last days with David at Bennachie, that she saw the first effects of a new and deadly virulent agent. She was greatly alarmed at the results before her. ***Something*** was massacring her cultured cells.

...

Her voice shook as she presented the information to the BMW delegation, "Looks like we have a ***Level Four...plus***, gentlemen."

"Exactly ***what*** is it, Dr Anderson?"

"Too early to say, but it's a new one on me... the scariest virus I've ever seen! Skin, liver and kidney cell cultures have all ruptured and disintegrated within five hours of infection. The vial code is ***BAG17***. Does that give us the source?"

"Shit!" Burnett turned towards Jason. "That's the Baghdad incident, Savage. A test tube was accidentally broken during the raid. One hundred and ninety eight troops have been potentially exposed."

Rose interrupted, "Then, I believe that the troops involved in the Baghdad incident may have unwittingly unleashed this microbe, that it is deadly, and that it may be sweeping through their ranks as I speak!"

"There is no need for melodrama, Dr Anderson. Just give us a ***factual*** report please," interrupted Colonel Burnett.

" OK let's be ***factual***.
One. This new organism is related to the common measles virus in that it causes a rash.
Two. It has similarities to a bad dose of the common cold, or para-influenza with respiratory malfunction and nausea.
Three. It is related to rabies in that it causes psychosis, and probably madness.
Four. It is similar also to respiratory syncytial virus, which causes pneumonia in AIDS patients.
Putting it entirely ***factually***, sir, this little demon appears to have developed the very worst elements of all these known viruses. It is a killer of unknown potential."

"What is its origin?"

"It has almost certainly been synthetically produced. It contains seven different, fairly large, proteins, three with known functions similar to some of the viruses I've mentioned. Four with unknown functions. However, they all seem to target the immune system."

“Without exaggeration, what do you think will happen of this germ is not contained?”

“If released, it is my opinion that this virus could cause a tidal wave of destruction. It could do more harm in six days than HIV could do in six years!
It is extremely contagious and can travel through the air.
It does not require contact through touch.
It is a powerful killer, and can pass from the dead to the living.
With our modern network of airlines, it could shoot on a twenty-four hour journey to any large city on earth, causing an explosive chain of transmission throughout the entire human race!”

An awesome silence fell across the small seminar room. Colonel Burnett broke the silence by clearing his throat and asking Jason Savage to verify the accuracy of Rose’s report.

“I endorse Dr Anderson’s work and conclude that we are dealing with a very dangerous organism here, whatever its source. We must make sure that it does not get very far. However, let’s keep this in perspective... I believe we are dealing with only a single outbreak involving twelve affected troops who are now in Israel. There is no reason to suppose that we cannot contain this small outbreak.”

“That is so, Savage. To brief the rest of you, I should clearly explain what happened. As I said already, one hundred and ninety eight troops were involved in a raid on a school, following surveillance reports of odd comings and goings of heavy traffic. A well-disguised laboratory complex was discovered there. During this routine Military action, there was some damage to the building. I believe a sophisticated liquid nitrogen storage vessel was accidentally ruptured and a glass vial was broken. The school site has since been bombed and completely destroyed, so there is no further danger there. Twelve troops developed unusual flu-like symptoms shortly after the raid and they have been swiftly moved and are isolated in a Military Hospital just outside Tel Aviv. Three of them have died and the other nine are very sick. Their asymptomatic colleagues are also there, being monitored for any signs of infection. The site is well cordoned off and under Military guard. If necessary we could get a presidential order for a TS Operation on the Tel Aviv site?”

"What's a TS Operation?" Rose asked.

"It stands for Thorough Spring-clean. We would seal off and destroy the entire facility, including the inhabitants, if the risk is considered high enough to justify the sacrifice of a few to save the many."

"That won't help if the organism has got beyond the perimeter of the site!" Rose exclaimed in horror.

She went on, thinking aloud, " With such a short incubation period, at least we should be able to see if the virus has escaped confinement... quickly. I reckon that if no external person turns sick within, say one week, we could begin to consider ourselves in the clear. Besides, if you have already quarantined the hospital properly, the sick will all be recovered, or dead, within a week or two. If necessary, you can destroy any contaminated buildings then. In the meantime, we need to monitor the course of this new illness, and, most importantly, determine if there are any survivors. Remember gentlemen, that it is perhaps only through those rare individuals with immunity are we likely to secure a vaccine. In the meantime, can I make the suggestion that all of our findings are relayed to the medical teams dealing with the incident without delay?"

Professor Blair Spooner, who had been sitting with his head in his hands looked up and intervened in an authoritative voice, "I will be serving all of you with a further Restriction Order. There will be no information passed to any third party."

"Why restrict vital information? We must work together as one nation on this one."

Rose was cut off. Every protest she made was skilfully bludgeoned.

"This is information vital to the security of the United States of America. I have the power to classify this material."

"You're welcome to classify this little beauty, Professor Spooner. I've given it my best shot. But, with no disrespect Sir, you're a fool if you think that silence can help this situation."

“Rose, he’s just doing his job,” interrupted Jason, “Bear with him. I know you’re concerned. You’ve been working too many hours on this...”

Rose cut in again, “Look you guys! Don’t underestimate this danger! National Security? That’s a joke! This little bastard will not distinguish the USA from China or from... bloody Turkey! We’re talking about an airborne infection with exceptionally high mortality. Make no mistake Gentlemen... this may be the most lethal virus ever encountered by Mankind! At least let’s put out a special alert to health workers in USA and warn other nations?”

“Dr Anderson! Do you have any idea of the cost of putting out a special alert for 400,000 health workers? Do you know the panic it would cause if we over-react to this ***contained*** danger? Besides, the chances of this virus turning up in the USA are surely negligible if we deal properly with the current outbreak - as aggressively as we have to!”

Spooner deliberately turned from Rose and addressed Jason. “So, being realistic, just what do you advise, Dr Savage?”

Angered, Rose cut in again, “With respect, sir, you’re the bloody Science Advisor... what do ***you*** advise?”

“Well, first of all, watch your tongue, Dr Anderson. Let’s be rational about this. You will need to re-run all your tests. We’ll seal off this infection by whatever means necessary. I guess we need to adopt our top specification quarantine procedures for the known outbreak. We’ll call in the PPT3 Unit - that stands for Primary Power Team Cubed by the way - it’s a Special Forces Unit set up specifically to deal with transcontinental threats.” He paused, considering the correct words to use.

Then he continued, “I believe that one of the asymptomatic troops may have been allowed home on compassionate leave, because his wife was critically ill. We best track him down and quarantine his known contacts also. Get on the network, Savage. Instruct code ***violet***...

...and Dr Anderson, prepare to repeat ***all*** your experiments. We want no mistakes here. I need you to give priority to analysing another sample to rule out a match. Just a precaution you understand. It is being flown in now from Riyadh. It is probably quite unrelated but we must check it out nevertheless."

"I need also to see the infected patients," Rose volunteered, "Educated guesswork and second hand reports are just not enough here - I need to see the clinical symptoms and monitor a few actual patients. We should determine if this virus is stable or mutating rapidly. We must assess the survival rate and see if there is an opportunity to prepare a vaccine from any survivors."

"Yes, yes, of course, we'll arrange for Savage and yourself to fly over there to the Tel Aviv Quarantine Unit within the next few days. Please complete this analysis on the Riyadh sample first... and I want all information contained within these walls!"

Jason and Rose flew to Israel three days later.

A full Level Four Containment Complex was found within the purpose-built hospital on the outskirts of Tel Aviv. It was brand spanking new, state of the art... as if this disastrous state of affairs had somehow been expected.

Chapter 29 – Hot Zone

The building Rose entered was grey mass concrete, with no windows, just extraction chimneys leading well up into the high atmosphere. Jason Savage did not go into the Hot Zone. He was taking no chances. He stayed at the gatehouse holding building, fully protected by his Level Four suit, complete with his own personal filtered air supply.

Rose alone entered the separate suite of special laboratories, sealed for the containment of super-bugs, and passed through the various zones, well seasoned to this type of maximum security domain. There was plenty of time to change her mind. Her superiors had clearly impressed upon her that even the experts run scared of super-bugs. The best scientists had nightmares about them. This was considered a normal healthy response. Rose was renowned for having metal nerves, but for the first time, she felt a creeping cold fear as she entered the hot zone.

All around was evidence of the precautions taken to avoid bio-leakage. Heavy glass aquarium viewing windows linked the hot suites to the central control consul. Strobe light alarm systems were in every room, walls were painted with a thick, shiny plastic substance, and another type of rubbery goo surrounded every pipe, wire and conduit cable that penetrated the solid partitions between rooms.

There were no openings.
There were no cracks.
Yet, given that one hundred million deadly virus particles would only just cover a single grain of sand, even a hairline crack could become an escape superhighway!

Scientists with blue space suits and yellow rubber boots could be seen moving slowly and cautiously within the inner sanctum of the complex. Matching air hoses, like jaundiced umbilical cords, linked them to a filtered air supply. A sign on the door warned that the use of scalpels and other sharp blades was strictly forbidden.

She reached level 1 and a notice read:
INFECTIOUS AREA - agents in use = ***Salmonella***.
*
NO UNAUTHORISED ENTRY
To Open this door
Place ID card on sensor.

She fumbled for the ID card and swiped it over the scanner...
PROCESSING...
You are cleared to enter...

BIOSAFETY LEVEL 2 - Agents in use = ***Hepatitis. Influenza.***
A series of increasingly threatening doors were traversed:

*

SUITE AA -5
BIOSAFETY LEVEL 3 - agents in use = ***Anthrax. HIV.***
Chief: Col. Valerie Turner-King
Please proceed...

BIOSAFETY LEVEL 4. Agents in use: ***Ebola. Lassa. Hanta. UNKNOWN.*** **There are no known cures or vaccines for the agents in use in this area.**

*

Locker Room.
Status: FEMALE
Remove everything touching the skin.
Clothing; rings; contact lenses.
Change into sterile surgical scrubs.
Suit up - inner and outer layers.
Bot check for any weaknesses in outer suit.
Connect to air supply
Bot check of vital statistics - pulse elevated but acceptable, blood pressure normal range, temperature normal range

You are cleared to enter.

...

It was like a hellish bio-library. Various deadly viruses were immortalised in glass vials in a liquid nitrogen bank... ***Lassa, Hanta***... Rose focussed on the familiar label for ***Ebola Ziare***, the hottest filovirus so far known to man. She had pondered its origins many times. Nobody knew where in nature it could possibly live. Virologists gave it a feared and revered status second to none. The last epidemic stemmed from the deepest rainforests of central Africa, but whether from a fly, a scorpion, a tick, a bat, or a plant? One could only speculate.

Nobody knew the precise origins of this latest virus either, but it must be man made. Over the past decade, Iraq had simply refused to submit entirely to the Western interference. The 2003-5 war had been only partly successful. Iraq and Israel had been attacking each other with more and more fury and terrorist attacks in other countries were frequent. A few fairly pith-less bio-organisms had been half-heartedly released, but like the early anthrax scares in the USA, these were more of a psychological threat than anything else. Further use of ***Bio-warfare*** was certainly on the cards, but this particular virus had probably never been intended for release since the scientists who engineered it must have known it was potentially the most lethal weapon of all.

Had its creators kept it in reserve? - under Level Four storage conditions - within the structure of a concrete containment laboratory, similar to the one she was in now, until... she shuddered at the thought of the incident that led to the exposure of innocent troops. The irony was that a broken test tube the size of a little finger could have started the outbreak, accidentally. A hundred million tiny viral particles would have floated in the atmosphere around such a breakage. There could have been no escape from infection.

The reality was that all one hundred and ninety eight troops masterminding the raid were probably contaminated.

There had been no symptoms for several hours perhaps, allowing ample time for spread. They had moved them from the Baghdad site to this hospital complex near Tel Aviv during that time... and one had been allowed to travel home!

Jesus, how many contacts had been exposed? Were they all quarantined?

Rose walked slowly, sweating inside her suit, breathing fast and shallow. Around her, she saw patients in all three stages of the disease process. Locked within sealed Perspex bubbles, monitored by robotic arms. Dehumanised!

The Medical Team had done well. They were clearly professionally trained to deal with this kind of catastrophe. Rose was impressed with the organised information they already had available. There were a series of push button voice tutorials in number order as she followed the green safety line around the high security bio-wards, stopping to peer at the suffering behind the thick windows.

She pressed **Button 1**.

An American voice recording responded in clear crisp business-like tones,
" *This filovirus is a Level Four micro-organism. It is exceedingly difficult to control, having a major respiratory component and transmitting through the air. In* ***stage 1*** *there may be no symptoms for twenty-four hours. Maximum containment measures apply at all times. In the case of contamination, you will be automatically quarantined here and will not leave this building again unless you fully recover. The virus appears to have a very high lethality.* "

A few of the healthy troops were confined in a separate ward off the Stage 1 Area. They were not showing symptoms, but pacing around like caged tigers, terrified of their fate.

She pressed **Button 2.**

The same sugar-coated voice went on, " *This is* ***Stage 2****. The virus particles attack the lungs first, causing bleeding in the first space. There may be few external symptoms, but headache and nausea are evident. Then vessels rupture in the eyes, causing the whites to go bright* ***red****. These typical symptoms appear within three to five days of first exposure.*

Using a remote viewing microscope, Rose examined the blood-shot eyes of the early stage patients and braced herself to take several blood samples using the sophisticated robotic arm system. A macabre record of clinical photographs had to be completed. The samples were triple sealed in plastic bags, before passing them out through long wave ultraviolet surface scanners.

She pressed **Button 3.**

"***Stage 3** follows in a few hours. The intestines are now affected. The virus is in the exponential phase of amplification, replicating at an amazingly fast rate, converting all host tissues into more viral particles. This leaves behind liquefied flesh and massive internal haemorrhage. The patient will vomit vast quantities of an unsavoury cocktail of decomposing tissues and active virus. The vomit is dark red, turning rapidly **black**. The patient will become disorientated and may slip out of consciousness but only for short periods. Clots are lodging in kidneys, liver, hands and feet, like a whole body stroke. Pain can be severe. The patient can still walk at this stage. A small number of patients can show spontaneous partial recovery from this stage, although failure of several vital organs can complicate their convalescence.*"

She pressed **Button 4**.

"***Stage 4**. The final stage comes less than six days after first stage. The body is now saturated with virus from brain to skin and all tissues are broken down and converted by the predator life form. The patient shows complete depersonalisation since only a primitive core of brain activity remains. There is no pain at this stage. The patient will crash and bleed out.*"

...

Later, Rose's armour plated nerves were weak as she was subjected to surface irradiation to the depth of her suit. It had a special thin metal lining that deflected the precise wave radiation beams from penetrating her own living tissue. The discarded suit was incinerated. Then she underwent total body disinfection.

Naked and vulnerable she was scrubbed for a second time by a team of ***stero-bots*** in a sealed shower cubicle. It was a painful experience. The little brush heads probed every orifice and the disinfectant stung. She emerged crying. She could not get the bright ***red*** eyes and the demonic ***black*** vomit out of her mind. Her normal reserve had been seriously weakened.

A meeting with the medical team was scheduled.

“Jason, it is even worse than we feared. I believe the mortality rate is very high. We need to speak to Spooner immediately. He wants a full report within two weeks, but we can’t delay that long! He needs to call a crisis meeting of the BMW and PPP3 team right away!”

“He won’t like melodrama, Rose.”

“Look, Jason, I’ve run and re-run the tests. This organism is the same as the Riyadh specimen and there is now a suspected outbreak reported in Lagos, Nigeria! So, we already have two, possibly three sites to quarantine. We need to trace all recent movements from this place and... there is so much to do... we must contain this thing... and try to find a vaccine!”

Jason suggested a trial with the test vaccine that they had brought over from the States. It was based on an Ebola antiserum, but they had added an agent that specifically reacted with one of the structural proteins in the new virus. Rose thought it could only be of value to the stage one patients, but had doubts whether it would have any effect whatsoever.

“Look, Rose, let’s not get too involved here? We’ll finish our work on this batch of trial vaccine but then we’ll need to get out of here quickly. I fear the action that may be taken in the interests of National security. Besides, you must agree that we could do as much valuable work from a distance now.”

“I want to leave here too Jason, but first I need to finish the essential groundwork, without wasting time travelling. It may take a couple of weeks, but then I want out of this... I mean out altogether! I will agree to complete a total DNA and protein analysis of this virus and determine its rate of mutation, but then there are others in the team that are just as capable as me to work on finding a more effective vaccine. I want released from this position. I fear the worst has yet to come. I just want to return to Britain and lead a normal life. All that I want to culture from now on are... ***Roses!”***

"Rose, calm down! I've never seen you lose your bottle like this before. Where's my iron lady? It's not ***that*** bad. We'll sort it out. The world goes on you know. Anyway, you don't have long to go until your twelve-month secondment period is at en end. We do make a good team, you and I. Perhaps we can even start over when we're finished here?"

Rose let out a little hysterical laugh, "We ***are*** finished."

Chapter 30 - Pandemic

Within the following forty-eight hours, news came from the USA that seven outbreaks of the mystery illness were suspected, spanning five different countries.

Rose and Jason were trapped in Tel Aviv for a further three weeks, despite their frantic attempts to be permitted to leave. They needed special travel passes and there was a delay. They were caught in a bureaucratic nightmare. Rose made good use of the time by working long hours in the Bio-safety Level Four Viral facilities, determined to completely characterise the murderous capsule of DNA and point the way to a better vaccine.

The modified Ebola antiserum was disappointing. It prolonged stage one of the disease, but had no other lasting effects. It did not halt the process. There appeared to be ninety-five percent mortality, with or without the vaccination!

It was confirmed beyond all reasonable doubt that the lethal infection was an advanced form of germ warfare. It was invisible in onset and deadly in action, manufactured by the terrorists and now backfiring on them as well. It was not exactly a weapon of mass destruction, but a mass casualty agent, destroying only people. The earlier anthrax scares had been effective psychological weapons, but pretty damn useless for mass mortalities. There was no question about the killing ability of this one. It struck sporadically without warning and spread at a frightening speed. It was transmitted by air alone, requiring no touch. Its nearest living relatives were Ebola Excel and Ebola Ziare, both hot killers kept well frozen down and behind impenetrable steel bars. It made HIV seem like a toothless tiger. Because of its rate of replication, Rose suspected that it might have a unique ability to mutate more than usual as it jumped around the globe, like a black-hearted flu.

Freaks and Religious fanatics thought it had arrived from outer space and signified the wrath of God. The End of the World was forecast with more substance than ever before.

Developments occurred at an alarming rate as the infection spread exponentially. The Asian media, who represented the great majority of the world's population, were the first to broadcast the grim details of the deadly biological germ that was spreading like a virulent cancer. They published vivid photographs and an Armageddon scenario. Their impact was to escalate the global unrest. East blamed West and vice versa. International panic set in as the leaders of different countries tried to allay fears and to apportion blame.

Eventually, their travel passes came through and they were ordered back to Britain for an Emergency Summit meeting which was to be held in London with Western leaders and scientists from the USA, UK and Europe.

Two days before they left for Britain, the President of the United States made a short broadcast to the Nation. Rose watched it from her hotel room in Tel Aviv. American citizens watched from the streets on the large outdoor television screens.
"It is my sad duty to confirm reports that a mystery illness, possibly caused by a bio-engineered germ is affecting multiple sites in five different countries. There is no need to over-react. We have the situation under control. Our BMW and PPP3 teams are working on it as I speak. We have called an International Summit to discuss quarantine arrangements and to give priority to the development of a vaccine.
Meanwhile, I am putting this country on alert for a National Emergency. Troops are being recalled from active duty outwith America. Medical teams are being briefed on best handling procedures.

Because this is an airborne germ, International Air Travel will be totally restricted as from today. Until further notice, only authorised personnel will be cleared to enter or leave this country. I will keep you informed. We will beat this threat as we have always done before. God bless America."

Communication networks went crazy as clusters of infection broke out everywhere. Big cities were the ideal place for spread. Conditions were perfect for an invisible airborne killer that could colonise virgin territory with ease, living in airshafts and shopping malls for days before silently entering the living bodies of its next victims. The epidemic became pandemic as the virus began infiltrating the crowded cities of Delhi, Bombay, Tokyo and Moscow. Thousands fled from these cities. The Bombay sick went from 3,000 to 18,000 in two days. The television showed crowds of crazed people wearing gas masks and surgical masks. Journalists and television reporters went into emergency overdrive.

The main electronic secure communication lines linking Jason and Rose to the USA base could not be accessed. Under the circumstances, Jason authorised the use of public lines.

Secrecy lifted, Rose e-mailed David with a short explanation of her disappearance and a clear message that she was trying to get back to London in the next twenty-four hours and wanted to see him more than anything else in the world. When she arrived in London for the Emergency Summit meeting, she intended to stay in Britain, by fair means or foul. She needed his help.

He responded, "Thank God, Rose! I've been worried sick! I thought you'd disappeared deliberately - with Jason Whatssisname! Please be careful. This infection is terrible. There are outbreaks suspected in Manchester, London, Birmingham and Glasgow. It was reported last week that the Northern Isles have confirmed cases of contamination. It is thought to have arrived with an oil tanker from the East. We have a state of National Emergency here. There are masked troops in the city streets, warning anyone who has symptoms of illness or who knows of a sick person to report themselves to the Infection Helpline. Transport is restricted and the roads and trains are hellish, but I will meet you in London come hell or high water. This time, my metal lady, I won't let you go! I love you, David. "

Rose also contacted Richard to seek his expert legal advice. She might need a good solicitor to get her out of a forced contract with the US government.

He replied, "Darling, I'll give you my best, as always - but this is a tall order!"

Chapter 31 – Danny Ives

Jason, Rose, and Danny Ives arrived at the Airport in good time, armed at last with their official US clearance passes for priority air travel. Security was a nightmare with a thorough personal search and detailed examination of all hand luggage. In the past decade, there had been too many terrorist incidents, so most of the larger suitcases routinely went on a separate baggage plane, an entirely radio-controlled carrier with no staff or passengers aboard. Jason's computer case was taken apart and he was made to press all buttons and switches. Rose did not carry a computer, but had various discs and an electronic laser beam that she liked to use as a pointer. These were all checked out and demonstrated.

"What's this, then?" The ground-staff security man asked in a puzzled voice. He was rummaging through the contents of her briefcase: tissues, soap-bag, toothbrush, tampons, nothing was sacred. He had withdrawn the red metal rose that her grandfather had made sixteen years before.

"Oh, it's just a lucky mascot. It's made from an aluminium beer can, so nothing to fear there. It goes everywhere with me... been round the world that has!"

The guard turned over the flower, a little faded at one side where sunlight had been hitting it as it stood on her dressing table, but it was still pristine in all other respects. He scrutinised it... "Never seen anything like it... well made... unusual..." He shrugged his shoulders and placed it back in the bag.

Rose, Jason and Danny Ives were eventually cleared by security to board the Airbus.
Jason had foolishly spent the night with a bottle of scotch, ending up in a prestigious and select Tel Aviv gentleman's club looking for comfort. He regretted it now. His head ached as he re-read his notes during the early part of the flight. He needed new spectacles. There was a throbbing behind his eyes and aspirin had not helped in the slightest.

Rose was planning to meet David and Richard in London and was determined to secure her freedom... somehow! Good old reliable Richard had wangled an invitation to the Summit, as part of the World Health Organisation (WHO) team of lawyers, so that he could be on hand. He was indeed a true friend. It was fortunate that he had specialised in Medical Ethics and built up a rapidly International reputation during the past six years of worldwide crisis. He was now permanently employed by WHO. If anyone could secure her release from the forced contract with the US Institute, he could.

"You OK, Savage?" Rose asked as Jason refused the drinks trolley. This was very uncharacteristic.

"Fine, just a headache... probably living it up too much lately!" He smiled half-heartedly.

He reclined his seat and dozed for twenty minutes while Rose gratefully sipped iced gin and watched the other passengers, all fit and healthy, going about their business. The man in front had a tattoo of a lion on his forearm. He looked strong. A lady passed on her way to the toilet cubicle. She had a sad mouth with the corners pointing downwards. Rose felt her own mouth and forced herself to smile. She did not want to arrive home with a sulky look. She was thinking of David, and looking forward to the familiar comfort of him, when Jason next spoke.

"I feel a bit sick really, sorry." He just had time to reach for the sick bag before projectile vomit filled the air.

A shaft of cold fear pierced Rose's body.

She gently turned his head towards her. His lips were caked with dark blood. He had the typical jaundiced pallor, and the whites of his eyes were already ruby ***red***. Naked and vulnerable, she stared into the face of her worst enemy.

The reality of his infection passed between them wordlessly. Restrained terror broke in sweat droplets on his forehead.

The air in the aeroplane re-circulated constantly.

It was a double decker A380 Sonic Cruiser, Mark 2, travelling just below the speed of sound, with its 600 seats almost full. There were 593 passengers. The overhead screens in every row showed a pilot's eye view of take off and then speed and information monitors were superimposed.
The time was 18.17...
The outside air temperature was –68 degrees centigrade...
They were travelling at an altitude of 37,000 miles...

A range of on board purchases sought credit card details to be inserted into the screen display. Sid, the exercise man was busy telling everybody to, "Relax and have fun. Smile folks. That's the best exercise!"

Rose summoned the air stewardess and sought council with the captain.

The pilot immediately sent a text message on ACARS, company frequency, requesting assistance. He also consulted his Health and Safety disc, scrolling through the help list to find the exact procedure to follow.

The company instruction was to place an immediate Mayday call to Heathrow Air Traffic Control.

"Mayday... Mayday... Mayday...this is Flight Captain Brooks aboard A380 sonic cruiser, flight number 00592 from Tel Aviv to London Heathrow."

"Go ahead 00592."

"We have a ***contagion*** on board. Several passengers are seriously ill. Doctor on board indicates that this is a potentially dangerous situation requiring ***full quarantine*** procedures. Request an ambulance on standby when we land."

There was a silence for a full three minutes. Then...

"Flight 00592, we have several other planes coming in. You are not permitted to land at Heathrow. Please continue your flight path and descend to 10,000 feet and circle until further notice. Repeat. You are ***not*** permitted to land at London Heathrow. Over and out."

Some seven minutes passed. There was panic aboard the airbus.

"Flight 00592. We are diverting you to Stansted Airport. You are cleared to land on runway 07. On arrival, you must not vacate the aeroplane or open the passenger doors until further instruction is given. Stansted is situated further from population. A full emergency team will be sent to secure the runway. Good Luck, Sir! Over and Out."

The second sick bag ballooned with ***vomito negro***.
The cabin smelled sour, like a twentieth century slaughterhouse.
Danny Ives had raped her colleague.

Danny Ives was the nickname given to the super-bug. Formed from the letters **DNA** (deoxyribonucleic acid), **NY** (an eminent New York Scientist working on the team had coined the nickname), **IV** (a Level Four virus) and **ES** (Ebola similarities).
The little bastard was there within Jason Savage, splitting apart the very molecules of his DNA, replicating at its usual phenomenal rate, destroying its host, killing its benefactor.

Passengers wept and prayed as they were informed of the gravity of the situation only a few minutes prior to touchdown.

Old couples held hands.
Young girls were hysterical and clung together.
A mother sang a lullaby to her child.

They taxied to a remote part of the designated runway and awaited the arrival of assistance.

By the time the men in spacesuits arrived, Jason Savage was vomited dry and embroidered with the brilliant purple rash. He was passive, eyes drooping, but not yet delirious.

"Rose, I don't want to suffer. Will you see to it that I get hold of something?"

"Don't ask me that, Jason. Anyway, we've both had all the jabs available. We might make it through this."

In the sick yellow light inside the claustrophobic cabin, the full weight of ***Danny Ives*** pressed down on her. She imagined that she was wearing a rigid, Danny-proof vest. She tried to convince herself that she was not vulnerable, that her iron will would protect her.

Jason squeezed her hand and convulsed again with dry retching.

Chapter 32 - Quarantine

A white plastic tent was erected over the nose and passenger doors of the grounded A380, sealing it from freedom. A group of hooded figures, clad in bright orange biological space suits slowly oozed from a helicopter. The first action they took was to erect a large sign:

Danger - Hot Zone
Army In Control
Strictly No Entry!

Several armed guards took up positions on the tarmac. A second tent was erected nearby to house equipment and supplies and to act as a temporary barracks.

Some time later, another helicopter arrived, with the URAMRIID (US Army Medical Research Institute of Infectious Diseases) personnel.

Trapped in quarantine, nursing the sick and the dying, Rose frequently vomited herself. She was uncertain whether this was a manifestation of phase one infection, or just the terrible odours and pressures of the situation. She coped by shutting out the detail of what was happening around her and engaging her auto-mode. She functioned like a robot, doing what was necessary as efficiently as she could, keeping her emotions submerged. It was the ultimate test of her years of training in the Hot Zone. This was a just different kind of Level Four Containment and she had to adjust. She did not cry. She did not even speak much except to issue necessary instructions. She withdrew from the world she was in and concentrated only on the practical tasks in front of her.

A team of twelve volunteers came forward to assist with essential duties. They included a priest and two nurses. As members of this initial group fell sick, others stepped in to take their places. Following a consensus decision among the twelve, Class A drugs were distributed to the dying on request.

Rose listened avidly to the news bulletins over the following seven days... nine sporadic outbreaks reported... twelve... dozens... ***Danny***

Ives appeared everywhere in Britain within a frighteningly short space of time. The large cities, where there were International Airports, seemed to be worst affected. Danny was taking longer to infiltrate rural areas, although the Shetland Isles and Orkney had been infected at an early stage and the death toll was already high there. No place was sacrosanct. Rose thought about her brother and prayed that he and his family had escaped.

Quarantine centres were set up in all the major British cities, with harsh containment measures from the National Guard. Doors of suspect houses were marked and families were sealed in their homes. One of the first so-called "Treatment Centres" to be established was St Mary's at Paddington, followed by other public buildings... libraries... primary schools... some with barbed wire surrounds to prevent escape.

International trade and transport tricked to a halt.
Food shortages were caused by panic buying.

The whole fabric of society was crumbling away and it was happening too fast for the politicians to take meaningful action. Governments in the East went down like flagging boxers in their final round, saggy, confused, punch drunk.

Britain declared a state of Emergency.
The Doomsday Clock was moved on a full two minutes.

In America, New York was a ghost town, riots ravaged Los Angeles and residents of major cities breathed disinfectant air in all public places. Brooklyn had been sealed off as an isolation area. Unable to keep pace with the burying or burning of the dead, the office of Emergency Management declared Governor's Island as ***Morgue Island*** for the dumping of body bags by helicopter drop. A Biological Rapid Response Team was activated by an Act of Congress, but even their response was not rapid enough! Danny was a formidable killer with a low recovery rate.

Four days into their confinement aboard the A380, puzzling reports came through to Rose from URAMRIID sources that the survivors of ***Danny Ives*** included a higher than expected proportion of Gay men. It was postulated that there might be some sort of link to immunity built up through HIV exposure. Alternatively, perhaps the AIDS vaccine itself may have bestowed an element of resistance. Rose would have liked to have a closer look at the similarities between the two viruses, but that was not possible in her present predicament.

Michael, the Steward aboard the A380 was Gay. Rose noted that he was also sick. Then, miraculously, Michael started to recover after a prolonged ***stage 1*** of the disease. Rose herself remained unaffected, but then she had been pumped full of so many vaccinations. Could one or more of them be holding Danny at bay?

Jason Savage died on day five. He had also received every known vaccination.

The cabin interior was filled with stench and slime... and body bags. Rose and a few strong passengers, who felt able to replenish the team of twelve volunteers, had managed to keep the Executive Lounge free of the worst cases. The few lucky people who recovered from ***stage 1*** of the disease were moved there to convalesce.

World Leaders, including the Prime Minister and the President of the United States made similar announcements to their peoples. Folks listened in their homes and on the streets...

"We are declaring a state of Marshall Law... There will be a curfew. Meanwhile, go on as normal. Restrict your movements. Make no unnecessary journeys. Walk if you can to save energy. All prices and all wages will be frozen as from midnight tonight. This is an International threat. We will prevail. We will find a way through this horror..."

Rose was in regular contact with her external friends now, but even Richard Martin QC, could do absolutely nothing about getting her released from Quarantine. As fatigue and depression took a hold, she began to doubt if she would ever get out. The news of the outside world did nothing to lift her spirits.

*"Hello America. This is your President. To guarantee the survival of our species, one thousand selected individuals will be moved into the sealed **Bio-caves** that we have constructed underground in the soft limestone of Missouri. These people will be taken from areas that*

show no contamination and will be quarantined and medically cleared before entry.

*The unit is a Level Four Noah's Ark Complex. It has been there for some time in preparation for such an emergency. All those chosen will be under thirty years old with good breeding potential. The ratio of women to men will be 2:1. We already have seeds, animals and plants in these **Eden pods** and enough triple entry screening to exclude **Danny Ives**.*

*Now that the full scale of this pandemic is realised, all survivors following exposure should not be shunned through fear, but rather should be treated like **gold dust**! They are surely our future and may be our salvation, because only they carry the secret of immunity.*

*I will **not** be joining the selected group.*
I believe in God.
I offer a prayer for our survival..."

In desperation Rose sent another message to the URASMIID team. "Most of the other people in here are dead. Nine survivors appear to be recovering now. They may have developed valuable blood components. I seem to have some inexplicable immunity to ***Danny Ives***! I believe I may have built up unique antigens that may be beneficial in formulating a vaccine. I have taken samples from myself and the nine survivors and will pass these to the URASMIID team for detailed analysis."

Rose and Michael, the Steward, were two of only ten survivors to walk from the stricken aeroplane into a second Quarantine chamber. The entire aeroplane was sealed in their wake and incinerated. They were showered with strong antiviral disinfectant and dried off in a UV-irradiation unit. Then they were ordered to remain in the second chamber for one more week, before release could be contemplated.

Rose sent an e-mail to David." I am ***not*** sick. I have an unexplained immunity to ***Danny Ives***! I think the guards will release me in a few days. They realise that the survivors are precious since we hold the key to vaccination. I would dearly love to see you, but please do not come here... it is much too dangerous!"

"I'm coming. ***Nothing*** will stop me!"

"Well, please wait until my colleagues and I have been isolated and thoroughly cleaned up, and then allow three full days to pass to make absolutely sure that I have no symptoms. The main URAMSIID crew has gone. Stansted is fairly quiet. No planes are landing here now. It is not completely deserted though, and there are a couple of security guards left. Please be careful."

"You and your bloody rules! I'm coming ***now***!"

Travel by any means was extremely difficult. Many folk had fled the cities for the rural areas, inadvertently assisting the spread of ***Danny Ives***. Refugee camps had sprung up in the countryside, and farming had ground to a halt in many places. Danny was estimated to be killing around 200,000 people a week in the cities.

Scheduled transport was practically unavailable. At David's insistence, Richard called upon Alex and his private Cessna. Alex was not keen at first. Rose was not ***his*** lifelong friend, but he eventually agreed, for the sake of his beloved partner. He was afraid, but unwilling to show weakness. He was a little encouraged by the reports that Gays seemed to have some resistance to the deadly disease.

The gutter press vanished into thin air. The most diligent news crews promised to do their level best to stay on air throughout the catastrophe. They did a sterling job in the face of the enemy. They advised listeners daily not to panic, reporting the survival cases rather than dwelling on the blackest incidents. It was quite a re-education process for the Press. They ignored many of the fires, the rapes, the pillaging, the street fighting... in favour of confirming the positives... that ***some sectors of the population had a natural immunity***. It appeared to be higher among American Indians, Aborigines, and very much higher in the Gay communities.

The reformed and focused Press praised the Gay volunteers who had taken up the essential tasks throughout societies failing infrastructure. They manned the service industries, especially the hospitals. It was strangely appropriate that many of these Gay individuals had been in service jobs before and were already well trained for the ***caring*** professions.

The wounded human race was greatly in their debt.

Soon, the world dead was estimated at sixty million.
The infection continued to grow.

Chapter 33 – Rescue Mission

Being a private pilot, with his own aeroplane, Alex was often contracted by Aberdeen Health Services to fly VFR (visual flight routes), transporting emergency medical and drug supplies. Access to that little plane meant that David and Richard could avoid a nightmare drive of unknown length and difficulty and did not have to rely on the failed public transport system.

They boarded the Cessna caravan mark 3, at the remote Leslie airstrip. Alex explained that they might have some difficulty with getting clearance for anything other than a very short VFR. It helped that they were starting their journey at the private airfield in Leslie, but they must pick up fuel in Dyce, the main Aberdeen Airport. Alex figured that, as long as they stayed airside at Dyce, rather than crossing the barrier to the landside, they could avoid most of the awkward security checks. However, he really had no idea what the state of affairs at the main Airport would be. Perhaps there were no security guards left. Many non-essential service workers had simply abandoned their posts and were fleeing for sanctuary to remote locations. He also thought it best that they did not mention London, since crossing the border into England was temporarily out of bounds.

Alex took the usual time to go through his departure checks. The physical controls, right, left, forward and back. Rudders OK. Direction Indicator on the dash, functional. Compass, correct bearing. Engine temperature and pressure OK. Starter button... fired... and then they were off!

The first short leg of their journey went well. They put down in Dyce at the special landing area for small aircraft, and collected fuel. Alex then contacted Air Traffic Control using his regular call sign.

"Dyce Tower. This is Golf Alpha Romeo Whisky Romeo, requesting clearance for a short VFR. Destination Dundee. Urgent medical supplies to Ninewells Hospital. Three persons on board."

"Roger, Golf Alpha Romeo Whisky Romeo, you are cleared for VFR. Flight level eight zero (8000ft.) Your transponder code will be Squawk 0135. "

Their flight plan was filed in the normal way after take off.

Just south of Aberdeen they changed communication frequency and dropped to less than 1000 ft. The skeleton crew that were still manning Aberdeen ATC lost contact. They had a low and bumpy ride to endure until they neared their target. Much of it was around 500ft, below radar visibility, just clear of the treetops on some of the hills. They could see sheep grazing on the higher ground.

Knowing that there was no way they would be allowed to land at Stansted, and being familiar with all the small Flying Club Airfields, Alex headed for Stapleford on the edge of the M25, only a few miles from Stansted. He had landed there many times and knew the ground staff and the layout.

George Willis was an eccentric bachelor who lived with his mother. Many people thought that George was not the full shilling, but he was intelligent and hard working, just a little odd. George and his mother lived right next to Stapleford Airfield and seldom ventured far from home. He considered the Flying Club facilities as an extension to his property and this was both appreciated and exploited by the Flying Club. George was encouraged to take a pride in the place. He kept the windows clean and mowed the grass around the airstrip on a voluntary basis. He was keeper of the Flying Club Landrover, available for members' use. He was an excellent unpaid maintenance and security man. Sometimes, George was allowed to operate the radio, but usually under the watchful eye of a Flying Club member. Everybody knew George Willis, once met never forgotten. Some avoided close contact with him because he could speak for hours about his mother's ailments, his dog's diabetes and his own cataracts.

Alex contacted George's familiar voice on the radio, and, careful to avoid admitting that he'd crossed the border, he told a white lie.

"Hello Stapleford, Golf, Alpha Romeo, Whisky, Romeo - caravan out of Newcastle. Three persons aboard. Requesting permission to land for re-fuelling."

"There's nobody here, only me, George Willis. You got any of them bugs aboard, Mister?" He enquired, uncertainly.

"No, George, we're clean. But stay your distance if you like. We'll need the Landrover, though."

Alex had hired the vehicle a couple of times before, and George recognised him. Amazingly, George did not seem to be too aware of the extent of the pandemic infection and he was wondering why there had been so little activity lately. He did not watch television much. He was a bit of a hermit, totally dedicated to his gardening, his mother, his dog and the maintenance of the strip.

Alex volunteered to stay with the plane, and brave an overdose of George, while Richard and David proceeded with the next phase of the Rescue Mission.

They parked the Landrover in a quiet lane some distance from Stansted. It was easier than they predicted to approach the cordoned off airbus morgue, which was near the baggage area and surrounded by high chain link fences and red Danger warning signs.

There was a huge hole burnt in the fence near the place where the blackened remains of the A380 were scattered. She was charred to a crisp.

At the other end of the runway was the second Quarantine unit. Radio alarm fencing sealed it off. There was a standard gate, locked from the outside with a bar lock. The reduced level of security was in place merely to stop those in the final phase of quarantine getting out. It was not really considered necessary to stop people getting ***in*** since nobody in their right mind would want to enter what had been a lethal virus-infested death trap!

The space-suited isolation squad that had been tending the needs of the sick inmates was gone now. Only one guard remained, along with a simple-task robot, that carried most of the food and medical supplies into the interior of the second Quarantine chamber, and disposed of waste debris for burning. It was 17 .46. The robot was nowhere to be seen and the sole remaining guard appeared to be asleep, slumped over his desk, still clad in his bio-suit.

He was simply on call in case the interns should need anything. He had instructions to release them in two more days anyway.

The guard was nervous, anxious to be off this lonely duty. Unsure if negotiation with an armed guard would be a fruitful approach, David opted for the element of surprise, moving swiftly to disarm him. It was an unfortunate course of action. He frightened the man and in the ensuing scuffle, David was shot in the leg. The spooked guard immediately apologised. He was clearly not a trained combat fighter.

David swore and said, "Go on mate! Beat it! The world is falling apart anyway. Folk are dropping down like flies."

The guard looked uncertain, then picked up his gun and ran.

Richard opened the lock and released the weary survivors. Michael, the Steward, who had become Rose's right-hand-man, with his nursing background and cheerful manner, joined her escape team. The others were told that they would have to make their own way from there. They all had families on whom they wanted to check as well as private agendas of their own.

Slowly and uncertainly, they started to walk from the site, some heading for the Terminal Building, others avoiding all enclosures, just relieved to be alive and free.

There was nobody around to apprehend them.

The flight back North was uneventful, but several burning pyres could be seen from the air, near to major cities like Manchester and Birmingham. Judging by the vehicles that were visible, the Army seemed to be in charge of the disposal of corpses. When they drew close to Aberdeen, Alex tried to contact ATC, but there was no response. The communication channel had nothing but noise. They circled Dyce Airport and it appeared to be abandoned altogether.

Brief investigation showed that there were several body bags piled in a hanger near the Terminal Building.

The living had gone.

Chapter 34 – Heading Home

Returning to Oyne, via Leslie, the roads were deserted. Not a living soul peeped from a window or crossed their path. They stopped for the night at David's house. Rose fell into a shallow sleep of exhaustion.

Plying him with whisky first, Michael removed the bullet from David's thigh. He had lost a lot of blood and part of his right femur bone had been splintered. Michael feared that a lesser infection than ***Danny Ives*** might colonise the wound, but they had no more antibiotics. Michael cursed himself for not having a full medical kit.

Before the effects of the whisky wore off, David said, "Look, you guys. I am very grateful to all of you. I never thought I would owe my life... and so much ***more*** than that..." He glanced towards the sleeping Rose, "...to three woofters! Gentlemen, I am in your debt. I am thoroughly ashamed of my past bad vibes towards Gay people. I am a reformed character."

"Hey, man, we're used to it." Richard volunteered, " Just get back on your feet and take this ***woman*** off our hands."

There was a message from Kate on David's telephone answering machine: *"Hello, David. I hope you have found Rose and returned safely. This disease is spreading from the city out to Inverurie. It is much worse than the Aberdeen typhoid epidemic of the 1960s that I remember well. I have decided to take up my neighbour's offer to go with him to his remote holiday cottage on the West Coast. I get on well with Bob Sinclair and it seems like a sensible move until this epidemic has passed. You should also get away if you can. We've taken a heap of supplies and I'll give you a ring when we get there. Don't worry about me, David. Good Luck. Remember, I love you."*

At first, Rose feared that the authorities would still be after them, so they laid low for a couple of weeks. Rose had taken extra blood samples from all the survivors aboard the crippled A380, including herself and settled out the serum. She had no means of testing it for antibodies, but suggested that if Richard, Alex or David wished to receive a shot of the combined serum, in the hope that it might help bestow immunity, they must choose ***now***. She pointed out that Richard and Alex might already have some immunity, but that they could still get seriously ill.

They all accepted this weak prophylactic measure.

Richard and Alex returned to their flat in Aberdeen. Michael stayed with Rose, to help nurse the invalid. They all listened to the media broadcasts, expecting to hear that Rose was a wanted person. However, it soon became obvious that she was much too small a concern in the face of true global disaster.

By the second week, the television was dead, but radio bulletins gave them the grim details that the black-hearted killer infection was rife in areas all over Britain, including the North of Scotland. They were united in fear. Richard and Alex arrived back in Oyne towards the end of Week Two. Aberdeen was in chaos. Sickness was everywhere. They were thinking of flying off somewhere very remote, away from the city, to weather the storm of the infection.

They discussed what to do next.

Rose said simply, "I agree with Richard. We need to seek isolation. We also need to go where the infection has already swept through some time before us. I understand that the North Isles were first infected several weeks ago. Many of the inhabitants, running scared like us, would have left for the mainland. I would reason that Danny must have well and truly run his course among the others. There should be very few people alive there now."

The others thought this sounded logical. Encouraged by their positive murmuring and nods of approval, Rose continued her train of thought, "Also, there are very isolated spots in Shetland where we can hide out and wait till the plague has passed its peak in the rest of the country. Shetland is a place where we could be self-sufficient at least for a while, having the potential for both land and sea produce. Besides, if we are all going to die, I want to die at home, in Shetland. If we are destined to survive, I want it to be in a place of quiet natural beauty, as close to nature as possible!"

She wanted to go to the Whiteness croft.

All her instincts told her they would be safer there.

After rejecting several alternative plans, including the Western Isles and the Scilly Isles, they decided that it was indeed more prudent to go to a location that was already past the peak of infection and that was also very familiar to at least one of them. They remained three more days in Oyne, gathering some basic medical and survival supplies, including firearms. David's leg was beginning to heal, although he still limped badly.

David never heard from his mother again. He had no means of contacting her. He left her a note on the kitchen table, explaining where they had gone.

The five of them went back aboard the Cessna caravan, having taken what essentials they could carry and flew North into the wake of the killer microbe.

There was silence aboard the little aircraft, each of them withdrawn into a private world of contemplation. David's leg still ached a bit. Rose gave him a weak smile and put her hand on his shoulder. She was glad to have been granted this short time together, despite the bleakest of circumstances.

They flew low over the Old Man of Hoy, standing like a majestic beacon of Orkney, unaffected by the centuries and the holocaust. They passed low over Scapa Flow. The wrecks of the scuttled German Fleet from the last Great War could still be seen submerged in the clear waters, a Mecca for divers for decades.

There were no divers.

Oil leaked from a tanker grounded on rocks. Ten minutes later and the larger Orkney Islands were left behind. They did not talk much. Rose focused on the famous wall surrounding the whole tiny island of North Ronaldsay. It was designed to restrict the native hardy sheep to the meagre pickings of seaweed on the shoreline. When she was a child, she had gone through a phase of believing in Reincarnation, and her biggest fear was to die and be reincarnated as a North Ronaldsay ewe, facing a short life of strife and surviving on the very brink of starvation. She wondered if it might now be a preferable existence.

Breaking the painful silence, Rose said to David, "Did you know that Snakes and Ladders was originally an Indian game of Reincarnation? A game of chance: a reminder that one can be reborn in high or low positions in life, as an animal or a King."

"No, I didn't know that useless piece of information. What made you come out with that?" He looked at her with a puzzled expression.

She pointed to North Ronaldsay below and now behind them. "Those sheep on the shore, outside the stone wall." She fell silent again, wondering if they would ever feel like playing a board game again.

Leaving the cluster of Orkney Islands behind, they passed the tiny speck of Fair Isle off to the west, and within twenty minutes they were flying past Sumburgh Head. Rose noted where the Braer had gone aground in 1993. It seemed an insignificant incident, a lifetime ago. Sheep ran from the low flying Cessna as they flew over the lighthouse, and a man and child were seen diving for cover behind the white walls. The sign of life lifted their spirits.

Flying over the main town of Lerwick next, they were less optimistic. Chaos covered the ground: discarded cars blocked main streets; supermarket trolleys were abandoned on pavements and in the harbour.

Smoke rose from the burnt out remains of a church.
A tattered flag flew at half-mast on the Town Hall.

Going in quite low up King Harald Street, two scavenging dogs were arguing over scraps and a shoe could be clearly seen on the road, with part of a purple leg still attached to it. It was a lonely sickening sight. It jerked at their hearts.

Several fishing trawlers and a ferryboat were aground in Lerwick harbour. A plague of seagulls squabbled over piles of miscellaneous rubbish. There was no sign of living human activity in the town. Leaflets littered the ditches.

Mark turned, at Rose's instruction, and they headed towards the Tingwall airstrip some seven miles distant. An ominous silence again filled the plane.

Chapter 35 – The Co-op

They settled in the renovated croft house in Whiteness where Rose had spent so many happy childhood days. Except for the distinct lack of population, the topography of the area had not changed much in the past decade. She considered that they were safe there. It was home. She still felt her grandfather's generosity of spirit there, blessing the house.

They did not travel far during the first week, merely inspecting the neighbouring houses, in parties of three, and confirming that they were abandoned. There was no sign of Rose's brother or his family. She hoped they had escaped to another place.

It was fortunate that Shetland had been a pioneer in sustainable energy sources. The small windmill power plant serving the croft house worked fine. The private water supply was fresh.

Rose was exhausted and slept a lot during the early days. It was the first place for weeks that she had been relaxed enough to sleep through a whole night. Nobody was making demands of her. Still, she dreamed, as she had never done before. She had a frightening and repetitive nightmare.

She felt something mechanical trembling against her, like the engine revving up aboard the A380 morgue plane. She was surrounded by unearthly light. In the centre of the light was an undulating area of perfect blackness. It was shaped like a gigantic viral structure although it kept changing morphs. It was flawlessly black in the middle and seemed to have inky depths with no trace of any light or form. It was certainly a three-dimensional structure but not a solid one. Her eyes peered into the primordial blackness, straining to pick out some detail, but she perceived only the static speckling of mindless staring. Her logic told her that this could not be real, but it felt too detailed to be senility or imagination. She tried to alter her level of focus with one eye using the technique Richard had taught her years ago for viewing the magic multi-coloured dot pictures, but it did not work here. It was truly a living hole that constantly altered its shape at the edges but had a dead core. There was no movement at all in the middle, but always the expectancy of movement.

Her heart thudded and her skin crawled as she put her hand out to touch the thing. Her fingers tingled at the edge of the moving shape. It felt silky damp, like hair conditioner. Then her flesh vanished into the infinite depths of the centre as if drawn into another dimension.

Something unknown but immensely strong seemed to seep into her arm.

She woke up in a cold sweat, every time, feeling altered in some way.

Each of the five of them contributed a vital skill to the group: Alex, the pilot; Michael, the nurse; Richard, the chief cook and light-hearted entertainer; Rose, the local expert and strategic planner of expeditions. Of all the men, David was the only one with typical male skills, like chopping driftwood, making fires, breaking into locked premises and getting equipment to work. Yet, more and more, he appreciated the complementary roles of the three Gay members of the group. David became a tower of practical strength on the land now that his leg was healing.

David was also Rose's lover: she clung to him like a limpet every night, although it was not always a passionate embrace. Often it bordered on desperation, but it was interspersed with laughing and crying and sometimes the violent animal coupling reminiscent of any species threatened with extinction. They each drew comfort from the other. Together they felt a little security but realised there may be no lasting stability. Both of them tried to maintain their own inner strength, but it was sadly depleted. Rose was no longer made of metal.

During the early days, they did not see anyone out in the open. Nobody attempted to approach them or contact them. They heard the engine of a boat in a nearby Voe, yet they never actually saw the vessel. No doubt the survivors were scared, perhaps even crazed, by their recent ordeals and were very wary of any strangers.

It was almost two weeks before they ventured forth to visit Lerwick. Desperate for supplies, having already pillaged the surrounding crofts, they found a Landrover Discovery that David managed to get jump started by running it down the hill. It had half a tank of petrol, according to the gauge.

They all went together on this foraging trip because nobody wanted to be alone and curiosity was strong. They glimpsed a few frightened faces, mostly peeping from closed curtains on the outskirts of Lerwick. There were signs of burnt out funeral pyres at the North end of the town, and a massive pit had been recently partly filled in, the bulldozers still in position. Despite these clear attempts to clean up, there was still the occasional decaying body here and there, although parts had been trailed away by scavenging animals.

The harbour was not a place to go swimming.

The Co-op building was eerie and deserted.
It smelt bad.

There were several cats wailing inside but they scarpered when Rose and the four men entered.

It was cold and dark inside the supermarket building. Richard and Alex went in search of an emergency electricity supply.

"There is always a reserve supply, to give a few more hours in a real crisis situation," Alex insisted, "I don't think they would have had the time or the inclination to use it though. We only have to find the trip switch."

Rose and David walked up and down the aisles of the shop, peering at products, selecting tins and dried pulses. Michael went off on his own, whistling a tuneless melody to keep his mind off what he was doing.

The freezers were green with mould. It looked as if human remains were intermingled with the fungal growth. Rose put her gloved hand over her nose. David put an arm around her shoulder.

Nobody spoke.

Suddenly the strip lights flickered and there was the sound of a motor. A strange female voice said "*Today's Bargain Offer -*

Midnight Sun butter - Buy one, get one free - Pepperoni Pizza - 30% off... Tenants Lager...6 for..."

Rose jumped and her heart ran a marathon. David laughed nervously.

A distant, "Shit, man!" Followed by rumbling and footsteps running could be heard from the depths of the back shop. Several fluorescent lighting strips now floodlit the squalid store. Looking up at the strange sight, Rose focused on the grey cemetery of dead flies trapped inside the casings of the lights. She had always hated these insect catchers. They cast a cold stark light, too frank and real.

Everybody needed make-believe, not reality.
Now, more than ever.

The light made the stench worse, so they quickly helped themselves to tinned soups, beans, fruit, wine, soap, disinfectant, toilet tissue, bleach, detergent, and socks, lots of socks. Michael could not resist putting a bottle of hair gel and a couple of deodorants into his pocket! Rose's luxury was a tin of macadamia nuts while David picked two jars of lemon olives and a ball of string. As an afterthought, he went back for a couple of bottles of Malt Whisky.

It was while they were stowing the mass of supplies into the Discovery that they heard the singing. It was high pitched and tuneless. They crossed the littered car park. David stooped to pick up one of the numerous leaflets. They were religious fliers, warning that Doomsday had arrived and that Repentance was never too late.

They followed the eerie melody which came in sporadic bursts, towards the Skipidock, where a few sad fishing vessels were still tied up to the pier. On the deck of the second boat sat a ragged child, about nine years old. She was rocking a pile of blankets in her arms. Her yellow hair was tangled and her knees black. She had a bruise on her temple. She seemed unaware of their approach until Rose spoke.

"Hello, there."

The child screamed.

Her name was Vaila.

She had been alone, with her baby, for a long time.
Her family was all gone away now.
The school was dark.
The shops were not nice any more.
She was looking for her father.
This was his boat... but he never came here now.
Chocolate, crisps and Coca-Cola still tasted all right.

Rose put her arm around the child and led her away.

Chapter 36 – The Matchbox House

Rose could still hardly believe it herself as she stared at the thin blue line on the third positive test. There was absolutely no doubt about it. She placed the plastic wand into a disposal bag and hesitated before dumping it in the waste chute. She buzzed with sweet excitement and bitter reasoning crept up her throat like nauseous bile.

Why was she spared the deadly infection?

She had been labelled infertile and this had coloured her attitude all her adult life. A barren Rose; yet life was stirring within her now. Oh, Joy! She was a real woman! Her wild thoughts ricocheted between the crazy impossible and the pragmatic. What was this thing Fate? She'd never really believed in it... but now?

She recalled her grandfather's words of wisdom, "***Mr Fate Esquire***, is a fine old gentleman, Rosie, for whom I have the greatest respect." Jim had been dead over five years now, but she heard his voice with a perfect clarity.

Was "***Mr Fate Esquire,***" a ***Divine*** being, synonymous with ***God***?

What a bloody world to take a child into!
Would it be all right?
Did it have only 45 chromosomes like herself?
Would he be phenotypically normal?

It was a "he" she had decided. Round and round went the dizzy thoughts in her head. Her stomach churned and she leapt towards the toilet cubicle and spewed into the pan... it was not bloodstained... there was no black tinge... it was ***just*** morning sickness. She laughed aloud.

She stood there motionless, holding her breath, trying to control the inner turmoil and stop the waves of nausea. She splashed cold water on her face and dabbed it dry with the fish motif on the end of her towel. Staring at herself in the bathroom mirror, she noted the flushed cheeks and the unkempt hairstyle. She had a small haemorrhage in her right eye, but it had been there a week and was just a tiny burst vessel. It was nothing to worry about. She was such a mess! Not ultra-attractive at the best of times, she fared worse than usual: she had a spot on her left cheek and her eyebrows were bushy and shapeless. They needed plucking. Her hair showed the ancient remains of multi-coloured streaks and reminded her of a stained public lavatory brush.

She did not look into the gentle face of motherhood.
Maternal wisdom was not etched across her worried forehead.

She resolved not to tell David until it was past the red alert stage of the early trimester. Should she test the amniotic fluid herself to check the chromosome constitution? Would there be enough working equipment? Could she remember how to use it anyway? She decided to leave it in the hands of ***Mr Fate Esquire***. He had served her well up until now.

"Oh, you poor little mite!" She said to her abdomen, "What will become of you with a mother like me? I can't cope with my own life! Oh, ***Mr Fate Esquire***, help me out here? If you're there? Please, pleeeease, don't take this away?"

"It'll be all right, It will, I promise," she said out loud to her belly.

She sat down of the edge of the bath and wrapped her arms around herself, desperately protective, rigid with willpower. She was full of nervous energy, restless, like a chained whippet in sight of rabbits. She felt the tenderness of her own slightly swollen breasts and squeezed harder, glad of the comforting pain. Moisture leaked from her eyes. She did not weep then. There would be plenty time for real tears.

...

"I'm sorry I didn't tell you earlier, David, but I needed to be certain and past the first stage. I needed to come to terms with it myself."

"What is there to come to terms with? It's marvellous, isn't it?"

" I guess I thought it just wouldn't happen... but oh, now I do want this baby, more than anything I've ever longed for before."

Her eyes misted over and she stared fixedly into the distance.

"I feel like the first woman on earth to ever have a child inside her. I know I've watched my friends swell and drop babies for years and I have pretended like it was no big deal, but it all changes in perspective when it's you yourself with new life within you... especially now, when there is so much misery. Death and decay everywhere. We are going to be alone, like frontier settlers. Can you deliver babies?"

He took her hand and rocked it backwards and forwards, like a tired playground kid.

"I'm an expert at all aspects of childbirth. I will boil all the water you need and have hot towels ready and... what else is there? Oh yes, the inevitable mood swings. I shall tactfully ignore you when you are bad tempered and illogical!"

She shook his hand free and stamped her foot gently in a mock temper.

"I'll have you know that I am ***never*** illogical. I leave that to you non-scientists. I have perfect logic and I know exactly the ***five*** things I'm getting myself into.

One, I will grow about 16 kg of blubber and stretch marks.
Two, I will end up with flaccid boobs like spaniel's lugs.
Three, I, no ***you***, will smell of milk puke and have stalactites down the back of your jumper.
Four, The baby will inherit all my good points, including my perfect logic.
And Five..." She paused a little too long.

"What's the matter, Sweeto, do people with perfect logic only have four fingers?"

"Piss off! I hate it when you talk down to me!"

" I've got only two words to say to you"

"Not three little words?"

"No two."

"What two?"

"Bad tempered!"

"Nyaaagh...." she pulled a face at him. "Smartarse! Sometimes, you have the emotional sensitivity of an amoeba, David!" Tears were trickling down her cheeks.

There was a hint of a smile on his rugged face. He opened one eye, and asked, "What's an amoeba?"

...

Richard and Alex moved into the town after a month in Whiteness. They did not like the permanent rural isolation. The town survivors gradually came out of their retreats and started again to mingle, to rebuild their society.

Alex started teaching, not history and geography, but survival techniques. A group of ten children, of mixed ages came to his classes, held in the Town Hall. Vaila, who had been living in Whiteness with them since they found her, was one of the pupils. She was a sad little child. She did not sleep much and bed-wetting had been a problem, but like all children she adapted to her new environment steadily and a manageable stability crept in. She made nine new friends at the makeshift survival school.

There was absolutely no call for legal services, but Richard attempted to assist people with tracking down their next of kin. Nevertheless, he was particularly discontented with life in Shetland and soon persuaded Alex to take him for short reconnaissance trips back to Aberdeenshire. They decided to move back to the Mainland once it looked as if people were going about their business again there.

Rose and Michael set up a basic Health Clinic in the empty and echoing corridors of the Gilbert Bain Hospital in Lerwick. Rose worked part time there and part time at home assisting David to manage an old-fashioned working croft. While in Lerwick, she was able to alleviate the worst of the minor complaints and explain the widespread infertility among the survivors.

She shielded the life within her with a reverence, like a Holy Being.

David was content to stay at home and do manual labour. When not at lessons, Vaila followed him like a puppy. With her help, although it was sometimes more of a hindrance, he resurrected the croft and they worked the land again. He rounded up and fenced in a hundred ewes, wild from their freedom on the Peninsula, and two surviving cows. He took a great delight in snipping the yellow plastic ear-tags off the beasts, rejoicing in the fact that mindless bureaucracy had been exterminated and there were no animal passport forms to fill in! The stock had to be tamed again with kindness. There were some dry concentrates still to be found in the Farmers Agricultural Store, and grass was plentiful. With the exception of the area at the very point of the Peninsula, which was guarded by a mad crofter with three unfriendly dogs and a shot-gun, he was at liberty to graze whatever land he liked!

Spring came and Wildlife appeared in great abundance. Nature had taken over the land. Meadows were filled with deep smelling clover, flag iris, red campion and marsh orchids. Wild fowl nested in the rushes and long grasses. Otters occupied holts along the shoreline and seals lazed on offshore skerries in the dappled sunshine. The song of the curlew rang out across the heather knowes and ***tirricks*** swooped noisily in the ***shoormaal.***

There was comfort and stability in all these things.

Michael realised a lifelong ambition after studying medicine from books for years.With Rose as his mentor, he pronounced himself Dr Michael King after six months. He was happy to be the head of the Clinic, having found his true vocation. Then, romance came along for him in the form of a young man who had been a trainee chef in one of the Lerwick Hotels. Michael loved Shetland.

He chose his own dwelling house within Lerwick itself. The folk of Shetland had called it the Matchbox House, although the Matchbox was now the shed and an enormous new harled mansion dwarfed the original whitewashed cottage. It nestled on the rocky shore at the southern edge of the town, a remnant of the past, surrounded by modern monstrosities and the chaos of abandoned cars and rubbish that had accumulated in the windy ditches. The old road had acted only as a parking place for the last owners and it led directly on to dual carriageway. Rose thought how the town had grown in all directions... and yet distances themselves had shrunk, and so many folks had gone.

When Michael had first seen the Matchbox house, while walking with Rose along the shore from the Slettes Pier to the Clickimin Loch, he had been fascinated with it. The back door hung on its hinges and creaked in the gale. They had gingerly entered the abandoned house and wandered around, picking over the detritus of a family's home… He had loved the place, with its history, its wild sea views, and it was within easy walking distance of the Clinic.

Communication with the outside world began to grow steadily. At first there was an interactive radio service and small numbers of survivors from all over the UK started talking to each other. Then there was regular contact with similar groups from all over the world, using good old fashioned CB radio, exchanging ideas, slowly but surely rebuilding infrastructure, ensuring a future for Mankind.

Rose lent her expertise to a Medical Consortium with the aim of trying to establish Hospital Services in Scotland. Their priority was to set up Reproductive and Fertility Clinics.

Rose and David had no desire to leave Shetland. However, once there was an option of easy and safe travel. they settled for regular trips to the Mainland, especially to Bennachie. In the meantime, they were at peace with each other and had found a real and solid little space to share. Michael was needed and busy and seemed also to want to stay. Alex and Richard were less settled and returned to Scotland as soon as a better network of communications was established.

After six months of silence on the commercial radio wave bands, a single UK station started broadcasting daily, reporting progress in every corner of Britain, with some news from other countries.

Michael took a great interest in Rose's growing pregnancy, reading medical books and fussing over her diet. As the pregnancy advanced, she gave up the Clinic in Lerwick and did her share of gentle outdoor croft chores. Voar was approaching and there was much Spring work to do. In the greenhouse, it was time to cut out all the dead wood and encourage the fresh new growth. She even found some herb seeds that were still fertile and had coriander and basil growing under glass. David did most of the cooking. Fish and mutton were plentiful. He had dug over the old planticrub and soon filled it with kale, turnips and garlic.

David liked to watch her bathe. Wee Oliver McKay, as they had already named the intern, came alive like a ceroc dancer when surrounded by steaming hot water. The marled skin of Rose's abdomen stretched out in all directions, contorting into magnificent shapes, mimicking a live chicken in a plastic sack. There seemed to be far too many feet and elbows and knees for only one small fellow. David could pinch the skin-clothed toe as it was kicked boldly outwards where no man had been before. Wee Olli would respond instantly to the pressure, withdrawing into his liquid sanctuary. Rose loved the attention and wallowed in it.

"I'll give you precisely ***fifteen*** minutes to take your hand off my belly!"

Chapter 37 - Birth

There was a great joy for them all in Rose's pregnancy.

It signified ***Hope.***
It signified how being ***different*** can be an advantage in some circumstances.
This improbable conception, that was difficult to perceive as a purely chance event, signified the future of the human race: the first of ***a brand new species***, with 45 chromosomes like his mutant parents!

Michael was particularly attentive and caring, making sure all was ready for the child and that they were well prepared for the delivery. He kept telling Rose that it was fortunate that he was now a trained midwife.

With the trauma of the past months, Rose was not exactly certain of her dates. However, according to Michael, the expected date of delivery was pinpointed sometime around 2nd November 2007, give or take a week. The baby chose a bad time to announce his arrival. It was the 18th of September, a clear bright day. David had taken Vaila and Michael fishing in the little boat. David had overhauled the outboard motor and they had found plenty of petrol in the Lerwick garage tanks. Shoals of mackerel could be seen boiling in the Voe, schools of porpoises in hot pursuit. Mark hated fishing, but liked the wildlife, and he responded to necessity in this new, "back to nature" style of life.

Richard and Alex had moved to the Scottish mainland, and were not expected to visit for a while. Rose had refused to travel far until the baby was born. Richard was meantime representing her at the Northern Medical Consortium. The Fertility and Prenatal Diagnostic Facility was to be called the Rose Anderson Unit. Rose had agreed to spend more time there, establishing new and improved techniques, once Oliver was born.

Rose was at home alone with the animals. She was pottering in the greenhouse. David had repaired the broken panes of glass, and after a gap of two decades, roses bloomed again in the microclimate behind the windbreak. Persephone, or Sephy for short, was the name they had given to their newest stray cat, who was very independent. She had been called after the statue of Persephone, at Chapel of Garioch, on Bennachie. Sephy had kettled under the staging in a cardboard box full of shredded paper. Rose was having some difficulty trying to coax her out to check that all was well.

It was hard to bend without the acid indigestion burning her throat and saliva running in her mouth. Her sciatic nerve was under stress and giving her pain with each attempt to kneel down and poke around beneath the staging. Sephy had picked the most inaccessible location, behind the wooden legs of the makeshift bench and fronted by plastic plant pots. Rose could hear mewing.

"Sephy, pusso... come on lass... let me have a peerie look?"

Kneeling with no elegance, legs apart, she probed the mouth of the box, knees pressing into her bulging abdomen. She felt the gush of water on her feet first, warm and frightening, like urine.

Her heart leapt. "Oh, my God, Sephy!" she uttered to the cat, who had poked its nose out in wide-eyed curiosity to investigate the commotion. She struggled to get up, knees also wet as a steaming puddle gathered on the concrete floor.

Holding a hand between her legs, trousers saturated, Rose dribbled her way to the house, saying repetitively "It'll be all right... pleeese God... it'll be all right..."

She noted the time on the wall clock. It was 1.19 p.m. The fishermen would be back before dark, she thought... no more than a couple of hours.

She ran a bath, added a handful of salt in an attempt to be sterile and gingerly stepped into the warm brine. The seepage from her womb looked pink against the pale brown peaty bathwater and whirling patterns appeared in the tub. She got hold of David's razor and a bar of soap and attempted to shave off her own pubic hair.

"Shit!" she muttered as she nicked her inner thigh. She was not much good at this shaving blind. Red blood mingled with the thin primordial broth surrounding her. For the first time in years, she longed for her mother. She had little idea of exactly what to expect now, only the cold clinical details of childbirth were etched in her mind. Emotionally, she was in shock. Romantically, she wondered about proceeding with her plan of a natural childbirth, perhaps in the water, but it was dirty and going cold. She could not remember where she had put the bloody candles.

She abandoned all ideas of water-birth. She dried herself with cool and steady hands, belying the trembling within, and put on a loose dressing gown. She made a makeshift nappy to catch the remaining small leakage, holding it in place with the biggest, baggiest pair of knickers she could find.

"Really sexy!" she thought as she glanced at her misshapen silhouette in the hall mirror. She put a plastic cover over the mattress of their bed and a spread a single clean sheet. She did not lie on the bed, but paced around, peering out the window for signs of their return. It was getting dark now. They would arrive soon. Her contractions came fast and furious, crippling her with excruciating pain for short bursts.

Between contractions, she sang to herself, completely off key:

"Yellow Bird... up high in banana tree
Yellow Bird... you sit all alone like me.
Has your lady friend...
Gone away again...
That is very sad...
Mak-a-me feel so bad... aargh!"

She picked up her talisman and kissed the red Shetland rose, willing it to work its magical powers now, thinking of him who made it and for whom it was made. Through the metal petals, she imagined them with her now. The pain was very bad. Nothing had prepared her for this incapacitating agony. She fetched Michael's case of medical supplies and placed it on the small table near the side of the bed. He had assured her that there would be monitoring aids and pain relief, but she had thought she would not need drugs. So what? She had changed her mind! She did not know what to do or what she could safely take.

Panic filled her breast.
Sweat stuck her damp hair to her scalp.
Cold fear prickled her back.

David heard her screams from the foot of the drive. He was laden with a box of fish. His old leg injury had stiffened up from sitting too long in the cold and cramped conditions of the little boat and he could not run easily uphill.

"Go on ahead you two! Something's wrong!"

Michael appeared first in the doorway of the bedroom and quickly became the Consultant. It was a long time since he had delivered a baby, he said. Rose was uncertain if he ever had! However, he had done his revision and was ready. The room was dark. No lamps had been lit. It was cold. Vaila was sent to find kindling and light the stove.

"David? Are you there?"

"It's Michael, Rose... I'll try to help you. David is just coming up the path now."

"I don't care if you're the devil him***self***... ***aargh***! Where's the pain relief you promised? I'm shit scared and sodden wet and I want every god-damned A-class drug you've got in that case, Mister!"

"Not yet, Rosie, I need to examine you first...how long...?

"***Now***...I need it ***now***, you cruel, woofter ***para***medic!"

"Now, now! I'm hardly the perpetrator of cruelty madam... perhaps even the victim?" He said in a perfectly calm voice with more than a touch of amusement, "Roll over on your back... knees raised..."

"How dare you be so calm and frivolous. I ***hate*** you! Where's David?"

"Here, Rosie!" He took her left hand and she dug her nails into his flesh and screamed for her mother, then her grandfather, then God, then Sephy the cat!"

Michael minced around efficiently, switching on the generator and light arrived. Vaila completed her tasks and the stove was lit. Water was put to boil, although nobody was quite sure why. It seemed to be the traditional thing to do.

Rose felt like the epicentre of a volcanic eruption, surrounded by order and normality. A drip was inserted into her arm. She did not notice the needle but longed for oblivion, even to die right then so that the pain would cease.

"What about an epidural?"

"Sorry, doesn't exist these days. I wouldn't like to administer a spinal injection anyway, I'm not ***that*** experienced, but I can give you a half dose of ***Wundural,*** a very powerful pain-relieving cocktail. It is injected straight into a vein and it's better than the old epidurals, so I'm told."

"You can stick it ***any***where... just ***giiive*** me some, ***pleease***!"

"Not yet, Rose, when you're a little more dilated. It will slow down your labour."

"I don't care! Slow it! Stop it all to-bloody-gether! Jeeesus H. Christ, ***help*** me!"

"Hey, Michael, there's an air bubble in this drip!" David announced with frantic concern in his voice.

"Go boil a kettle, man! It's fine! Leave this to the experts!" Replied Michael, checking again her pulse, her blood pressure, and her eyes.

"Go boil your fucking head, I'm staying right here! Michael! See this air bubble in this drip?" He stood up and tapped the plastic tubing.

"Give him a shot of that ***Wundurel*** stuff too, will you Michael?" Gasped Rose, in the tiny lull of normality between contractions.

Wundurel seeped like an ice cold Messiah into her bloodstream and down to her toes, instantly obliterating the acute agony and transforming the thorny lunatic back into a docile mother-to-be, pink faced and lucid, full of instant remorse. ***Wundurel*** was indeed a wonder drug, the closest thing to pure magic she could ever have imagined. She thanked God and then Michael. She felt mild discomfort in her right hand and remembered her talisman. It was clutched so firmly that she had to prise her own white fingers apart. Her palm was bleeding, punctured by the metal petals. The rose was misshapen and one solitary petal had detached itself altogether from the body of the crushed flower.

The mandatory pushing and panting became a quantum leap easier then. She meekly followed Michael's instructions. Armed with silver cutters that could have trimmed the hooves of a carthorse and a thing like a metal spoon, Michael's head hovered in the small visual space between her raised knees.

"We're almost there... one more mega-push... When I say. Swear away! I'll have to cut you to stop you tearing," Michael announced in his matter of fact voice.

The final shove seemed to crack her coccyx and sharp toothache spread down her legs from the hips. She heard a crunching noise and felt sharp stinging like a paper-cut and then a massive movement as if she had been disembowelled.

"It's a... ***boy***! Looks... ***fine***! Not too premature... bugger... I must've got the dates wrong...Well done, Rose!" Michael whistled and did something effective with cords and cloths and disinfectant. She heard the clatter of instruments being discarded into stainless steel containers. Michael held the mewling scrap of angry reddish innards by the ankles. There were two feet, she noticed. He yelled loudly... a strong call of distress. Her heart stopped, then hammered furiously out of control.

Michael placed the naked infant on her empty flabby stomach skin and said, "Feed him. It'll help shut him up and your milk should be in around now!"

Her breasts were swollen and veined like never before and each one the size of the tiny damp head that lay beside them. A soft spot on the crown beat a fluctuating pulse. Two bright eyes, sparkling blue, wandered around searching the wilderness and fixed on her. She was amazed how easily the infant managed to latch on to her nipple when his pouting little mouth was placed there and how strong the suction was. A small curled hand nuzzled the side of her breast. Perfect fingernails glistened like rainbow sequins.

David counted toes and fingers and laid his head on the bed, one hand on the baby's bottom and one touching Rose's cheek, asking nothing more. Vaila tentatively crept into the foot of the bed beside them, just needing not to be excluded.

Rose tasted the sacredness of motherhood.
David tasted salt.
The room was filled with great joy.

They used the boiling water to make a cup of tea!

Rose was only vaguely aware of the clean-up operation around her genitals and the burning sensation of sutures being put in place. She felt quite detached from the lower end of her body, as if it had come away with the child. Before she drifted into sleep, she heard Michael say to David.

"Hey, man! where d'you think this ***flappy bit*** goes? I'm not an expert on the fine details of the female anatomy!"

Chapter 38 – The Word

Some brave Shetland folk had remained on the island when ***Danny Ives*** had arrived. Large numbers had fled, thinking they could escape infection elsewhere. Gradually, the Islanders had returned to claim their homes and their land. From the local population of 24,000, there were less than 1,000 of the original inhabitants who had survived the holocaust and who came back to settle again.

However, these survivors had represented a good cross-section of professions: teachers, nurses, fishermen, crofters, electricians, plumbers, engineers, musicians, and civil servants…

A register of skills had been organised at the Town Hall by two men who had been local Councillors. Gradually, Shetland had picked up the pieces and rebuilt a community.

…

Mr Fate Esquire did not grant Rose a long life, but he granted her a happy decade. With David by her side, she watched her son Oliver grow tall and strong. Oliver McKay was sunny-natured from the day of his birth, entirely contented with his surroundings. Although both Rose and David had been sickly as children because of their rare autoimmune disorder, Oliver was never ill. He had a natural immunity to all forms of childhood disease.

The Earth's radiation levels were high in the year 2021 due to the progressively thinner ozone protection. Skin cancers were common among the older people who had survived the holocaust. Clinical tests had shown that Oliver had a higher natural tolerance of this radiation. He was exceptionally well adapted.

He was only an infant when the first signs of another brand new hybrid characteristic became evident. Before he could walk by himself, toys moved to him! The power of telekinesis grew stronger with the years and he gradually learned to control this new gift.

It was only one such new development in the strange modern world. Many things were radically different. Values had changed. The materialistic society of the early twenty-first century had been obliterated in one fell swoop.

Man had shuddered and fallen, against a more lethal enemy than himself. Billions had died in the slaughterhouse wake of the superbug, ***Danny Ives***. The tiny microbe had killed more folk than any previous weapon of war. Less than 5% of the World's population survived. Many of the survivors had been rendered ***infertile.*** The lucky ones with the lucky genes were synonymous with minority groups. Pockets of humanity that had been ***different*** from the majority before the holocaust now became the survivors. The new normal. The ratio of Gay to Heterosexuals was two to one! The Gay community seemed to have had a greatly heightened immunity: more lucky genes.

A new religious group had sprung up, called the ***Bio-Evangelists***. They believed, as before, that "In the beginning was ***The Word,***" but now the Word was seen as synonymous with the thread of life itself, that marvellous filament of nucleotides and ribose sugars, that faithfully carries its coded messages. ***The Word*** written in the universal four letter alphabet of bases, the gene language that is common to all life on earth. ***The Word*** was a linear language: digital, just like English, but written in a simple code of chemicals.

They believed that it was, without doubt, the most profound scientific and religious discovery ever made. The same clear and sophisticated Word documented precisely the detailed instructions for life that was shared by man, mouse... and microbe*!* ***The Word*** that could copy itself perfectly and *ad infinitum*. ***The Word*** that had persisted for four thousand million years of earth history and evolved into five million different species. Man was one of these highly evolved species, and Man ***was still evolving***. Variations in the Word and survival of the fittest had resulted in several new sub-species of man, many with only 45 chromosomes. There was likely to be a period of very rapid evolution of the human species over the next generation.

Other religious zealots said, simply, that "*the meek have inherited the earth.*" There seemed to be a grain of truth in this.

Small groups of unassuming Aborigines from the Southern Hemisphere and several families of Jews and American Indians were among the survivors. A single black African tribe had a 75% survival pattern. Other small groups had been analysed genetically and appeared to have unusual chromosome constitutions. A few other individuals with t(15:15) had been located in this way.

All those with reproductive capability were now listed in Genetic Registers and Bio-banks. It was a simple matter to obtain a printout of suitable mating options.

The "***Rose Anderson Unit***" in Aberdeen had played a major role in setting up the very first of these Registers. Rose then acted as an International Advisor, although she did most of the work electronically. She steadfastly refused to travel outwith Britain.

Breeding programmes were started among all surviving groups. All fertile and healthy adults were encouraged to participate, to come forward and secure the future of Mankind, including the Gay population. Sexuality was considered no deterrent to reproduction and parenthood. Test Tube Techniques played a major role. Soon, there were five such centres, using the latest artificial placentae and taking babies to full term with a high success rate. Their genetic blueprint was known at conception, yet only those with severely deleterious characteristics were rejected. The main aim was to preserve as much genetic diversity as possible rather than to limit or delete the remaining gene pool.

The rules of the new emerging society were changing rapidly. The old bias against those that were ***different*** was long gone.

Chapter 39 - Seasons

Euthanasia by method of choice became an accepted part of the modern world.

Oliver McKay was only fourteen years old when he was called upon to perform the heavy duty required of him. He was brave enough not to flinch as he pushed his mother's wheelchair into the Voluntary Euthanasia Studio. It was a warm and welcoming place. Soft music played. Oliver helped her to swallow the lethal dose of barbiturates. He did not touch her hand, but his will lifted the useless arm to Rose's lips.

David stood beside them, in silent vigil.
He understood.

He endorsed the end that his Rose has chosen. It was documented long before she suffered the stroke that robbed her of her speech and her mind. The Rose that he knew and loved was long gone, only a shell of the person remained with the brain of a vegetable. Her eyes had acquired the affinity stare, deep, blank, and vacant.

They took her body home and buried it at the remote West shore, near the otter holt. It was her wish that she be laid to rest there, and not in the public cemetery, surrounded by concrete anonymity. She knew that such a cold and lonely place of traditional mourning would not draw ***her*** family for forced visits. Her essence, her spark, the vitality that defined her would be felt at the croft, in the haunts that she loved. She had a horror of cremation and had always thought it a waste. She wished to integrate with her precious microbes, so that the molecules of her body would be recycled into new life.

She had written her wishes quite clearly. "***Bury me in the ground for the micro-organisms. These wonderful life forms are the Architects of our planet and the Engineers of life. They conserve and recycle energy. They are the reason why we are not drowning in dead plants and animals. They make the very air that we breath. They are worthy of my body and my utmost respect.***"

A faded and crushed Metal Rose marked the place where she lay and a new generation of wild otters would play in her Voe.

Oliver held his father's frail hand as they stood together after the short open-air ceremony. Oliver shed no tears. He dwelt only on the memories. He had a complete acceptance of the procedure. It was required of him as a statutory duty. He would do the same for his father if the need arose.

Oliver and David went home to the wake with all their friends and neighbours around them. They spoke of Rose in her prime. They projected her three-dimensional laser recording on the electronic room spot. They thanked her for the time they had with her. They celebrated the whole person. They felt her love.

She was there in her son. He carried ***The Word*** and the intergenerational equity. She smiled from his face. She was there too in the heart of her David, deep in his bones, branded on his soul forever. Oliver was strong. He had inherited his mother's steel backbone. He had characteristics shared by his father and the grandmother, Kate, whom he had never seen. He felt that, "anything could be achieved with a strong will and determination."

Richard and Alex attended the funeral ceremony too. They had a three-year-old daughter of their own and they treasured her dearly. They had called her Eve. They were her true biological parents.

Eve was the result of a new technique pioneered by the ***Rose Anderson Fertility and Reproduction Unit,*** whereby a haploid chromosome set from one parent was micro-injected into an enucleated donor egg and then fertilised by the other parent in vitro. It was just a technique that has been refined from that used in the cloning experiments back at the turn of the century. There had been hundreds of such children born in the past five years. The method was first perfected in Scotland, then passed on to America and Italy a year later. There was no problem finding a surrogate mother to carry such test tube conceptions from same sex parents. Willing surrogates were State Registered for the purpose.

Richard's contribution to the funeral service was a poem he had written to celebrate the birth of his daughter.

"Seasons

Flaxen dawn, my Spring fairy, birth.
Life in all her pastels like rain,
Turning, changing, sinking, eyes as morning milk,
Pristine, she unfolds, new as leaf.

Brazen sun, my Summer princess, zenith.
Vigour like a blaze, intense,
Swirling, melting, burning, hair as flame,
Sparkle, she bursts, full as brass.

Waning moon, my Autumn queen, wilt.
Fade to brown, fallen, crisp,
Blowing, drifting, whispering, voice as paper dolls,
Wither, she cracks, dry as parch.

Darkest black, my Winter past, cold.
Smile like lost souls, numb,
Vacant, glazed, frigid, blood as ice,
Inert, she passes through.

Flaxen dawn, my Spring fairy, birth ..."

It was equally apt to celebrate the life of Rose Anderson, his dearest friend.

It was perhaps a celebration of life itself. A celebration of ***The Word*** that reiterates through the living, because wherever one looks in the kingdom of life, whatever person, plant, animal or microscopic viral entity that one examines, if it is alive, it uses the same Word code and the same master dictionary.

All life is one.

The Author

Jessie Watt was born in Shetland, to a long family lineage of fisherfolk. She obtained a first Degree in Genetics and Biochemistry, followed by a Postgraduate Degree in Medical Cytogenetics.

Following a decade of Regional Service to Hospitals in the West Midlands and Grampian, and publication of some thirty original Research Papers in the field of Medical Science, Dr Watt was invited to become a Fellow of the Royal College of Pathologists in 1999. She then received the Honour of an MBE in 2000, for "***Services to Fishing and Agriculture in Shetland and Orkney.***" She does not consider this a personal achievement, but rather ***an accolade for Shetland***, due largely to the team efforts of numerous friends and colleagues.

Through popular fiction, the author now strives to bring a measure of scientific understanding to the ordinary man in the street.

Her first novel, "***Holm Sweet Holm,***" ISBN: 0 95244130 0 6, achieved a Literary Award from the Shetland Arts Trust.